Balancing Act

Balancing Act

Barbara Howell

HODDER AND STOUGHTON
LONDON SYDNEY AUCKLAND TORONTO

British Library Cataloguing in Publication Data
Howell, Barbara
    Balancing act.
    I. Title
    823'.914[F]   PR6058.092/

    ISBN 0 340 36909 4

Hodder and Stoughton Editorial Office: 47 Bedford Square, London WC1B 3DP.

For Alan,
with love and thanks

Even a thought, even a possibility can shatter us
and transform us.

Nietzsche

London

The hardest thing is waiting.

Waiting and waiting while he rolls feverishly around in that bed. Will he ever get well? Of course he will. Malaria stops. The doctor has told me this a dozen times. But when? And once he has recovered, will he realize he is in love with me?

I am downstairs writing this in the study. He is directly above me in the guest room. We can both see the garden in Eaton Square which, it being spring, is in full bloom. In between bouts of fever, does he notice the tops of the flowering trees? Or does he just lie there staring at the walls and brooding?

Yesterday, I decided to use this time to write an account of everything that happened in Africa. What I did was wrong and a statement must be made.

I could buy my way out, of course. Many women in my position would. But being a former journalist, I choose to write about it instead.

There's a chance that the world will forgive me. Though everyone will say I should have acted differently, thought less of safety, more of honor, found better advisors. But I did my best.

The doctor says that since the malaria has been complicated by hepatitis, he'll probably be in bed for three weeks at least. That gives me plenty of time to finish.

It feels good to be bent over a pad of paper again. The top of my desk is covered in old leather and my chair has just the right amount of springs for hours and hours of sitting. And when I open the window, the breeze coming from the garden smells of fresh new grass and hyacinths.

The odd thing is that today I feel rather happy. How could that be when I failed?

11

Because I also succeeded.
I tried.
Like Icarus.
There is a place in heaven for the likes of Icarus and me.
But before I assign myself a place in heaven, surely the end of any human story, I must describe Cy. For he was the beginning of everything.

1

I had no idea how rich he was. He was too simple and too subtle, plus there were the Naugahyde cushions on the chairs, the ill-fitting seersucker suits, the love of a good bargain. When he spoke of "my place in London", I pictured a little *pied-à-terre*. Assumed that the Boys, who called him from Chicago, were his partners, not his employees. And that when he said: "I've made a little money", that was what he meant. Which was terrific, but not what I was thinking about. I was too busy giving and getting rid of guilt.

We met in Crete five months after my mother died. It was April, off season, and the island was blanketed in violent spring winds. I had planned to do nothing but visit the Minoan ruins, which I knew something about, and let the clear Greek sunlight into my mind.

He was the only other American staying in the hotel in Aghios Nikolaos, which was one-third full. A wry, kind, perky gentleman with a dimple in his chin whose name was Cyrus Cavanaugh. From Chicago, he said, visiting Crete, to close a shipping deal and rest a little.

He invited me to dinner. We talked for hours. No question of romance. Just liking and listening to each other. He was smart, knew that I was too, and liked that fact. I told him about my mother, my work, the magazine and so many other things. A feeling of coming home. Maybe the father I never knew.

Days passed. We sailed around the bay. Visited the museum in Heraklion. Joy everywhere: in the colors, the painted flowers, the small ancient ornaments. Saw the little goddess with the leopard on her head. Looked for male gods, found none, which delighted me. Decided to see the ruins, where we discovered more beauty and low, labyrinthian buildings.

But then, one afternoon, climbing around the Palace of Knossos, he stopped. Couldn't breathe. Shaking.

His driver, very worried, asked if he should call an ambulance. Cy, ashamed, not looking at me, said no, not necessary, and took some pills.

I hated seeing him in pain. What I felt was not love, but something important was there, pushing its way to the surface. Perhaps because of his kindness. Or maybe just knowing how lonely he was.

The next morning, he was a little better and told me he was only fifty-eight. "I just look very old," he said.

The day after that, he confessed: "I'm dying." Three months was all the doctors gave him.

We were sitting on the veranda overlooking the Gulf of Mirabello. I looked at the wind raising his clean white silk hair, the sea glaring back at us under the fierce spring sun and said nothing, silenced by my horror, his horror of death.

And then – as if struck on the back – he barked out his request: "Would you spend the next three months with me? Could you?"

His son was gone, he said. His son, a thirty-five-year-old addict with no soul, living somewhere in India, was lost.

Three months was all he asked. "Just hold my hand. We'll go back to the South of France and Mrs Obie will take care of us. It's so beautiful there and I need . . ." he paused, stared at the sea, then back at me, "someone there."

Eyes waiting, no begging. Blue.

I looked into those eyes and the magazine didn't exist; my apartment in New York didn't exist; my friends were insubstantial memories. And I said, "Yes, Cy, yes". And to my mother: "If I do this for him, will you forgive?"

No human being should die alone. Though many do. My mother did, lying on sterile sheets, entwined in gurgling tubes. Alone in New Hampshire, except for my aunt who was usually somewhere else, and all those doctors with Johnny Carson smiles who came and went in shifts.

I thought it was just another hospitalization. For my mother, sickness and frequent, non-specific illnesses were a *life* pattern, had nothing, *nothing*, to do with death. But she was dying and I didn't go to New Hampshire. Because I was too busy. Too hard and too busy and heartless.

14

It went like this: I was working in New York at *Woman's Work* and, just before my thirtieth birthday, had turned full editor. My mother, a widow for twenty-six years, was a former school teacher. She had a pension, a house, lived alone, contentedly, more or less. I had just been given an assignment to interview Mayor Jane Byrne of Chicago when my aunt wrote that my mother was ill again.

I thought: first Chicago, then New Hampshire. But when I was having lunch at the Palmer House and my aunt was down the street buying a hat for the funeral, my mother died of a stroke. Alone, listening to beeping steel machines. Her last contact with humanity: the starched white hip of a nurse.

Five months later, still numb, still fighting off the guilt, I used some of the money she left me and went to Crete: a prayer to St Geography: get me out of this horror. Make this pain go away.

And I guess Cy did.

The following day, I called my boss at *Woman's Work* and asked for a leave of absence which he granted petulantly (he liked me), if I promised not to be gone longer than six months. That afternoon Cy chartered a plane and we flew to the South of France.

His villa was on the low side of a mountain that cast long, interesting blue shadows. Inside the house, room after room of sun-filled, white stucco space. Madeleine Obie, who had served him since his first wife died twenty-three years earlier, was in command. She looked at me and seemed to understand.

He asked me to marry him a week after we arrived in France. It would be a short marriage, he said, but would give him, me, dignity. "Then, too," he said with a terrible smile, "the doctors will feel better having someone to report to."

The marriage banns were posted in the *mairie* and the next day, I moved into the room closest to his. And slept there alone, in that uneasy no man's land somewhere between virtue and guilt.

What bound us together most was the fact that he needed me. (As my father never had, as my mother always had.) He was helpless and suffering and underneath his wry acceptance of what was happening to him, desperately afraid. I was strong, filled with vitality and hope and for the first time in my life conscious of the meaning of charity towards another human being. Yes, I admit it was occasioned by my remorse and guilt over my mother. But perhaps most good deeds start with a sin.

I began slowly to love him. Not admire, *love*. Not just his wisdom and incredible courage, but also his curious attachment to *me*, the least suitable person in the world – I would have thought – for a man of his age and scope to want to spend his last days with. But he did and it made me glad. It made me love him.

Meanwhile, without telling Cy, Mrs Obie frantically sent letters and telegrams to Wylie, the son, telling him to come quickly – for the marriage as much as for the death. But not a word in reply. She even called all the US Consulates in every major city in India, but still nothing.

Three weeks later, we were married in French and then, the real dying began. He had the best doctors, the best drugs, the best wines, and nurses around the clock. His lawyers came and went; his phone calls to Chicago slowed down to two a week.

Every day I smiled and made sure my hair looked right. Carried in trays, put the Frank Sinatra tapes into the stereo and filled his room with flowers. We played Scrabble on the bed and honeymoon bridge. When he couldn't sit up, I taught him Botticelli.

I cannot, will not, describe the last days or the end.

But the day after he died, the *morning* afterward, all I could think of was the life still in me. A lot. Grunting, juicy, all-I-had life. And of sex. The dark, flickering candlelight, passion and glistening flesh. Sex and food and running. I wanted to run to the top of the mountain and shout.

That afternoon, the Boys arrived: three middle-aged Irishmen from Chicago, wearing knit ties, cracking their knuckles in grief. The body had to be taken home, they explained. There was this mausoleum near Chicago. A crypt near his first wife. His last instructions. I understood, didn't I?

The funeral mass was brief. Mrs Obie wept and wept. The Boys, who did not really like her, held her up. Some villagers who had known Cy since he built the villa, came with their hats in their hands and bowed to the priest.

And Wylie? Surely now, he would come. But no, still somewhere in India. Unreachable and unloving. Ungrateful and hating.

Later, the will was read. A few pensions and large gifts for charity. Tidy settlements for Mrs Obie and an old widowed aunt in Chicago, Cy's last caring relative. The rest for me.

Total: $236 million. Or $272 million. Depending on market fluctuations in land prices and other variables which I didn't understand. Whatever the amount, it was mine.

All of it.

Nothing for the son.

Shock. Followed by a reckless, mind-searing glee. Then panic. Real fear.

Why? How could? What had? *Tell me what this means.*

No answers. Just the Boys standing with their arms folded, mouths clamped shut, eyeing me; Mrs Obie's cold British back turning and leaving the room; the lawyer grimly slipping his papers back into his briefcase.

I ran out on to the terrace: mountains, red tile roofs and a killer-blue Mediterranean sky, but no reasons. Just the incredible fact of Cy's inexplicable deed.

How could he have done this thing to his son? To me? Who were we?

Had he acted out of love for me or out of a terrible unforgiving hatred for Wylie? He hadn't seemed like a man full of anger. That slow, resigned smile. Those amused canny eyes. But how can anyone know what is inside a dying man's heart?

Still feeling the panic coming in waves, I went over in my mind the few things Cy had told me about Wylie. The last time he had seen him was in a small house in Goa some time in 1974.

During their half hour together, Wylie had spent most of the time boasting about having been to an opium den. When Cy objected, Wylie patiently, condescendingly, said that after Vietnam, he had made himself look at the whole spectrum of human existence and come to the conclusion that the only way to truth lay in experiencing either the highest or lowest ends of that spectrum. Mysticism, which he viewed as being at the highest end, was beyond him. He had neither the calling nor the discipline. That left only degradation to explore.

"In bestiality, Dad," he had said cheerfully, reclining on his bed, wearing sandals and the Hindu holy man's loin cloth, "I will ultimately find some sort of meaning in life."

Cy fled from the house, followed by the sound of his son's weird string instrument. Stumbling over mud ditches and pushing small begging hands and sewage-eating street pigs aside, he shouted for his driver who had disappeared. How many times had I thought of that miserable, middle-aged man, racing across the subcontinent, crying and pleading for help?

"Why, why does Wylie do it?" Cy had asked me, more than once, his mouth trembling, his wasted, yellow face, radiating pain. "What answer to life is there, except that there is none?"

Then one morning after a sleepless night: "Oh Janet, he was so repulsive. That dead white skin and brainless talk. And so handsome when he was growing up. Full of mischief, artistic. First he wanted to be an actor, then a writer. Shy, but smart, a good boy – at least until his mother died."

Covering his eyes as they filled with tears: "He said I killed her. That she died of a broken heart. But she had cancer, like me. *Nothing* to do with her heart. And I was a good husband. Maybe preoccupied by business. What man isn't? But not cruel. Nothing that would make a woman die."

I turned away, fussed with his bed tray, poured him more juice. "Don't think about it Cy, it won't help."

"The prodigal son came home, didn't he? They put his story in the Gospel for a reason, for fathers like me. Sooner or later, he got fed up. Wylie will too, you wait."

"Of course he will. Tomorrow, I'll bet you there will be a letter."

"No, he won't come. He won't forgive me."

"If he knew you were sick, he'd be here," I said, holding his orange juice up to his lips and hating Wylie for what he was doing to this kind, unhappy man. "I wish you'd let us hire some detectives to find him."

"No, never. I won't hire detectives to find my own son."

And so it went. He wanted Wylie to come and he didn't. Or if

18

he did, he wanted him to come of his own accord. He would have been furious if he had known about all the letters Mrs Obie had sent.

All that day, I plied the Boys with questions about Wylie, but they knew no more about his recent past than I did.

As I listened to them tell me how, after being discharged from the army (honorably, they believed, but they weren't so sure), he had begun to experiment with low-life, "hippie-thinking" and poverty, then followed some guru to an ashram, all I could think of was how much he would despise the middle-American career girl with whom his father had chosen to end his life.

When I asked the Boys to speculate on why Cy had chosen me to be his heir, they had no comments at all. As far as they were concerned, Cy's last wishes were Cy's last wishes.

"Just accept the will and be grateful," Moriarty said softly, throwing his great square head back on the Naugahyde sofa, revealing a neck that would give any bouncer pause for thought.

All things considered, it seemed to be the best advice I could get.

Later that evening, I had dinner with them in a restaurant near the old port. Over *bouillabaisse* and chilled wine, they relaxed and grew merry as they told me about Cy when he was young. Of the fun they'd had. The successes they'd known. In those days, Cy was a different person, they said. Tough, driven, boisterous, liked the girls too. A winner in every respect.

The son of an electrician from Oak Park, Illinois with maybe-maybe-not a high school diploma, he demonstrated his genius for trading from the first day he hit the commodities market. Later, when he went into speculative real estate and started setting up his various companies – Cavanaugh Southwest Industries, the CCI Company and the Chicago Mining Company – none of which he ever took public, he developed his uncanny instinct for land-buying. Which led to the main killing: the acres and acres of barren Oklahoma fields, under which oil was still quietly seeping, waiting for someone to come along and drill it.

And all of that land, every parched, scrubby inch of it, Moriarty reminded me for the third time that evening, was mine.

"You want my advice?" Tom O'Riley asked. Tall, bony, the leader of the three, he poked his narrow, sweat-drenched forehead in front of my eyes. "Enjoy it. Have a fucking ball!"

I tried. I honestly tried to enjoy my incredible reward for three months of kindness to a dying man.

But what had emerged from the rubble when Cy's money rained down on me like shrapnel from the sky, was a person whose values had nearly been destroyed.

Filled with a loneliness I'd never experienced before in my life, I clung to the nearest lifeline: my job. The first thing I did when I went back to New York was go to see Fred Hirsch, my boss at *Woman's Work*. Surely he would have insights, advice, a plan.

But after I had told him the whole story, all he said, looking at me as if I were Anastasia returned from the dead, was that I should forget about working – I couldn't possibly concentrate on the magazine – and buy myself some decent looking clothes. "If you don't mind my saying so," he said as I was leaving his office, "that raincoat you're wearing sucks."

Newspapers called me up when word of the will got out. I evaded them as best I could and refused to give any interviews. Nevertheless, I imagined people staring at me and that salespeople knew I was buying designer clothes for the first time in my life.

I did not feel I was in a "gilded cage". That term comes from an era when wealth seemed to grow out of the natural order, still had some beauty and graciousness attached to it and women who had it were known as "gentlewomen".

Whereas the heir to the hard earned oil and real estate money I had inherited was far more likely to be called a "rich bitch" and the prison this wealth produced was closer to being a Lucite one. A suffocating box: impenetrable, isolating and as oleaginous as my friends' eyes slipping away from mine as I tried to explain how inadequate I felt or asked them what they would do in my place. I was counting on them to help me. But they couldn't, wouldn't reply.

Before Cy, they had been the most important people in the world to me. All of them – journalists, photographers, a few advertising people – were honest, striving, respectable people. Like me, active in the Anti Vietnam War movement. Now mostly just liberal and ambitious, but kind, fun to be with, share problems with. But none of them, not even my copywriter friends, who were supposed to be gifted with extraordinary imaginations, could identify with my strange, ungainly problem.

As far as I could make out from their vacant stares and failure to return my phone calls, I had ceased to exist for them, vanished, as it were, from their consciousness and floated up to some mystical, higher strata of glamor where they dared not tread, nor even think about. Much easier, they apparently decided, to put me out of their minds than deal with the ugliness of envy or the awkwardness of awe.

Filled with a loneliness I'd never felt before, I flew to Chicago and telephoned Cy's widowed aunt. She invited me to tea. I talked. She stared, burst into tears and stared some more.

Still wondering what to do, knowing I should get guidance but not seeking it, trusting no one, I fled to London to check out Cy's *pied-à-terre*. It turned out to be an eight-room duplex on Eaton Square, beautifully decorated by a mistress of his in 1974 or thereabouts. Although it already contained a butler, I needed more bodies to fill it, so I rehired Mrs Obie and decided to settle there. And submit, at least for a while, to that anxious, fun-filled condition of being a woman who has everything.

Everything. Let me tick the list: my flat on Eaton Square, a villa in France, Cy's gloomy five-story townhouse in Chicago, an unfurnished apartment I bought in New York during that first trip home, cars in all those places, a 72-foot boat, moored in St Tropez, that I planned to hire a crew to sail if I ever got around to organizing such a thing, a Lear Jet sitting in a hangar in Chicago, closets and closets of clothes, an embarrassing number of fur coats and, rolled in a ball in a bottom drawer, a red fox jacket I'd bought on sale before I had left for Crete, for which I felt no nostalgia whatsoever.

In addition: Nigel Draycott, my English lover with impeccable blond hair and the body of Michelangelo's David. And a crowd of other Davids waiting in line at Annabel's, who longed to gyrate and tremble before me on their long elegant legs: "Let me show you my act, Mrs Cavanaugh. Just give me a chance." Panting, sweating, driving muscles, promising to pulsate inside me. No footmen for the Empress Catherine ever tried so hard to please.

2

It was the Queen of England who brought me to my senses, though she has no idea of this. It happened after I had been living in England for two years.

I had stayed on at Eaton Square, because London, unlike New York, had accepted me. With a little help from Lady Whitmore, a public relations person who "handled" rich, presentable foreigners who didn't know anyone, invitations poured through the mail daily. And like many multi-millionaires of lowly origins, I quickly discovered it was much pleasanter to be rich in a foreign country where one had never been poor before. The French call newly rich exiles like me *parachutistes*.

I went to almost all the parties I was invited to. Mostly because I was lonely, but also some grotesque, childish part of me loved the swift bustle of interest I created when I entered a room. "So that's Cyrus Cavanaugh's widow!" I felt them thinking. "How young she is! Will she marry? How much money was it exactly that he left her?"

I told no one the exact amount. It wasn't only the fear of kidnappers. It was the embarrassment. Nevertheless, I was delighted to be the center of their attention. My response was always gracious. I smiled. My eyes gleamed. The Merry Widow who was also Narcissus.

When I expressed a desire to see the Queen, Lady Whitmore, who knew one of the Queen's ladies-in-waiting, arranged that I be invited to a garden party at Buckingham Palace. She had also promised that I would be "presented", but that had fallen through. "These things take time, darling," she shouted through the phone in her majestic baritone, "but go anyhow. It will be a su-pah experience." Thus, I was just one of the throng staring at the Queen from a respectful distance.

Everyone, including myself, was wearing a hat. The sun was blazing. I spent most of the time sitting on a folding chair behind a white line painted on the Palace's emerald lawn which barred us from coming within thirty yards of the Royal Tent. When the Queen completed her descent through the garden, she would pass into her tent and receive her special guests. They were already lined up with blue cards in their hands and waiting patiently for her arrival.

"Do you think the Queen will be coming this way soon?" I asked the woman sitting next to me. Her eyelids were smeared with sparkling turquoise grease.

"I think so, but it takes a while for her to get through that mob around the Palace steps." Her accent was not one most Americans would associate with garden parties at Buckingham Palace. Beside us was an assortment of diffident old men with raw, ruddy faces and some women who looked like nannies.

Standing on the broad patch of lawn which separated us, the seated ones, from the Royal Tent were two men in impeccably tailored morning suits with smiling, fine-boned faces, trying not to look like watchdogs, which is what they were. They were guarding the lawn in the unlikely event one of us suddenly bolted across the white line and charged the Royal Tent.

There was a flurry to our right. The beefeaters guarding the Queen were approaching. Finally, finally, her short, waxen figure moved slowly, wearily, across the verdant enclosure. She was wearing a lavender silk coat with a matching dress, shoes, purse and what looked like lavender stockings.

The people leapt to their feet. The equerries bowed. It was impossible not to be impressed by this tiny country with its big empire-style queen. Pomp that shamelessly exceeded the circumstances, but no one minded. With her up at the top endorsing the ancient, pyramidal order, a whole nation could dream that the twentieth century wouldn't sink them.

You could see the love in the people's eyes. Their will. "Don't do, don't think, don't speak", they seemed to be saying to her. "Make us believe there are still reasons for things. With you up there, we hold on."

Her face was white, her expression, remote and solemn, but not serene. Silenced by her nation's dreams and imprisoned in privilege and class, how could she be serene? When had she ever felt free?

Whereas I, easily the second richest woman at the party, was awesomely, chaotically, unnaturally free. A member of no class, an orphan with no responsibilities and limited by no one's dreams, I could, without consulting anyone, do anything I wanted to do with the money, my time or my heart.

I was not in a Lucite box. I, not the world, had created that stifling image to keep myself from facing my incredible freedom.

And for one tense, crystalline moment, I realized that was why Cy had left me the money: to see what would happen if he made someone as free as me.

His wry, humorous smile and dimpled chin flashed through my mind. Was his gift to me some private metaphysical joke? His last challenge to humanity? Through me?

None of these were answerable questions and didn't matter. Cy was dead and I was alone on a palace lawn. What mattered was that I take hold of that freedom and use it. Fast. Before I smothered to death.

When I raised my head, the Queen was a blur of lavender silk passing into her tent; the people with blue cards were pouring in after her and my contact lenses had become grainy from squinting. Saying good-bye to the woman with turquoise eyelids, I walked quickly past the Diplomats' Tent (also barricaded with white lines), to where tea was being served in the Commoners' Tent. This is not its official name. I have invented it going on the premise that all descriptives of objects in the environs of Buckingham Palace support the class system. I picked up a cup, put it down and left.

Walking up the endless Palace stairs, trying to get used to my newly discovered freedom, I realized that I could easily give a tea like the Queen's. I could just take over Central Park and invite everyone I knew. Instead of painted white lines, a few electrified barbed wire fences where I didn't want the muggers to walk.

But why?

They called my name through the loudspeaker at the Palace gates and my limousine slid in front of me. I took off my hat, opened the rear door before anyone could do it for me and jumped in quickly.

Should I start a religion?

Buy a small, bankrupt African nation and become a queen myself? Janet the First, weighted down with beads and animal bones, thumping my foot to tribal drums?

We were caught in traffic near Hyde Park on the way over to Nigel's club in Mayfair. There was another anti-nuclear bomb rally going on in the park.

Before the bombs come, I thought, looking at my driver's red, responsible neck, I should go back to New York and start a magazine. The magazine I always wanted to work for. Original, beautiful editorials. Stunning photography. Everything I've ever wanted to say. Did it matter that millionaires' magazines always foundered?

"Save us from a nuclear holocaust!"

"Support Unilateral Disarmament!"

"Stop Deployment of Cruise Missiles in England!" It was impossible to ignore the marchers' passionate shouts and jagged placards as we drove up Park Lane. Impossible not to think about the bomb at least once a day, to dream at night of fireballs and children raising their arms to fall-out.

All over England, idealists in sports clothes and worn-out shoes were demonstrating and crying out against the arrival of cruise missiles in England. "The world is about to be annihilated!" they warned, pleaded, screamed over and over again on television, in parks and in leaflets.

And of course, they were right.

How could you argue with them? Forty years ago a mad man had created a holocaust which destroyed six million Jews. What hope was there that another maniac wouldn't screech his way to power and exterminate billions? And if not a maniac, what hope that there wouldn't be an accident in a world where statistics on human error proved that accidents were as inevitable as the passage of time?

What hope that this world – this beautiful, shining place that Cy had put at my disposal – wouldn't be blown up before I died?

Oh God, I thought, closing my eyes and the car window, how can anyone living between holocausts find a reason for doing anything with a quarter of a billion dollars?

3

"Those weren't nannies at the garden party. They were civil servants' wives or women who have done a lot of work for charities and things," Nigel said. It was five-thirty and we were alone on a sofa in the upstairs bar of his club, surrounded by gold-framed oil paintings and sinking in downy, velvet cushions. "The Queen invites a different batch every year and sprinkles a few aristocrats about." He was the third son of a baronet and prided himself on his knowledge of royal cunning. "It gives them a feeling of rubbing shoulders with their betters."

"Betters?" I asked, tediously American.

"Well, weren't they better?" His head was cocked. Mockery in his almond-shaped eyes. Asian blood somewhere which he refused to admit to. Swore he was pure Yorkshire English, but long ago, I'm sure, a Mongol nomad strayed into the British Isles and a great, great grandmother dallied too long in a field. I had ceased to bring it up. In any event, he was tall, graceful and his long, slender nose had not been affected by the secret Oriental genes.

"I don't know. I couldn't see into their souls." I loved annoying him.

He sniffed, leaned his golden head against the tapestried wall and sank deeper into the velvet cushions. *Luxe* and *volupté*, but no *calme*. He was thinking of leaving me and would never know how much I would miss him.

We had spent almost a year together. No one approved of him. But he had suited me perfectly, for he was sensual and generous and had made me happy.

"What have you and Horace been up to? Did you buy any more night clubs? Are you going to take a business trip with him?" I asked. Horace Leone was his new business partner and, Lady Whitmore had intimated the other day, his lover.

He tugged at the cuffs of his Savile Row jacket and looked

27

distracted. Before he met me, he owned one suit. Now he had four, a gold cigarette case and a Mercedes. He deserved them. "We might go to Rio," he said. "On the other hand, there's an Arab he wants to see in Monaco. When are you going to America?"

"When I decide what to do with my life."

"You could marry me."

"I mean decide what to do with the money. We could all be blown up before I find something to do."

I would have loved to have told him all the things I'd been thinking of at the garden party, "tried out" my new insights on him, rolled the word freedom around, considered Cy's motives. But Nigel and I didn't have that sort of rapport. In truth, the only person with whom I'd ever experienced that sort of intellectual intimacy had been Cy.

"You could also walk outside and get run over by a car. But you can't let thoughts like that stop you from making decisions," he said irritably. His cheeks were flushed a deep rose shade I find even more becoming in the men of England than in the women. "Why won't you believe I love you? Why can't you trust me?"

"Because I have a deep-seated, free-floating intelligence which, when provoked, I use." And suspicion growing round me like a second skin.

"It isn't because of your money."

"Of course."

He turned away wearily. Didn't even bother to argue the point through two or three more rounds. In the beginning, he would go on for an hour about how it was my body, our great sex, even my intelligence and wit, that attracted him and made him want to commit himself to me for ever. Nothing, nothing to do with the money.

Not that he knew how much there was any more than Lady Whitmore did. No one knew except Mrs Obie, who was there when the will was read, and the Boys. The latter still managed it and served "Cy's last little lady" even though they thought I was too attractive and too poor to have ever loved him. For what was there for a young woman to love (they thought), in that unhappy, agitated, slave-driving bag of old bones?

28

They were wrong. I did love him.

"Nigel, is Horace Leone in love with you? He calls and calls. Why?" I asked.

"I told you we have a new deal going."

"Carrying heroin from Burma to Teheran?"

"Nothing like that. Just buying into a few night clubs and fronting for this Arab. It's very confidential. Horace has a million fingers in every pie."

"Pudgy fingers."

"Why don't you like him? He speaks well of you."

"Men who want to steal away a woman's lover always speak well of the woman."

"Do you really want us to end?" His voice was resigned.

"No, but I'll have Dempster pack up your things. Shall he send them to Horace? Do you have his address? I've lost his card."

"Hold my things. I'll call and give you an address when I'm ready. Can't you see that working with Horace makes me independent?"

"Oh Nigel, stop. Please. Just leave me here."

"It's my club."

I rose, picked up my hat and headed for the door. My feet ached inside my English shoes. The English will never understand American feet. Near the threshold, I staggered from the pain of a blister forming near my Achilles' heel.

Nigel's long, irritable sigh traveled across the room. "What's the matter with you today?"

"Ask the Queen."

4

Dempster opened the door when I returned to Eaton Square. Cy's apartment is truly wonderful: two floors filled with graceful English antiques and grinning orientalia, all of it swathed in fading Persian rugs and heavy silk, tasseled curtains. Cy's 1974-76 mistress had not only been English and upper class, she had known her way around Sotheby's and liked her rooms heavily cluttered with priceless *objets* and nineteenth-century paintings, of which two were Turners.

"Did you have a nice time at the garden party?" Dempster asked.

"Very nice, thank you."

"You had three calls. The messages are near the phone in the study." Thanks again to the mistress who hired him, Dempster had been watching over the flat and its inhabitants since 1975. Except for his enlarged pores and rather sinister black hair, he was perfect.

"Could you bring a whiskey and some cashew nuts into the study?" I asked.

"Certainly Madam. Anything else?" He made the tiniest bow with his neck. He had thin shoulders, a high forehead and a big British jaw. Without him, I never would have learned to be a rich woman.

Two of the phone messages were from Nigel which meant he had started calling the minute I had left his club. He was not therefore impressed by my harsh words about Horace Leone and had interpreted them as proof of jealousy, which in his circles, was, I suppose, the only proof of love there was.

The third call was from Susie Raintree. She was an American in her mid-forties who was more or less happily married to an English stockbroker – pleasant friends, a pretty Georgian house in Chelsea – when this cruel debutante came along and she was abruptly dumped.

She wanted me to marry her younger brother, Lawrence Klimpt, a playwright, also in London, who was trying to write for the British stage. Unfortunately, once he had heard of Susie's plan, his creativity came to a full stop. All he could think about was his IBM going tap-tap all day in the large roomy Victorian house in Hampstead I would buy him. I am off to the side somewhere, in another room, reading quietly, brushing my hair (long, red, my best feature), waiting for him to finish the wonderful, avant-garde, soaring, non-commercial plays he has been carrying within him for years and never dared to write before. At night, after I have written all the checks, we make love in front of the fire.

Susie picked up on the first ring and invited me to dinner. Her father was in town and she had just found herself a new unattached, marriageable man, an American.

"He works at the Pentagon and is sensational." There was too much hope in her voice.

"What's he doing in London?"

"He's here to talk about the bomb of course. All the demonstrations in London have got the Pentagon climbing the walls."

"Did he tell you that?"

"No, he's very secretive, but I know I'm right. And he's rather handsome too, in a way, but very tough. All-man. I'm dressing and the men are wearing black tie. Can you come?"

I accepted with pleasure. She was a *cordon bleu* cook and, though I would have preferred her new beau to be someone less intimately involved with the possible annihilation of humanity, I wanted to be with Americans. I'd had enough of baronets' sons and tradition for one day.

Since there was still enough time to rest before going to Susie's, I went upstairs to my bedroom. The mistress had done it up with red velvet hangings on the bed, paneled walls and trailing curtains. On the fireplace, she had put two Italian painted candelabra. It reminded me of a chapel.

When I was a child, I was a Catholic, mind-beaten, doubt-infected, soul-stirred, but still living up to the Church's laws, wearily heaving my twelve-year-old body out of bed on Sunday mornings. Such agony, such drama to get to Mass rather than commit a mortal sin and invite eternal damnation. Not knowing

that, even at that age, I was opting – so innocently, so calcu-
latingly – to believe, if not in God, at least in Pascal's wager: if
there is a hereafter and the possibility of damnation, better to
abide by God's laws for one brief lifetime, rather than risk an
eternity in hell.

After four years at the University of New Hampshire, not
even Pascal could tempt me back to virtue. I became convinced
that, if I was lucky, I'd live sixty or seventy years or so and then,
like all the other organisms occupying space on this globe, I
would move on to a more boring combination of molecules and
minerals under the earth's crust. Nothing could change that.
Not all the money in the world, not a million smiling Dempsters.
Nothing except, of course, a few large bombs.

I was tired. The Queen was also probably tired after such a
long day, but she was dressed in lavender silk and had a way of
life. Respect and self-respect. No freedom, but also no doubts.
She got up in the morning and did her job and a whole nation
thanked her.

I took off my horrible shoes and garden party clothes. Should
I call Nigel at his club? Should I go to dinner at Susie's? Should
I take a hundred Nembutal?

Lying down on my bed, I closed my eyes. For months, Nigel
and I had amused ourselves there. Straight, sincere sex in the
beginning. Then every position and experiment we could think
of. He was endlessly inventive. I, endlessly willing.

"Janet can't get enough of it," Nigel had undoubtedly con-
fided to Horace Leone, shaking his head wearily, perhaps
happily.

One of the reasons Cy liked me: "You're such an animal.
Beauty *and* Beast." But capable of great restraint, he knew. I
knew. For how could the marriage be consummated? It was too
late; he was too weak, too old and dying. The best: letting my
hand rest gently in his. The most: kissing his chest, growing
thinner, feebler and more liquid, as he forced himself to animate
that mind that never stopped being grateful to me for being with
him.

"See me to the end, Janet. It won't be much longer. Can you
do that?"

"Oh yes, Cy, love, yes." Holding him as ounce by ounce,

breath by breath, he passed from urbane, witty, wise, amusing man to misery and unspeakable pain.

Oh God, I prayed, if there is a God, have Cy and my mother meet one day. On a great, white, scented cloud, with angels cascading about and sweet Mozart violins. "Hi there!" Cy says to her. "Your daughter saw me through to the end. I asked her to be with me while I faced death. I think she did it for you. To make up."

And my mother, beautiful and beatified, capable now of a great celestial forgiving, looks at him and says: "She neglected me and I was bitter. But now I have forgiven her. She was a sweet child, some of the time." (When?) "And I love her still."

There was a knock on the door. "May I come in?" It was Mrs Obie.

I jumped quickly from the bed, straightened my hair and let her in. Her eyes had blue rings and her hair was fluffed-out white. She was English with a tough, square-boned face under soft, wilting skin. Hands thickened with arthritis that belied a towel-wringing strength. Married once, she claimed, to an officer in the merchant navy. Ran away from her or died? I was never able to pin her down. She was purposefully vague. An old woman who wouldn't let me into her mind, but had promised she wouldn't leave me. In spite of the trust Cy bequeathed her, she wanted to keep housekeeping and bookkeeping. As long as there was staff, of course. Why? No real reason. She just did. She loved Cy, I believe, knew what I did for him, thanked me for that and hated Nigel.

"Dempster is leaving. I thought I should tell you before you went out," she said, walking into the middle of the room.

"He's quitting? Why?"

"Hired by an American. The domestic employment agency rang him a week ago. They want an English butler to run some think house in Colorado. Can you imagine?"

"But he's irreplaceable. We'll never find anyone as good as he is." I motioned her to sit down. As she passed, I caught the usual faint odor of Scotch. "Why didn't he tell me himself?"

"He's waiting to sign the contract first. Then he's telling you. He says he'll be working for very important professors and intellectuals. Apparently all they do is sit around and think. The whole thing sounds absurd."

"What will we do without him? He knows everything: where to buy wine, how to get caterers and drivers. What cleaners do we use? Where does the window washer come from? Do you know?"

"Obviously I know, since I pay their bills. But it's his grasp of all the details that I'll miss. And who will drive me to the chiropodist?"

"We'll double his salary. Why not? He's worth the price of two butlers."

"You don't understand, Mrs Cavanaugh. His head is completely turned. He wants to see America and be called Mr Dempster. He's going to have a staff of five under him."

"Oh shit! It isn't fair for them to steal him away." I slapped the top of the Georgian chest of drawers near the fireplace and started to pace about the room.

One can only appreciate the absurdity of this scene if one realizes that before marriage to Cy, my salary as features editor of *Woman's Work* was $15,000 a year, less taxes, which was enough to purchase my clothes at off-season sales, paint my furniture with those antiquing sets and make chicken curry dinners for my friends.

But better off. For all my economic and social constraints, I had a nebulous sense of purpose. Something to do with getting ahead so I could better myself. Always busy. Maybe a little driven. Taking night courses at New York University in political science and philosophy. Thinking of going on for a Master's degree in one or the other. Maybe disappointed that the articles I had to write and edit for those working women so like myself had nothing to do with reality, but at least getting paid for them, making money, getting promoted, *going somewhere*.

And two years later, I was stomping around yards of bedroom on Eaton Square and carrying on like a Saudi princess because I couldn't keep my butler. Money doesn't corrupt, it enrages.

"Well, it's not the end of the world," Mrs Obie said, appalled by my lack of control. Before she went to work for Cy, she was a housekeeper for Viscount someone or other. The poor woman had gone from a viscount to Cy to me. "How can we ask him to give up a brilliant future to stay here and take care of two women and . . ." She looked down at her bent, swollen hands.

"Nigel and I have broken up. He won't be staying here any more."

She looked at me with tired, skeptical eyes, but said nothing. Between her and my sexual life was a white line she would never think of stepping across.

"Oh Mrs Obie, I'm so sick of myself," I heard myself moaning. "When I saw the Queen today, I realized how unfree she is and how free I am and how awful it is that I'm so useless."

She looked distressed. "Maybe the best thing is to go back to New York," she said at last. "It might be better for you there."

"And call up my friends who will come to dinner once and never call back? That's a wonderful idea."

She bit her lip and looked at me warily. "Maybe a holiday in France would do you good."

"A holiday? I've had two years of holidays. Why on earth would I want more?" I opened my closet and pawed through my clothes. "I want to be involved in something. Doing something. Susie Raintree says that if she had my money she would create a string of beautiful resorts all over the world like that Rockefeller did. But I don't know anything about the hotel business. All I've been trained for is writing articles for women who *work* for a living."

"You should get into the arts. That's where all the good wealthy people are. I told that to Mr Cavanaugh over and over again. But he never listened. He could have been a great art collector or trustee of the biggest museums."

"I don't know enough about the art world. I can't just go barging into the Whitney Museum and say: 'I want to give you a million dollars, please make me a trustee, please be my friend.'"

"You could start as a *docenne*. You're a beautiful woman. They'd be delighted if you volunteered."

"I'm not beautiful. I'm attractive. Please, don't you start flattering me too. Anyhow, you have to train to become a *docenne* and that takes for ever. I don't have *time* for that."

"You're worried about time?" She looked at me incredulously. When she thought of my future, she saw nothing but an infinity of candle-lit dinner tables, surrounded by chatting, charming lightweights.

And while she saw me, I saw Cy, looking down from the sky, his poor spirit in agony over the dreadful mistake he had made.

"Oh, how could I have been so dumb?" he asks the shade standing next to him, who happens to be my mother.

She shakes her head in dismay. "Poor Janet. She is so blah. Do you think there is anything we can do?"

"Nothing but take the money away from her," he says.

"Can you do that?" she asks hopefully. She is wearing a navy blue crêpe dress, is gentleness and vulnerability and loves me.

"Of course we can't. She has free will. All we can do is watch and hope she'll do something worthwhile with the money."

"Maybe she could . . ." My mother's voice faded away.

She had an idea for me.

What is it mother? Please, please tell me. Come back!

5

Susie Raintree's little dinner was not a success. To begin with, the Pentagon man was a half hour late. Thus, while Susie raced from the kitchen to her bedroom, her mind effervescing with last minute thoughts on how to improve her appearance and the meal, I had to make conversation with her father.

His name was Harvey Klimpt. He was a slim, inoffensive person, a retired American banker with dyed hair, trying to hide his irritation over the mess his daughter and son had made of their lives in London. But what was a man to do? He had his own problems.

"I'm so pleased to meet you," Mr Klimpt said to me when Susie introduced us. "My daughter has told me how kind you've been to her and Lawrence."

Kind? I had done little for them. At most I'd had them to dinner a few times in my flat. Was just allowing them to be in my presence kind?

"Susie has been kinder to me," I said. "When I first arrived in London, she introduced me to tons of people."

"I hope the right people," he murmured, sending me a flaccid little wink.

"Well, they were fun," I said distantly and thought: What is "right"? When I was poor and respected everyone because I was afraid of them, they liked me because I was nice. Which didn't necessarily mean I was "right". Now people seemed to fear me more than they liked me. And though I shouldn't have been, I was still afraid. Of what? Of freedom? Of Wylie Cavanaugh puncturing his veins in Goa?

When the Pentagon man arrived at last, Susie introduced him as John. His last name, it would seem, was going to be a private matter between her and him.

He had capped teeth, big shoulders and a tight-fitting, blue ruffled shirt under his dinner jacket. A hard stubble of beard. Cheeks that maimed.

37

Susie was embarrassingly smitten by him. The man negotiated deals for nuclear weapons that could annihilate us all and she couldn't care less. He was single and she was lonely and all that bomb stuff was exciting, if not glamorous, and really over her head, which was another way of saying it didn't matter.

"Before John came to London, he was in Africa," Susie said chattily. "In Zambezi."

"Where?" Mr Klimpt and I asked simultaneously.

"Zambia, not Zambezi," John said stoically. "Southern Africa. Copper mines."

"Ah yes. Don't they have uranium too?" Mr Klimpt asked, innocently enough.

John's dark cheeks stiffened and his mouth closed over his gleaming teeth. I was afraid he was going to get up and walk out. They couldn't all be that bad at the Pentagon, I thought. Some must look like George Bush.

"We can't discuss things like that with John." Susie sent her father a pleading, desperate look.

Trying to ease the tension, I said: "I've only been to Africa once, but I think it's the most beautiful place in the world." Which was true. I did. It was one of the few authentic feelings I had left.

"I've never been to Africa. John, the next time you go to Zambia, would you take me along?" Susie asked playfully.

He turned away, refusing to acknowledge such an imbecilic request.

Mr Klimpt looked dully at John, then at me. I was definitely the lesser of the two evils. "Tell us about your trip to Africa, Janet," he said.

"I went to Nairobi for *Woman's Work*, where I used to work as an editor. We were doing an article on the new African working woman."

"Did you go into the bush?" he asked.

"I only had time to go to Treetops. I loved seeing the animals, hearing the sounds at night, all that life . . ."

"Africa is the asshole of the earth," John announced abruptly. Then yawned. A soft pink tongue in a big gray jaw. How could they have let him out of America?

38

Susie looked at him anxiously. "Let's save Africa for later. Dinner's ready."

Susie was close to hysteria. To begin with, she had hired a waiter whom she could ill afford. But she wanted to sit serenely looking her best at the head of the table, as she did in the days when she had reigned as Raintree's wife. It was a memory she had to re-enact every now and then and required more than a little courage, but she would have been better off sweating over a stove in the kitchen, banging plates and pounding veal.

Like too many women I knew, she was at the breaking point. Oh, the pain. It does seem to me that women have more pain. This is not a complaint about my own life. I do not have the right to include myself in such a lament. I am – at least in the world's eyes – outside this pain. But I saw it in Susie that night, felt her despair, recognized her bravery and knew neither of the two men sitting beside her had any idea of what was going on in her poor frantic heart.

How awful to marry well, make the nicest friends, and then wind up with pillowy puffs under the eyes, a flat that was too small, alone, except when someone like John came along and interrupted that treacherous peace that comes from being useless and unscheduled. She hoped he would marry her. She thought he could *save* her.

Knowing this, I hated this man who hated Africa and loved bombs and hoped the British would spit in his eye.

"He's very high up in the Pentagon and an expert on those medium-sized missiles that America wants to put in Europe and aim directly at Russia," she had told her father and me in hushed, reverent tones before he had arrived.

Poor, lost Susie Raintree. She had as few convictions as Nigel, but none of his style. And no one to turn to except her father, who sat helplessly watching her come apart in front of that self-important, unshaven example of official brutality. And observing this, her new American friend, Janet Megabucks Cavanaugh: childless, free, ten years younger, but as confused by our inalienable right to the pursuit of happiness as she.

6

"So you're abandoning us, Dempster?"

"I'm afraid so, Madam."

It was the next day. I was with Dempster in the drawing-room and the July sky had turned a mid-winter gray.

"Do you think you'll be happy with those old men in their think tank?"

"The gentleman who interviewed me was very pleasant."

"You have no idea how awful it is in Colorado. Full of Colonel Saunders diners and cheap little ranch houses. The newspapers only publish local news and you can't buy double cream and no one respects anyone." I had never been to Colorado and was not sure all of this was true. But I wanted to worry him.

"I'm looking forward to eating American food. The steaks especially. And the countryside is beautiful. I've seen pictures of the mountains."

"They'll obliterate your dignity. You'll end up wearing shirt sleeves at the dinner table and chewing gum and all you'll think about is making money."

He smiled happily. Apparently I was describing goals and a life style he had been secretly cherishing in his soul for years – that same soul which, I had foolishly imagined, possessed the rectitude and consistency of whatever it is that animates grandfather clocks. How was I to know that all the time he worked for Cy, then me, his black pellet eyes were fixed on that distant dream of living in Sitcom USA?

"Look, I know you want to get to America early and tour a little before you start your job. I'll give you your salary for the month and you can leave tomorrow." Who was I to fight the American dream? I was one of its major beneficiaries.

"That's very kind," he murmured in funereal tones, but little blips of joy were visible in his right temple. "Will you be all

40

right? With Mrs Obie going to Ireland this August, I thought maybe you'd want me to stay on."

"I can manage. In fact, I want to be alone."

"I don't know how to thank . . ."

"By the way, Mr Draycott won't be staying with us anymore. Could you pack his clothes and get them delivered to his new address?"

Nigel had come to a few decisions the night before. That morning he'd asked to speak to Mrs Obie and told her that he had decided to go to Mr Leone's. This should have come as no surprise to anyone. But it did surprise me. I was expecting an interim address: a hotel or his family's house in Yorkshire. How can he travel from bed to bed like that? I had indignantly asked Mrs Obie. Oh, but he could. We all can.

"Is there anything else, Madam?"

I flipped the lid of the cigarette box in front of me. "Dempster, if I started a think tank in the United States, would you come and work for me?" The question and the thought came from nowhere.

"I beg your pardon?"

"I would call it the Institute for Magnanimous Thought." Also from nowhere. Or from my mother. Was I then going to start hearing voices? Better than silence.

He laughed, then froze. "That's very interesting, Madam."

"Would you come?"

"But I've already signed the contract with the other group."

"Job contracts can be broken."

"Yes, I imagine so. Yes, indeed." He did a little shuffle and warily waited to see if any more fantasies would come pouncing out of my brain.

He left and I wasted no time. *Magnanimous.*

Bumping my leg against a table in the hallway, I raced into the study and searched for the dictionary. This is what I read about the beautiful word that had flooded my mind:

MAGNANIMOUS. adj. (L. fr. magnus, great+animus, mind.)

1. Great of mind; elevated above what is low, mean or ungenerous.

2. Dictated by or exhibiting nobleness of soul; honorable.

When it's a question of values, I asked myself, suddenly excited, almost trembling, why not start at the top with magnanimous?

7

In August, shortly after Mrs Obie left for Ireland, Nigel came back. A man with whom one has enjoyed excellent sex always comes back. Unlike pain, a good orgasm is remembered for ever.

He did not telephone before he arrived. Just appeared one evening at nine. I was in a bathrobe, looking at television. No makeup, sallow skin, everything but my hair in curlers.

He was exquisite. Less swagger and more sweetness. Almost vulnerable.

"Glad to find you alone," he said, after I had brought him into the drawing-room. "Where's Dempster?"

"He quit and Mrs Obie is in Ireland."

"Who's taking care of you?"

"I'm taking care of myself. It's an ancient craft I picked up when I was poor."

"There's not a soul around. What made you stay in London during August?"

"I felt like being alone," I said, noticing that he was wearing one of the business suits I had given him in the days when I had hoped that I could talk him into getting a job. Why he chose that evening to wear this evidence of my failure, I will never know. "Lady Whitmore wanted me to rent a villa with her in Marbella so she could introduce me to all those deposed Middle European dukes and princes that hang out there."

"That might have been nice."

"With the understanding that I pay for everything, of course."

He raised his eyebrows.

"Well you don't expect her to like me for myself, do you?" I left him to get a bottle of champagne from the refrigerator. To celebrate.

"What do you do with yourself all day?" he asked when I returned.

"Sit through movies twice, walk through parks, look at the people demonstrating against the bomb."

43

"I'm so sick of hearing about the bomb."

"You'd be twice as sick if you met Susie Raintree's new man. Susie told me that he's in Germany right now helping to organize the new Pershing 2 missiles that can get rid of Russia in eight to ten minutes."

"As fast as that?"

"Not before the Russians retaliated, of course. I'd say that, all told, it would take about an hour, maybe two, to finish off the whole world or at least the northern hemisphere."

"It's appalling."

"I feel like joining the marchers."

"And waving a manicured fist?" He uncrossed his pin-striped covered legs and sighed. "I hate this city in the summer. I've got to get away."

"And leave Horace?" I asked, irked that he had changed the subject, but not saying I was, realizing I was as vulnerable as he was. Did I also look sweet?

"There's a chance we might go to Rio together. On the other hand, he has some business to do in America. I'm not sure where we'll go."

"Whither thou goest . . ."

"I would have gone with you anywhere. I would have devoted my entire life to you. I loved you."

"Nigel, don't toy with your emotions or mine," I said as calmly as I could. If he was telling the truth and I refused to believe in his love, what did that make me? What new sin – new isolation – was waiting out there for me?

"There are only two people in the world who ever loved me, Cy and my mother, and both of them are dead."

He walked over to where I sat. His hand landed on my shoulder and rested there. None of the pleading, kneading movements he usually performed so skillfully. Just a solemn plunking of a male hand on a trembling female shoulder. "I meant what I said. I love you."

"Enough to go to an anti-nuclear bomb demonstration with me?"

"Those people are fools," he said petulantly. "And so shoddy. Half of them have pink hair."

"But they're *right*. Sooner or later there will be a nuclear war if there is no disarmament. One day there will be this earth with green trees and animals and Horace Leone on it, and the next day, because of a finger on a button, there will be this gray spinning thing, which after a few years of smoking and belching will look like the moon."

"Not likely though. Deterrence works," he said, sitting down and slipping his ankle around mine. "There hasn't been a world war since 1945."

"All that proves is that no one has come along who thinks he can win a nuclear war."

"Reagan and Andropov are rational men."

"Possibly. But what happens when another mad man comes along?"

"Like Qadhafi in Libya? He doesn't have the power to do any real damage."

"I don't mean in a little country. I mean a maniac in Russia or America or China, like Stalin or Hitler. What guarantee do we have that one of the big nuclear powers won't produce another one, who, because his little band of scientists has achieved some technological edge, thinks he can *win* a nuclear war?"

"Because no one will let a mad man get his finger on the button."

"*If* they know he's mad."

"Look, if we didn't have the bomb, England would be a communist satellite by now and America probably would be too. How would you like to see your money being used for the betterment of the Russian people? Aren't you happier being one of the prettiest capitalists in the world?" His hand stole around my shoulders and deftly encircled my breast.

"Horace doesn't amuse you enough?"

"Horace is not my lover. You were the one who decided he was."

"You never denied it."

"Of course I did. You didn't listen."

"You didn't deny it with any verve. You just accepted my accusations. Another man might have threatened to kill me."

"I didn't feel like fighting. Either you trusted me or you didn't."

"Well, I still don't trust you."

He shrugged. I wanted to shake him. Sighing, he stood up, lit a cigarette and wandered over to the fireplace.

Finally: "Horace calls me 'tiger'. That's his name for me." He took several melancholy drags from his cigarette. "Tiger."

"Did the name apply to your behavior in bed or your aggressiveness in business?"

"I don't know." His voice was desolate. "I think he means 'tiger' in general." He looked at the stopped tortoise shell clock over the fireplace. His hair had just the right waves around his ears, which were just the right size. His long hands, long body, long and fine, made me frantic with ambivalence. And, of course, passion.

"Could I ever stay the night?" he asked softly.

So sad. Him and his request. But sad in the way the death of animals is sad. We don't like it, but we accept it without rage.

"Oh Nigel, I would like to but, but . . ." I was stuttering. Perhaps he wasn't a tiger, but one thing was certain: I was a rabbit. A rabbit with a pink, twitching nose, searching for tidbits of love.

"Did you really love me, Nigel?"

"Maybe. Maybe I just said that. I know I love all this." He waved his hand around the lovely drawing-room. "But Horace has almost this much wealth and I don't love Horace."

"So by a process of elimination, you figured you loved me?"

"Is that awful?"

"Yes, Nigel, it's awful, but come to bed. Let's take the champagne and go upstairs. Isn't that what you want? In the morning, I'll send you back to Horace. You waited until Horace left London before you dared come over here. Isn't that true? Please don't answer that."

I held out my hand to him and we went upstairs.

His arms glided around my waist and undid the sash of my robe as I lit the candles. It was easy. You live with the thought of the nuclear holocaust the same way you live with the thought of death. You put it in the back of your brain where it can't contaminate the other cells and you get on with things.

He popped the champagne cork, undressed me, then himself.

He filled up his tiny gold spoon with cocaine and his noble, slender nostrils tightened and collapsed inward as grain by grain, the magic flared through his body.

Oh Nigel, beautiful tiger Nigel, so new to me, as new as my red velvet room. Nothing too animal, nothing too moist. Affirming our bodies over and over again, enclosing ourselves in a universe that was getting smaller and smaller until soon, our minds would inhabit only that space our limbs were able to fill and we had nothing but flesh for words and flesh for thought.

After he left, promising to call me that evening (he didn't), I got dressed and went for a walk in Hyde Park.

Hardly anyone was around except the unemployed and tourists in shirt sleeves, plodding through aging chrysanthemums, spoiled grass and the detritus from yesterday's anti-bomb rally.

I was as sick of thinking about the bomb as Nigel was. Then why couldn't I stop caring? Why couldn't I accept it the way he and Susie and the rest of the world seemed to have done?

"If you don't like what you're doing, choose it," one of those self-help people in the 'seventies used to say. His theory: if you're doing something, you've already chosen it. So you may as well admit it and not add to your misery by claiming that you didn't.

Okay, I told myself, sitting down on a bench opposite a Japanese couple about to be strangled in camera straps, I *choose* deterrence. I choose to risk a nuclear holocaust rather than have the Russian boot in my face and be made to work a twelve-hour day as a street cleaner and live with four or five gray, drunken people in a one-room apartment that smells of cabbage.

I would rather risk blowing four billion people off the globe than live in a society which would, if I criticized it, have me sent to Siberia where I would face starvation, minus 30° Fahrenheit weather and probably flogging, because, never forget, the Russians are also wife beaters.

Because I *love* my money. I love my flat on Eaton Square, my yacht and airplane I never use. I love being a citizen of a free country and knowing I can call up John, the Pentagon man, and tell him to stuff it without worrying about being sent to an insane asylum. I love knowing that tomorrow I can start a new political party or a religion dedicated to God, the devil or, if I felt so inclined, myself.

When you're that free and that rich, it's *normal*, it's *correct* to want to keep your society as it is and not see it overthrown by a gang of thick-necked, bellicose, Slavic thugs who hate you.

So you sacrifice the world.

You say fuck you to the communists and shake your big nuclear cock at them and pay in dread as your country creates more and more ways to squeeze nuclear energy out of atoms which would make everyone's money, freedom and political philosophy terribly beside the point.

It started to rain. Big, warm, August droplets fell on my hands and skirt. The Japanese couple scurried away, shielding their heads with a London street map.

I didn't move. I *chose* to be rained on.

But I didn't choose the bomb. The trouble with that self-help exercise was that when it came to nuclear weapons, it didn't apply. They were chosen for me. True, I was helping to pay for them, but I did not choose them. Saying I did was not a way to relieve misery, but to add to it.

My choice was to see the bomb destroyed, *not* humanity. Most of all, my choice was to have the word "future" return to its old pre-Hiroshima meaning and not signify something which was contingent. Maybe other people could walk around thinking that sooner or later they'd be burnt alive or die of radiation, but I personally found it intolerable.

Was that so peculiar?

A taxi cruising on the road twenty feet from my park bench slowed to a stop. The driver pointed mournfully at my hair, which was almost drenched, and opened the rear door of the cab. I gave up and got in.

Back in the flat, the first thing I noticed was a hairpin on the floor in the entrance hall. Before we had gone upstairs, but after he had refused to march in a demonstration with me, Nigel had unpinned my hair.

Should I join the marchers? I asked myself again. Should I shout their slogans, camp out on air force bases, carry candles in the night, even though I knew, Nigel knew, everyone knew that demonstrating has no real effect on anything happening in NATO, the Pentagon or the Kremlin?

Surely a woman with a quarter of a billion dollars could do better than that. Someone must have a better idea for me than that.

But no one had a better idea.

What was needed was an idea.

A single true idea that would inspire nuclear disarmament in the West *and* the East. An idea as powerful and startling as All Men Are Created Equal. For hadn't that concept inspired the American revolution and dozens of other revolutions around the world, including the one that added the words, "and women" to that thought? Hadn't its success in the past two hundred years proven that nothing is as powerful as an idea?

Certainly the time had come for an even bigger concept.

But would it come in time? Would the maniac wait?

And who would discover it? Not a journalist from New Hampshire. Not the architects of NATO's nuclear policy or any of the friendly fellows in the Pentagon. Great ideas were produced by geniuses with brilliant, generous, disinterested creative minds. Not by frightened men facing an enemy's arsenal of weapons similar to one's own.

And that was when I had *my* idea.

Standing by the stereo, looking for a tape to play and thinking how nice it would be to see Dempster at the door asking me if I'd like some hot coffee, it came to me.

What if, I thought, a group of the most creative geniuses in the world were fed, lodged and cosseted for months and months so they could concentrate all their intellectual powers on finding that one beautiful magnanimous idea that could save humanity from exterminating itself?

What if I used my money to organize and finance such a gathering of geniuses?

Somewhere on this earth, there had to be brilliant, creative people who would be willing to perform such an experiment. I couldn't be the only person who believed in the power of ideas. And of those who did, some had to long for disarmament as much as I did. My idea wasn't absurd. It could be done.

The Institute of Magnanimous Thought, I had said to Dempster.

Had that been my mother's message?

8

"I've decided to change my life," I told Mrs Obie when she returned from Ireland in September.

We were in the drawing-room. After she had unpacked her bags, I had invited her to have a sherry with me. (Though I knew she had already had a couple of Scotches from the little flask she carried with her on trains.)

There was a strange new elated look in her eyes. The petal-soft skin seemed firmer, the cheeks a fresh pink color that did not come from alcohol. The sister she'd been visiting was sixty-seven. She was sixty-four. No matter how deeply felt, a relationship between two sisters of those ages does not put color in the cheeks. Had Mrs Obie met a man? Was she planning to leave me too? The only way to deal with that possibility was to ignore it.

"I'm going to start a think tank," I said, filling her glass.

"Like Dempster's? Why?"

"To analyze pressing world problems," I replied, purpose-fully vague, for I had also decided that no one should know the extent of my ambition until the project was well under way.

"But if you have trouble organizing your own life, how can you organize the world? I mean . . ." Her voice trailed off. She was rarely so bold. Yes, definitely, something had happened in Ireland.

She shrank back into her sherry and waited for my anger to emerge. I could fire her on the spot, but there was no danger of that.

"Because from now on my life is organized," I said calmly.

Her eyes wandered as she ran her finger down the leg of the side table near her. Discovering dust, she nervously began to rub it into a ball. "I shouldn't have left you alone. I'll hire another cleaning woman right away."

"Don't bother. We're going back to America soon."

51

"I thought you didn't . . . Where would this think tank be? New York?"

"No, I thought of somewhere in Connecticut or Massachusetts. I want it to be in an isolated spot in the country."

"Do you want me to be there?"

"Of course. I wouldn't dream of not involving you. You could run things. There will be a lot of staff: gardeners, chamber maids, typists."

Her face softened as she considered this administrative role. "It would be nice to be in the country. What sort of place would it be?"

"I want a large, peaceful, old estate that I can remodel. Most scholars have led Spartan lives and been deprived of luxury. I want to give them everything they've ever wanted: meals cooked by a French chef, large rooms, eiderdown quilts, big salaries. It will take a lot of money."

"Out of capital?"

"That goes without saying."

"The Boys will be upset." She chuckled at this.

"It's my money. In any event, I'm sure I can get some sort of tax break if I set it up as a non-profit corporation. That should appeal to them."

"What exactly do people in a think tank do?"

"Solve problems, write forecasts, think. At *Woman's Work*, we used to have brainstorming sessions when we planned new issues. Ideas would just pour out of us. Our minds worked faster. Why wouldn't it be the same for geniuses? Only instead of solving editorial problems, I'd be paying great minds to tackle the biggest problems of the world."

"Like Frederick the Great summoning Voltaire to Prussia!" Mrs Obie exclaimed. Not critically. A new biography of Frederick the Great had been reviewed in *The Times* that morning.

"Or Mad King Ludwig," I said. "A lot of people are going to say I'm acting on a spoiled, rich woman's whim or that I've gone crazy. Fine. I'm prepared for that. But the truth is I feel saner than I've felt in two years."

"What sort of people would you find?"

"Nobel Prize candidates. Eminent scientists. Political thinkers.

The best academics. Of all different nationalities." Anyone, I thought, not involved in existing anti-nuclear groups. They were too committed to lobbying and demonstrating to be interested in what I had in mind.

"But how can you get them to drop whatever they're doing to come and . . . talk?"

"I'll pay them more than they can get anywhere else. I'll offer them $80,000. That's twice as much as most college professors make in a year."

She frowned. "You said they lived Spartanly. Would money mean that much to them?"

"I rather think it does, we'll see. Maybe some would come just to get away from their families. Or maybe they'll be the most idealistic people in the world. Anyhow, the whole thing is an experiment."

"The Boys will try to talk you out of it."

"Why? Is giving these people money any stranger than Cy disinheriting his only son and making me his heir?"

"The Boys don't see you the same way as they saw him. He made his own money."

"Well, the money's mine now. I've already got a name for it, by the way. I'm going to call it the Institute for Magnanimous Thought."

"It sounds like one of those churches founded by Americans." She crossed her arms over her bosom. Her sherry glass was empty.

"Really? I hadn't intended that. What would you suggest I name it?"

"The vaguer the name, the more room for changing your mind later, like those corporations that Mr Cavanaugh used to have. One year they were involved in plastics, the next year it was refineries."

"I could name it after Cy. But what if it failed?"

"How can it fail when all you're producing is ideas?"

"How about the Cyrus Cavanaugh Institute for Magnanimous Thought?"

"Perfect! Only I'd leave out the last three words."

I didn't bother to argue. She was right. Magnanimity and nobleness of mind were *verba non grata* today. Something smaller

and more specialized was in fashion. Yet magnanimous was
what I wanted the geniuses to be, with minds opened wide, able
to think on a grand eighteenth-century scale. Like Kant. Huge,
powerful thoughts like the Categorical Moral Imperative. Other
ages had produced arrogance like his. Ours could too. *Must.*
Where had intellectual modesty led us except to the threshold of
death?

Mrs Obie looked pensively across the dining-room through
the French doors. The leaves on the trees in Eaton Square were
already turning yellow and falling. "You know, it's not such a
mad idea. I think Mr Cavanaugh might have liked it."

"Maybe the little drug addict in India won't have the last
laugh after all," I said.

She sighed a directionless, old-woman sigh that made me
think of the moors of England.

9

The nice thing about being a very, very rich former magazine editor is that, not only have you learned how to delegate, you have the money to hire the people to whom you can delegate. Thus, when you come up with a weird, unwieldy goal like starting a think tank, you can move into action right away.

My first step was to tell the Boys about it. Not convince them. Not plead for their understanding. Just tell them.

Since Tom O'Riley was the strongest and most argumentative of the three, I called him first. If he bent gracefully to my will, Moriarty and Byrne would follow suit.

"I'm going to be spending about three million dollars more than I'd planned."

"You buying a couple of castles or something?" He groaned. "We were planning to buy into a venture in the Western Sahara. You know pink mealy tomatoes? Well, we found out we can grow an old-fashioned red tomato in Egypt for practically nothing. If we put enough money in this year, we could control the United States tomato market by 1987."

"Tom, I think tomatoes are wonderful, but you'll have to invest a little less than you planned. I'm starting a think tank. Since I'll be hiring and lodging some of the best minds in the world, I don't intend to stint."

There was a long pause and the sound of a cigarette being lit. Then, from a great spiritual distance: "This a Woman's Lib idea?"

"No, it's a much bigger idea than that. I want to meet you in New York and talk about it."

"Is your New York apartment furnished yet? You're paying a lot of maintenance on it, you know."

"I'll furnish it later. What I'm talking about now is more important."

"Whyn't you just enjoy yourself?"

"I am enjoying myself. After I hang up, I'm calling Dr Heilbronner, a professor I had at university, and asking him to find a researcher to write up a detailed report on think tanks – their capitalization, size, salaries, results – everything. I'll have a copy sent to you, Byrne and Moriarty. Then we can have a meeting in New York to discuss it."

Another tired pause. "What kind of problems do you want to analyze?"

"I'd like our meeting to be three weeks from today. I'm going to call it the Cyrus Cavanaugh Institute, by the way."

"Reminds me, I just got a letter from Wylie Cavanaugh. He's in the us and wants a loan."

"We haven't finished talking about the think tank."

"Yes we have. You're having a study done and in three weeks we all meet in New York. What else is there?"

"You mean you'll help me?" I was stunned. Until then I – and certainly Mrs Obie, too – had expected him to try to talk me out of it. But both she and I had forgotten that three million dollars simply wasn't enough money to matter.

"Sure I'll help. I like the name you've chosen for it by the way. It can't do any harm. We'll – I mean you and I – will make sure it doesn't."

"Good. Now tell me about Wylie. His letters are always a delight and a surprise."

We received his first letter after Tom hired detectives to track him down in Nepal and tell him of his father's death and the terms of his will. Writing in a tiny, precise hand, that I doubted was his own, Wylie had informed us that he would honor his father's last wishes, had no desire to contest the will and would spend the rest of his life in the East. Two more letters arrived during the two Christmases that followed. In the same neat handwriting, he sent his best wishes to me for the holidays, adding that he hoped I was continuing to enjoy my inheritance. No threats, no overt malice, but the sight of those missives made my skin shrivel. My reply to each was to have $10,000 sent to him. Not out of generosity.

"He asks that we deposit $50,000 for him in a bank in Bermuda."

"Did he give any explanation why he wanted so much money? I thought he slept on a bed of nails and wore rags?"

"He didn't say why. Moriarty said he heard from someone else's nutcase kid in India that Wylie was making movies, but I doubt if it's true. If you ask me he wants the money to pay for drugs. Question is, do you want to support his habit?"

"I don't have much choice, do I?"

"Sure you do. Just say no. He drove his father crazy for thirty-five years. He'll do the same to you."

"Tom, giving him $50,000 is not driving me crazy. Send it before he tries to come and get it. But tell him that if he contacts me in any way, we'll never give him money again. No, don't tell him that. He'll know I'm afraid of him. Say nothing. Just keep him away from me."

Even though I had never seen a photograph of him (Cy had destroyed all pictures of him in a fit of rage after the Goa meeting), I had a clear mental picture of Wylie: a tall, limp-muscled man in his mid-thirties with bad skin and the sly, self-indulgent look of the heroin addict. For it had to be heroin. Cocaine was not destructive enough for someone with his determination to drive his father mad with grief.

Not long after Cy died, I had a recurring nightmare where I come home, open the front door on Eaton Square and Wylie is sitting there, with his white, crazy face and glazed, jealous eyes. He reaches a fluid, snake-like hand into my purse and laughs, weeps, screams out his hate for me, his father, and the world that had cheated him of love.

Addicts terrified me. Wylie Cavanaugh terrified me and the further the Boys kept him away, the better.

"Want me to find out what Wylie is really up to?" Tom was asking me.

"No. Just give him the money. But you can tell me one thing: how well did Mrs Obie know him?"

"Pretty well. She came to work for Cy when his wife died and Wylie was only about twelve. Why?"

"I was just wondering. She hates it when I talk about him. Did she like him?"

"I guess so. We all did in a way. He was a cute kid. It was when he became an atheist at goddamn Chicago University that he started to change. After Vietnam, he was a different person. Horrible to see."

"I hope I never do."

"Mrs Obie was as fed up with him as we were when he came home from Vietnam. You worried about something?"

"No."

"You don't have to be afraid of him, you know. He was like a vegetable."

"I'm not afraid."

"Good. So, we'll see you in three weeks."

I hung up and gazed dully at the dark green walls of the study. Glee was first. Then confidence, great gusts of it, pushing me forward out of the study into the hall.

"Mrs Obie," I shouted, running to the foot of the stairs. "We're on. Tom's going to help with the think tank."

I ran back into the study to call Dr Heilbronner.

Life had begun again.

I was rising on wings.

New York

1

You can't help loving New York when you cross the Triboro Bridge on a sunny day. You're cruising along in a car and suddenly you're part of that great leap of steel reaching into Manhattan's stone madness. And all around you, you see that glare bounding off the river and the asphalt, and finally, in the whites of your eyes, gleaming at you in the rear-view mirror. And somehow, anything seems possible and nothing too late.

Leaning back in the heavy, navy blue limousine, the length and power of which were as mad as the island we were approaching, but also comfortable and reassuring, I crossed my legs and grinned at Mrs Obie.

At last, I was a woman with a purpose and a plan. I had spent my last weeks in London buried in books and articles on nuclear weapons. Even though I had been dutifully skimming the reports on the nuclear situation for years, there were hundreds more things to learn. But no matter how deeply I delved into that gruesome and opaque information or increased my vocabulary of lethal, technological terms, the more convinced I became that whether you knew what particle beam weapons were or how many warheads could dance inside an ICBM, the larger picture didn't change. The truth remained that the destiny of the planet was in the hands of a few men who hated each other more than they loved you.

"Are you glad you came?" I asked Mrs Obie.

She nodded stoically. She hated flying and did not look forward to seeing the Boys who, if all went according to plan, would be coming to the Regency the following morning for a breakfast meeting in my suite. We would have hot coffee, croissants and some delicious jam from Fortnum & Mason which she had packed in her suitcases between the folds of her sensible underwear, along with pencils, pads and a tape recorder.

"Did you find a stenographer?" I asked. Whenever I attended

a meeting set up by the Boys, there was always a girl present who took notes in shorthand and answered the phone. I had decided to have a stenographer too and give my meeting the same formal business-like tone.

"It's done. I called a secretarial agency before we left London." She had also hired a French couple to watch over the apartment in London while we were gone, had had a new burglar alarm system installed, flown to France to make sure the villa was okay and arranged for the boat to be chartered. She was indefatigable and I didn't know what I would have done without her.

"Tonight, I'll have dinner sent up to the room and we'll read the opus on think tanks," I said, referring to the report that Professor Heilbronner had farmed out to a young researcher. It would be waiting for us in the suite.

"How long is it?" Mrs Obie asked.

"He said about seventy-two pages."

She winced.

"We've got to hire someone to start looking for property right away," I went on. "I favor Long Island because of the ocean, but it doesn't sound as serious as Connecticut or Massachusetts, does it?"

"They're going to have even more trouble believing it's serious when they see you."

"I know. I'm sure people would prefer me to be the bony, haughty widow of some elder statesman. But it can't be helped. I'm nice looking and a redhead. If I weren't, Cy would never have noticed me and I wouldn't have millions of dollars to spend on humanity."

The chauffeur swooped the limousine into the shortest lane as we approached the toll booth. Mrs Obie tapped the window that separated us from him. "Get a receipt for that please," she ordered. She loved receipts. I had no idea what she did with them.

"Those geniuses are going to be suspicious of you," she said. "You're so terribly young."

"And lonely. They'll smell that right away. Too bad. I want to participate. When and if they come up with their idea, I want to be there, on the premises."

"I hope you don't get involved with any of them."

"I won't. I promise you that. If I start feeling deprived, I'm sure I can find myself another faithless Englishman."

She looked away in embarrassment and clutched her pocket-book in which was her usual flask of Scotch.

The suite at the Regency Hotel was more than adequate. Thick, silencing carpeting. A large living-room with a Queen Anne style table that opened to seat six. Decent sofas. Two bedrooms and three bathrooms.

After waiting forty-five minutes for drinks to be sent up, Mrs Obie suggested that she run around to Sherry Lehmann's to stock up on Scotch, vodka, and cognac, "for guests".

We had dinner in the suite while I read the report, passing her the pages as I finished them. It was typed double space. All very dry. Miss Ellen Taylor, the researcher who had written it, was no journalist, but she would go far in the business of dream deflation.

The most depressing conclusion in Section One was that think tanks were out of fashion due to their failure to predict the oil crisis in 1973. After this enormous loss of face, their credibility had deteriorated remarkably.

The think tanks most in the news in the 'eighties were conservative ones like the American Enterprise Institute and the Hoover Institute. Ronald Reagan was an honorary member of the latter which was founded in 1919. Its original goal: "to demonstrate the evils of the doctrines of Karl Marx". Its archives contained "the files of the czarist secret police and documents on radical political movements in Europe, Asia and Africa".

I looked up from my too zestfully peppered pepper steak. "We need archives, Mrs Obie."

"Archives?"

"They'd give us a lot of prestige." I noted the word, archives, on a small pad I had placed near my butter plate and read on.

Liberal, Democratic think tanks like the Brookings Institute and IPS were respected but not getting the same media attention as their Republican counterparts. Whereas our military think tanks, which were funded by the government, got almost none at all. Nor did they want it. Little was known about them except that they employed thousands of people, had yearly budgets that exceeded $40 million and that germ and nuclear warfare were their main concerns. Worst fact: they were not accountable to Congress but to the Pentagon.

"Would you mind if I read this later?" Mrs Obie asked. "I'm awfully tired."

I looked up from the manuscript, surprised at her plaintive tone. Her face was mauve with fatigue and too much wine. "Of course, yes, you need your sleep. I'll tell you everything that's in it." I put my hand on top of her gnarled, red one. I liked her more and more. She had no idea, but it was true.

She looked at me gratefully. She felt she needed my permission to go to bed, which unnerved me.

Picking up the report, I went into my room. It was decorated with gleaming Louis xvi facsimiles in a great bath of celadon green silk. Even the walls were of the same serene, comfortless color.

It was an effort to keep reading. Miss Taylor's prose was as pale and uniform as gravel on an empty road. On page forty-two, however, my interest picked up when she described "independent" think tanks. Unlike the big conservative and liberal institutes who were financed by specific power groups, these smaller tanks claimed to receive their funds from several clients with differing political views. Of these, the best known was the Hudson Institute, founded by the great, obese "futurist", Herman Kahn, who had started his career at the government-controlled Rand Corporation and thought up the idea of creating a "doomsday machine". This inexpensive, easy-to-make military contraption would automatically launch a retaliatory strike in the event the Russians attacked and we suddenly got too soft-hearted to push the button that would annihilate the world. Kahn did not recommend the creation of such a machine (that was not his job); however, he did estimate its cost and carefully consider its viability.

The Center for the Study of Democratic Institutions in Santa Barbara was another independent think tank. It had always fascinated me because its founder, Robert Maynard Hutchins, who was once president of the University of Chicago, had spearheaded a movement to revive Thomist philosophy in the forties. I had always pictured his California think tank as being dedicated to the purest of thought, motivated by the highest of intentions.

But according to Miss Taylor, Hutchins used to raise money by laundering it. Bernie Cornfield, the ios swindler, financed one of the Center's meetings in Geneva. Hutchins himself was no prize either. "The failure of the Center," she wrote, "is directly attributed to Hutchins's arrogant personality. As long as he was running it, the country's most brilliant thinkers would not have anything to do with it. Its most notable scholar was Alex Comfort, author of *The Joy of Sex*."

I put down the report and stared at my face in the mirror opposite the bed. It had turned celadon green. The euphoria I had felt on the bridge was fading. If Hutchins couldn't put together a decent think tank, how could I?

I flipped impatiently through the rest of the report. The biggest spender in research in America is the United States government. The total Research and Development budget projected for 1982 was $41.7 billion. Defense and military research received $20 billion of that. Little health and human services received $4.2 billion.

Also: the correct name for think tank was Research Institute.

Overall, it was a dry, influence-peddling world Miss Taylor described, thoroughly infested with bureaucrats who moved from government jobs to think tanks with each changing administration. She called the men at Brookings, "the Democratic government in exile" and reminded the reader that the majority of Reagan's second-string advisors had been recruited from conservative think tanks in Washington and California.

It wasn't difficult to picture these ponderous, opaque-eyed civil servants, moving in and out of think tank and government circles, supporting the ideologies of the monies that funded them, their minds like briefcases, bulging with facts, their smiles as masked and ambiguous as the names of the places they worked for: Center for Strategic and International Studies of Georgetown, Institute of Contemporary Studies.

Not what I had intended at all, that evening in my drawing-room on Eaton Square. For my think tank, I wanted independence and wit. Blasphemous, cutting minds. Plato, surrounded by brilliant pederasts. Lace elbows jostling one another at Madame de Staël's. Voltaire defying the King of France from his outpost in Switzerland. In my dream, the world of ideas was alive and full of hope, nourished by geniuses as bold as *conquistadors*, as confident as saints that, today, this year, *now*, was the time to recreate the world.

The report ended with a dreary statement which paraphrased a book appropriately entitled *Think Tanks* by Paul Dickson. "A think tank's primary function is to act as a bridge between knowledge and power; they are closer to being *agents* of knowledge than creators of it."

A bridge? Agents? Why wasn't the creativity of all those brilliant minds being used? Was the point for it *not* to be used?

That night, I dreamed I had a huge cube of lead in my mouth. I wanted to bite down on it, but knew that if I did, my teeth would crack into a million porcelain pieces.

I woke up at dawn and there was Dr Freud, sitting on my bed. "Your dream, young woman, signifies that you fear you have bitten off more than you can chew."

2

After breakfast, I put on a navy Chanel suit and a green silk blouse. I had long since discovered that it paid to wear the symbols of wealth around the Boys. The less I reminded them of the bewildered person they'd met in the South of France two years earlier, the better we got on.

Mrs Obie, bleary with jet lag and hungover, stumbled into the living-room as I was putting up the flaps of the dining table for the morning's conference.

She picked up the phone and ordered coffee and rolls for the Boys who were expected at 9:30. Her voice sounded like Walter Cronkite's.

"The two most important items on the agenda today are the tomato venture in the Western Sahara and Janet's folly. Guess which they'll want to discuss first," I said chirpily. I felt reckless and endangered, the way I used to feel before exams at school.

I didn't know it then, but a decision had already begun to form itself inside me.

Moriarty was the first to arrive. Cy used to refer to him as the Mother Superior. No brains, but great witnessing powers. His face was an almost perfect square with a broken cube for a nose, a straight jaw that merged with his chin in one hard line and a body that repeated the same square theme.

"Good to see you back. You ought to stay in America for a while. Great things are happening," he said, saliva gushing in all directions, landing, I hoped, on my navy suit and not the green silk blouse. "The Republicans are finally giving us a break."

"I thought the recession was affecting everyone, even big business," I said.

"Mustn't read the papers too carefully. The press deals with a different set of facts than thou and me."

"You used to be the kind of people I hated. Coffee?"

"God yes, thank you. Long night. Flew in and went straight to goddamn P. J. Clarke's. Everytime I go there, I realize how old I am."

I walked to the window. Outside, Park Avenue was alive with bumper-to-bumper traffic. The city was as unmanageable as ever. Frantic, well-dressed white collar workers dashed down the pavement, turned back every now and then to see if there was a taxi, found none, but waved all the same. Most of them women. Me, as I was two years before. A bit of female energy pumping life into the space I whirled through, ambitious, broke, crazy with hope, scuttling about in an anguish that nibbles and pricks.

"Did you and the others take the same plane?" I asked Moriarty.

"No, Tom left Chicago at noon yesterday. I don't know when Neil came. Brought his wife."

"Where are you staying?"

"The New York Athletic Club."

"Do you like my think tank idea?"

"I think it's very interesting. Actually, I've been more taken up by the tomato thing. More my line."

There was a sharp knock at the door. I opened it and saw a stout red-faced woman in thick cowhide boots, steaming with that formidable energy and stamina peculiar to New York middle-aged women.

"Hello, I'm Mabel Serubin. From Knox Typing? Sorry to be late." Her face was shining from exertion. She had turned right, walked passed our suite and all around the building at least twice, which was why she was late, she said, as she entered the suite and put her shopping bag against the mirrored wall in the foyer. Lurex threads coursed through the fuzz of her angora sweater.

Mrs Obie guided her to a chair at the conference table where she settled in immediately, placing pencils and a spiral note pad on the table and flinging a gold eyeglass chain around her neck. Spread across her forehead like commas were flat dyed brown curls.

"I just wait here?" she asked, staring at us with her knees

clamped together and her thick-booted ankles a foot apart, not bothering to hide her impatience to find out what this assignment in a hotel suite was all about.

"Mrs Obie, would you tell Mabel what she'll be doing this morning and how to take calls? I'll be right back." I left them and fled to my celadon green womb. Some of the anxiety I'd felt the night before was threatening to invade again in spite of my serene Chanel exterior.

My usual source of tension in the Boys' presence stemmed from my ignorance of finance. Somewhere in my brain, there was a large airy space where economics should be, which I could not fill with knowledge. A simple procedure like selling short had me baffled. I'd have it explained, understand it for a few seconds, assure my instructor that it was now quite clear, and then forget it ten minutes later.

I had always forgiven myself for this weakness. I was a journalist, an intellectual *manquée* who once loved Pascal. Wasn't that enough?

Buried in Miss Taylor's report was a quote by Herman Kahn: "We define intellectual as anyone who deals with secondhand information."

I looked into the mirror over the bureau, slid my contact lenses into a more comfortable position on my eyeballs and realized that no, being intellectual was not enough. Neither was putting together a group of brilliant minds who might or might not come up with a great intellectual idea that would provoke disarmament. For an idea to have any impact on the world it must be backed by *power*.

Which I had. 250 million dollars worth. Though it was a widow's mite compared to America's $20 billion military research budget, if it were used to support a truly innovative idea, it could be very powerful indeed.

Until then, I had not been willing to assume the power inherent in my money. Not because of greed. Greed didn't make sense when you were talking about such figures. One twenty-fifth of that fortune could satisfy every greedy impulse I ever had. It was fear.

Fear of being different.

Fear of not joining the rest of the lemmings in America and

Russia slouching towards annihilation, their hearts filled with resignation, like warm gray soup.

Fear of using the money to challenge that massive authority represented by John, the gray-faced Pentagon man, that said we ordinary people, who paid their salaries, should not upset the natural, suicidal order of things.

Fine. A lot of people were afraid of challenging authority. That was my weakness. Many women's weakness.

Which could be overcome.

My hand shook as I reapplied my lipstick and combed my hair. The Boys weren't going to like it at all.

When I returned to the living-room, Tom O'Riley and Neil Byrne had arrived and were sitting at the long table as far from Mabel as they could get. Mrs Obie was pacing up and down. Her tension around the Boys stemmed from their suspicion of her. They had always thought she had had too much influence over Cy. It was a complaint and a compliment she could never possibly live up to since, to the best of my knowledge, no one had ever influenced Cy.

Tom uncoiled his long-drink-of-water frame and rose to greet me. Moriarty and Byrne bobbed up two beats later. All three had wrinkles in the crotch area of their trousers. They were not the sort of men who carried an extra suit for a two-day visit to New York. A fresh shirt on top of their files in their attaché cases was the most they would concede for Cy's last little lady.

After exchanging greetings with them, I sat down and began the meeting. "The two most important items on the agenda are the tomato venture and the think tank. Is there anything else?" I looked at Tom.

He leaned forward, bringing his head more than half way across the table. "Well, there's next year's budget and profit projections, but we can get through that quickly and leave the papers for you to study and sign later." His narrow, sweat-covered forehead glinted at me reproachfully. Which meant he knew about Ronnie Lopez, the MBA from Fordham, whom I had engaged the year before to check up on their reports and profit statements. It should come as no surprise to anyone that I did not trust them. Three Irish cronies organizing the finances of one female interloper with a dumb spot in her brain, could hardly inspire trust in the female interloper.

"I'd like to discuss the think tank first. Then tomatoes. I realize the latter is a serious investment possibility, but I'm sure you'll understand my limited interest in it. By the way, did you bring any of the Sahara tomatoes?"

"Yes, they're over there," Byrne said. Mabel's eyes slid across the room to the fake empire sideboard where a much-traveled, wrinkled, brown paper bag was perched.

"Good, we'll have them with lunch. You are staying for lunch, I hope?"

There was a general murmur of disgruntlement as luncheon obligations to mothers, cousins and elderly sisters spilled from their mouths.

"Mrs Obie, would you call room service and tell them there will only be three for lunch? You'll stay, Mabel, won't you? We'll have some letters to do." Mabel smiled her joyful acceptance.

"So that's settled. Have you all read Miss Taylor's report on think tanks?"

"Sure did. Hell of a good job," Byrne said gloomily. His facial muscles, weakened by gravity and excess water retention, reflected his deep pessimism. Even his eyes, brown leather slabs on yellow chamois, were doom-filled.

"One of the facts I found most reassuring is that other millionaires have created think tanks," I said. "I'm sure you all noticed that Samuel Rubin, the owner of Fabergé, founded ips and that Mr Coors, the brewer, started the Heritage Foundation. So what I am proposing isn't that far-fetched, really, is it?"

The only sound was Mabel's pencil racing down her steno pad.

I went on: "The down side, if we are to believe Miss Taylor, is that a think tank is of no earthly use unless it's linked to some sort of power base."

"Well, Janet, that seems to be the way it is," O'Riley said, leaning back in his chair. "I was talking to this man I met from the Brookings Institute. He says a think tank's got to be tied into the system to be effective since their main purpose is to back up policies that have already been established by people in power. Give you an example. Say you want to sell grain to the

Russians. What you do is tell your think tank to put together some graphs and forecasts proving you're right. Which you then show to your Congressional committees. In other words, think tanks are more like high-class lobbyists."

"Who do everything but think."

"Yeah, well . . ."

"Therefore we can classify my project as pure, quixotic folly." Other men would have exchanged glances at this. These three only vibrated.

"At first I was discouraged by this, but it doesn't really change anything," I continued. "My goal remains the same: to put together fifteen or twenty brilliant minds to solve pressing world problems. Until I read Miss Taylor's report I thought it was enough to discover a few great creative ideas. I now see that ideas have to be backed up by power."

"Well no, not necessarily. Sometimes just stating things in a book or report can be very effective," Tom said, possibly suspecting where I was headed.

"Look at Karl Marx or Darwin. They changed the world with a few books," Byrne said, following O'Riley's lead.

"But let's say I'm not lucky enough to find a Marx, who, by the way, was very active politically, or a Darwin. What if my scholars only come up with a practical idea that needs to be implemented?"

They looked at me blankly.

I went on. "What if the problem we're tackling is population growth in South America and we decided that the quickest way to curb it would be to give the Pope a couple of hundred million to convince him to change his stand on birth control?"

"What does that mean?" Moriarty asked sharply. Of the three Catholics there, he was the most practicing.

"It means that, if I thought it would be effective, I would consider bribing the Pope."

Mabel's glasses dropped off her nose and dangled from a chain on her angora bosom as her pencil raced down the pad. Bribe the Pope! A couple of hundred million! Unthinkable, sacrilegious, delicious! What luck to fall in with a bunch of nuts like this!

O'Riley's chin was three inches from the table, but his voice

72

was calm. "You mean you'd throw away Cy's money on some hare-brained scheme like bribing the Pope?"

"I object to the word hare-brained. Who knows if the Vatican is incorruptible? In any event, I would never put *my* money, not Cy's, *mine*, behind an idea that hadn't been adequately analyzed and studied. I used bribing the Pope as an example to show the actual power the money could have."

"So that's what you plan to do. Find an idea that will give you an excuse to dissolve your entire estate."

"Sell all your goods and follow me," Byrne said in the strangled voice of someone in the middle of a nightmare.

"Not *all* my goods. I'd always make sure you got your pensions and that I'd remain a rich woman. I'm not Mother Teresa. But let's face it, there's a lot of money left over that I don't need and will never use that could have a real impact on the world."

O'Riley clapped his hand over the documents on the table. "Well, then, I guess we won't have to talk about this year's or any year's financial plans."

"No, proceed as usual. It's possible that one great break-through book will be sufficient. I just mentioned what I might do with the money, so you'll know what I consider my options to be."

I smiled at them over the bow of my green silk blouse while they rubbed their brows, clenched their teeth and jabbed at their cuticles. They had expected silliness, vagueness, garrulity, but never, not in their most anguished projections, had they foreseen such sickening altruism.

3

"I don't know why they put you down when you said you'd consider bribing the Pope," Mabel said after the Boys had left and she had begun gathering up the coffee cups and emptying the ashtrays without being asked. "It might work! But those guys are all Irish, right?" She grinned.

Some time during the meeting, the thought had entered her mind or subconscious – wherever feelings of inferiority are stored – that I was no better than she. From this, two corollary thoughts had flowed: I was up against a tough bunch of men and needed her help.

"I think it's wonderful you want to do something good for the world. But you can't expect guys like that to get it. They're looking to find out what your angle is. Right?" She turned for confirmation of this view to Mrs Obie, who was still coming to terms with the fact that I had invited this angora-clad person from Queens to lunch. Have I mentioned that Mrs Obie is a snob?

I liked Mabel. She was one of those New York battleaxes you most frequently meet in coffee shops or behind cosmetic counters who, for the price of a few minutes of straight talk, is willing to swim around with you in whatever hostility you're feeling towards men, the system or New York weather on a particular day. The sort who might get on the back of the bus during rush hour but would always help a blind person across a street, never missed a funeral, had all her friends' birthdays marked down in her date book, and never lost a battle in Macy's complaints department in her life.

Over lunch she wasted no time zeroing in on the one issue to which I had given too little thought: the scholars themselves. "How are you going to recruit all your geniuses?" she asked as she sliced up the delicious red tomatoes the Boys had gloomily left behind. "I bet they're really clickish."

"Geniuses are everywhere and usually underpaid," I said. "Anyhow, finding a place to put them in is my first priority. I have to hire someone to scout for a location in Connecticut right away. After I've found a headquarters, I'll look for the talent. It may only be a matter of going through the list of Nobel Prize candidates for the last five years, sending them a long, thoughtful, well-written letter and making them an offer they can't refuse."

"It sounds vague," Mabel said, patting the comma-like curls on her forehead to an even greater flatness. "I worked in my husband's store and in borough politics for twenty-five years and if I've learned anything, it's that you don't hire people by throwing out a net and pulling in what you can get."

"What kind of store?" Mrs Obie asked.

"Kitchen appliances. Best store on Queen's Boulevard until they took our lease away. My husband passed away six months later. It was terrible. So I took up secretarial." There wasn't a trace of self-pity in her voice. She was a woman whom calamity did not overcome.

I rose and walked over to a sofa. My two assistants followed. Had old Mr Coors or Mr Rubin of Fabergé had more sensible people around them? Did the President? Surely these women, with their sagging chin lines and widow's humps were more humane, maybe even superior, to the experts who sat at the feet of the powers who managed the century we lived in.

"Mind if I get out of these boots?" Mabel asked, pointing to her scuffed cowhide boots with their huge iron zippers squeezing against her calves.

I nodded yes. Sighing with relief, she undid the boots' heavy zippers. "I think I've got some slipperettes in my shopping bag." Mabel padded confidently across the room. All she needed was a frying pan in front of her.

"Whyn't you get someone else to do the hiring for you?" she asked when all three of us were seated.

"Brandy, Mrs Serubin?" Mrs Obie asked, opening the Courvoisier bottle she had brought over to the coffee table.

"No thanks, dear," Mabel said. She had barely touched her wine at lunch. Decaffeinated coffee would be her drink of choice. Didn't Mrs Obie see that?

Mabel turned to me. "I don't think you should let those intellectuals know a young, good-looking girl like you is behind this thing."

"But I want to participate. Half the joy of forming a think tank will be in the interviewing and hiring."

"I don't like it."

Mrs Obie poured herself some brandy. "Well, since it's really not your problem . . ."

"If I don't interview them, who will?" I asked.

"You could get a headhunter to screen them first."

"I hardly think there are employment agents for think tanks," Mrs Obie sniffed.

"There must be a pipeline you can tune into," Mabel replied. "Like there is for doctors and lawyers where the winners know the winners and the losers know the losers." She withdrew a powder-covered mirror from her satchel and blew on it.

"In Miss Taylor's report, she mentioned a few smaller think tanks," I said. "I wonder if one of them would be willing to do the recruiting for me."

"You got it! Hire a tank to hire a tank," Mabel said decisively. She unfurled a flat lipstick tube and smeared an hallucinogenic blue-red color across her mouth. "Let them screen out the dregs. You interview the cream of the crop later."

Mrs Obie stared in horror as each stroke of the lipstick passed jaggedly across Mabel's mouth. But we both knew she was right.

Two days later, I called Mabel and offered her a job as a secretary. Her minutes of the meeting, though erratically typed, made sense. I also liked her quick grasp of the fact that I should start acting like a person with power and her willingness to show me how.

Mrs Obie said I would live to regret Mabel. I didn't. But what I did not see then (how could I?) was that her approval of what I did later had nothing whatever to do with moral approval.

4

A week later I was sitting across from Hal Palmer of Hal Palmer Associates in his Sixth Avenue offices, forty-four floors above Central Park.

He spoke in slow, deliberate tones, like a doctor repeating the details of a psychiatric patient's fantasy. "Now, let's go over it again. You want me to recruit about fifteen or twenty researchers of different nationalities, working in various disciplines for a think tank whose sole purpose is to come up with a solution to the nuclear problem. That right?"

"That's right," I replied crisply. Rather than waste his or my time, I'd decided to bite the bullet and begin our interview by telling him the true purpose of the think tank. He was still absorbing it. "Would you like to handle it? Or is it too absurd an assignment for a professional of your standing?"

"I'm not sure." He rocked his chair back until it was almost touching the rain spattered, bullet-proof window behind him.

He was a dark, chain-smoking man with gleaming black hair, sharp, Sicilian good looks, and horny. The horny was only a guess on my part, but I am invariably right about such things.

I had discovered him in Miss Taylor's list of independent think tanks still extant in the 'eighties. He was the ideal person to do my recruiting. He had had his initial training at the Rand Corporation, one of the oldest, most respected research institutes in America, was not connected with any political pressure group and had worked on projects as varied as the elimination of the drug traffic in Marseilles to the creation of a shopping mall in the Persian Gulf.

Tom O'Riley checked Palmer out for me. "A fellow at IBM who hired his outfit tells me Palmer's a maverick, but responsible. Brilliant record. Ph.D.s in engineering and physics and a Masters in anthropology," O'Riley growled into the phone.

"They say he's a good guy, whatever that means in that crowd, and has a staff of about seven top-drawer researchers."

Palmer scrutinized me through a cloud of cigarette smoke. He was an intelligent man, accustomed to making quick, accurate evaluations of people, situations and things. An anomaly like me was making him irritable.

"The recruiting can't be too difficult," I said, "considering that I'm willing to pay researchers $80,000 to work in a beautiful location with complete comfort, good food – all the luxuries they never had on the job before."

He smiled sorrowfully at my tactlessness. Although his offices were in an expensive modern building, they were shabby and sad. The top of the conference table was formica; the walls were covered with green blackboards and Rand McNally maps framed in plywood, and the chair I sat on was upholstered in a scratchy, thigh-puncturing tweed.

"You can tell them we'll be discussing the nuclear problem, but they mustn't know I'm willing to contribute most of my estate to implement one truly great idea. I don't want to attract hustlers who only want to sell me a contract with Boeing to build a better beam weapon or something. I want people willing to work only on ideas."

He grimaced.

"I also plan to create a great library with prestigious papers and original manuscripts of, say, someone like William Blake."

"William Blake?"

"His *Jerusalem*. It's pertinent to the problem. Do you know it?"

"No. Can't say I've read it." Until he figured out what to do about me, he wasn't going to give me an inch.

"Well, never mind. Political papers like . . ." I groped in my mind for any political name. "Cyrus Vance's."

An elaborate shudder coursed through him. "Mrs Cavanaugh, we've got to have a long talk about what goes on in the us. Cyrus Vance's papers are some of the most valuable documents in America. Money doesn't buy those things. Power does."

"Of course. I was exaggerating to show you the caliber of papers . . ." My voice trailed off as I groped for one reasonable,

78

intellectually sophisticated remark to make, but none came. I was out of place in this world of professional scholars and green blackboards and he was mercilessly aware of it. Yet, if I were to employ Hal Palmer (not possibly the name he was born with), the balance of power had to be redressed. It was my earth too that was being threatened.

I put my purse on his desk, crossed my legs, sat back in my chair so my pearls fell over my breasts and looked straight into his dark, smart eyes. "Mr Palmer, you have come highly recommended and I'm willing to give you $100,000 to recruit people for this project. However I can't tolerate being patronized. I have well over two hundred million dollars to spend on humanity. That alone gives me more personal power than you will ever have in your life-time. I'd appreciate it if you would remember that if we're going to work together."

His rose-beige lips parted as he stared at the map behind me, then at the smudged white walls, and finally at my pearls. Dust, silence and cigarette smoke billowed between us as he patted the table with his fingers. Little cushioned multi-thuds, like a very experienced drummer.

"Agreed," he said at last. Then grinned. The confrontation had pleased him. "You've got a lot to learn, but I think we'll get on. In an odd way, it's appropriate that someone like you would want to do something about the bomb. People could be intrigued."

"If you had $250 million given to you, would you be tempted to take on the bomb?"

"I don't know. I might just have fun and forget about it. But I'm not you, am I?" He rubbed his lips with his thumb. "You realize, of course, that the recruiting is going to be very difficult. Though, I suppose we could try to get people from the Freeze Movement."

"I don't want to involve them, even if they are dedicated and selfless. Most of them are just reworking old pacifist ideas and only want to see nuclear weapons *limited*. My experiment is about finding a completely new, fresh, universal idea that could inspire disarmament on both sides."

He nodded and drew a little square in the air with his hands.

79

"It's got to be positioned as an exercise in pure thought. It sounds . . ."

"Impossible?"

"A bit, but still, I kind of like it."

"Good."

"Let's start with people, then we'll tackle the library, okay? I've got files on about one hundred and twenty top independent researchers in the United States. Most of them have worked either at the Rand, the Hudson Institute, Brookings or one of the better conservative places like the Center for Strategic Studies in Georgetown. Why don't I go through the files this weekend and meet with you again on Monday to discuss the most likely candidates?"

"I also want you to look into outstanding academics and Nobel Prize candidates."

He sighed and let his head drop. We were back to the doctor-patient relationship. "Academics, maybe. Nobel Prize candidates, well, it's just not in the cards. I'm sorry Mrs Cavanaugh, if you like I'll try, but . . ."

"Well, do your best. There's no harm in aiming for the top."

He smiled limply.

I rose from the tweedy chair with relief. "While we're discussing names on Monday, maybe you can teach me everything you know about research and the subtleties of power that I have to learn."

"I'd enjoy that very much," he said, getting to his feet. His smile was sincere. Maybe he was a good guy after all.

5

Shortly before Thanksgiving, the check for $50,000 that we sent
Wylie Cavanaugh was cut into two pieces and returned to Tom
O'Riley. The typed letter accompanying the mutilated check
was forwarded to me:

Dear Tom,
Please thank my stepmother for her kindness. Events have
taken a turn for the better and I find that I will not be
needing the loan I had requested. Do wish her well in all
her endeavors. Sincerely,

Wylie

No return address, just a Washington DC postmark. What did
he know about my endeavors? Why was he calling me his
stepmother and writing in that finishing school prose?

It scared me. A disinherited child who won't be paid off is not
to be ignored. Sickly addict or not, he was a human being with
a powerful reason to hate me. I was tempted to give him the
money and be done with it and him for ever.

Why should I be the instrument of his father's wrath?

What had that vast fortune ever given me but loneliness and
a feeling of responsibility not towards my class, country or sex,
but towards the whole earth?

If it hadn't been for Hal Palmer, I might have persisted in my
fantasy of handing the money over to Wylie. But things had
radically changed between Hal and me. Clamoring, sexual child
that I was, I had gone to bed with him. Perhaps I should hate
myself for that, but if I hadn't reached that final intimacy with
him, it's possible that he would never have had his great idea.

It started with too many drinks, Mrs Obie staying overnight
at an inn in Connecticut and me, missing Nigel more than I ever
thought I would. And there was Hal, alone with me in my suite,
his dark, complicated eyes gleaming at me across a table,

murmuring his clever, seducing words. How could I not have ended up in bed with him?

On the physical level, the experience was good. Thoug,. forty-seven years of age, he was still an exuberant, passionate, even limber, lover. But the situation between him and me was not correct. A scholar-Rasputin in my bed, who was also my employee, was out of the question once the think tank was launched and I had moved into Little Middletowne, the pristine, pastoral spot which I'd chosen to be the Cyrus Cavanaugh Institute's headquarters.

Mrs Obie and I found it without the help of a real estate agent. We had been driving toward Litchfield on a narrow country road, bordered by ravines and ancient fir trees, turned left where we should have turned right, and there it was: an old, fieldstone, former boys' school, nestled in mellow, rolling hills that had once been pasture lands, with several smaller, ivy-covered buildings scattered about the grounds.

I showed so much enthusiasm and determination to buy the place that the owners wanted 30% more than it was worth. O'Riley told me I was crazy to choose a place so far from New York and Moriarty threatened to quit if I didn't let him negotiate the price down. Only Hal, who had always longed to go to a private boys' school, gave me his unqualified approval. When he saw it, he said I had just discovered paradise.

His support in the Little Middletowne matter, the zest with which he reported on the interviews he was conducting with the scholars, and the several dinner meetings we had had together, did much to increase the warmth between us, but what endeared him to me most, that night we went to bed, was the disappearance of his arrogance.

Unfortunately, this was due to his failure to recruit anyone at all for the Cyrus Cavanaugh Institute. He had interviewed forty of the people whose names we had selected from his files and no dice. A high salary, the promise of luxury in Connecticut and the freedom to work on the world's most pressing problem were not enough to entice them away from their underpaid, bureaucratic jobs.

"There's no status in working in a research institute named after a millionaire they've never heard of," he said mournfully.

"The project is too vague. Possibly dangerous. Maybe even ridiculous. They'd much rather work in one of the established institutes or even in a government-supported tank. It gives them a feeling of snuggling up close to power and getting nearer to the truth."

"They're looking for the truth from government?"

He nodded slowly. "Well, isn't might right and doesn't might make history? And isn't history all we have to go on?"

He looked away, drained his glass of cognac and began to laugh. Some private vision had transported him miles from the Regency Hotel.

"Tell me what you're thinking," I begged.

Chuckling quietly, he waved a hand in front of his bright, mischievous eyes. "I was just seeing it all. After about six months of looking, I finally dig up a group of men willing to work for you, pack them into limos and drive through a snow-storm to Little Middletowne.

"They walk through this huge entrance hall with moose heads on the walls and there, at the top of the stairs, is a beautiful redhead with green eyes and emeralds around her throat and plucked eyebrows."

His face fell and his voice was filled with sadness. "They're standing there in their shabby suits with cheap pipe tobacco in their pockets and don't notice the puddles forming around their rubbers. All they see is this movie star person who wants them to think about doing good for the world.

"A butler comes to take their coats. And hats. These guys all wear hats in the winter. And you say: 'Drinks and canapés will be served in the library at six. Meanwhile you can go to your rooms and look at the heated towel racks and bidets in the adjoining baths.'"

I laughed. If I hadn't, I would have cried. It did seem ridiculous. My idea of seducing them with luxury and high salaries was absurd. Hal was right. And damn. Oh damn, damn, damn.

He stirred his coffee and shook his head. "They're not all that bad. I mean, not all of them. But imagine their suspicion and fear as you walk towards them, your perfume coming closer and closer."

"How can men who can talk in a perfectly relaxed way about a first-use policy and the megatonnage of icbms be afraid of a person like me?"

"You'd be life as they've never seen it. An angel with no power base, a whore with a heart that's literally made of gold."

"How could I ever imagine they could think freely about the bomb when most of them have spent their whole careers working for people who support it?"

"Much safer to think about blowing up the world than to analyze their feelings about you."

"Are you sorry now that you got involved?"

"No, but it would help if you were a little older or had some education in physics, some background . . ."

"I don't want any background in the world that created the nuclear problem," I said, or maybe shouted. "It's 'background' that's going to kill us. It's because your men in galoshes are enmeshed in it they can't see the forest for the trees. My function here is to be a normal human being. *Vox populi.* An ignoramus who sees the nuclear problem in black and white: either humanity continues along on a path that will lead to its eventual obliteration or it doesn't. The only difference between me and the rest of the ignoramuses is that I happen to have some money and can act on my very unneurotic, rational desire not to go up in a fireball."

"It would help, too, if you weren't so goddamn sexy," he said in a tense, uncomfortable voice. His eyes, normally so black and multifaceted, had turned opaque and his forehead was covered in sweat. His hands stole across the table and slipped around my wrists.

"The trouble, Janet, is that you want to upset almost four decades of resignation to the nuclear threat. All the best minds – at least all those outside the disarmament movement – are resigned to it. Even the anthropologists are. Man is aggressive and will defend himself with the best weapons he can make. It's in our genes. Period."

"Not in women's genes. Women defend themselves with sex and reproduction and gentleness."

"Silly Janet." He shook his head and poured himself more cognac. "Men *are* women's weapons – their guns and bombs.

Why else do women feed and nurse their warriors? They're like GIS oiling their guns."

"Or do women *provide* men with weapons each time they give birth to a boy?"

"Women are just as aggressive and paranoid and protective of their territory as men."

"I don't believe that. I think that's what men say."

"Look at the way women vote."

"If women, not men, controlled the world, there would never be a thermo-nuclear war," I declared recklessly. My mind was racing. Everything was assuming an incredible clarity and simplicity which I should have known to distrust. Nothing about men's and women's differences is ever simple or clear. "Look at ancient Crete. A rich, happy civilization with only female goddesses, magnificent art and trade and no signs of war. Women aren't violent. They never would have created nuclear weapons. They just don't *think* that way. That's why I hate the male intellectual establishment. In fact, I'm delighted you weren't able to recruit any of them."

"You've just given me an incredibly brilliant idea." His eyes danced with self-congratulation. "I think I may have solved your recruiting problem."

I didn't ask what it was. All I could think of was that sitting across from me was an excited male with an interesting, interested body who had, earlier in the evening, told me that I was beautiful and sexy. And because so much that happens to me is invariably linked with sex, I wanted to go to bed with him.

I rose, walked dizzily across the room and fell on the sofa. My wraparound skirt fell open, exposing my right thigh.

In seconds, he knew where his priorities lay. Flinging off his jacket, he whipped over to the sofa and stretched out beside me. His face was flushed and hot looking, but his slender Mediterranean hands running swiftly all over my body were dry and confident.

"I'll tell you my idea later," he muttered. "Oh Christ, you feel good. You're so beautiful. I think I might be in love with you."

And many more adulatory adjectives and expressions of incipient love which I quite like and ordinarily listen to with fierce concentration, but then his arms, which had been chival-rously supporting his body above me, collapsed and his full weight fell upon me. Growling and panting, he buried his head in my breasts and wrapped his legs around me.

"Would you like to go into the other room?" I gasped, fighting for air.

"Yes, oh, mmmmm, hrrmph, hrmf." And other manly, animal grunts. It is not true that intellectuals are not in touch with their pre-literate, primal nature. He was reveling in reverting to it.

Which should have taught me something, but didn't.

6

The next morning, while Hal was still sleeping, I ordered breakfast and sent his suit out to be pressed and the lining of his jacket sewn up.

I gave him my silk Japanese kimono to wear while we had breakfast. He had never had pure silk next to his skin before, he said wistfully, as he stumbled rather than walked, to the breakfast table.

He was not at his best. To begin with, he was forty-seven, hungover and suffering from an excruciating headache. Added to this was his guilt for having said he loved me when he didn't. But the main agony pressing on the fragile, brilliant matter of his brain was his fear – well-founded – that he had jeopardized his professional relationship with me, and good-bye one hundred grand. His best memories would probably be of the silk slinking across his shoulders.

He couldn't touch his eggs, but two cups of coffee and three aspirins cleared his head enough to get back to business. All things considered, the safest place to be.

"Remember when I said the recruiting problem was solved?" he asked.

"Yes, I wondered about that this morning. What's your idea?"

"I have a feeling you're not going to like it."

"Try me."

"Hire only women scholars and researchers and make it an all-female think tank."

"Only women?" Because I had gone to bed with him, did he think he could turn my think tank into some sort of intellectual seraglio for himself? "That's the corniest, most limiting thing I've ever heard."

"Really? Last night you said you hated the male intellectual establishment."

"I did?"

"Of course you did. You do. Everyone does."

"I was exaggerating."

"You were telling the truth. Admit it. Men, your weapons, have brought the earth to the brink of possible annihilation and it's time for women to redirect them. And if you come up with a real solution, think of the great publicity you'd have."

"Which would be negative. Do you realize how much money I spend to keep my name out of the paper? The circumstances of my marriage make reporters salivate. If they got wind of my starting an all-female think tank to solve the nuclear problem, they'd go wild. They'd make it sound like Brigitte Bardot and her little seals."

"Not if the women were real heavyweights. Not if we reminded the press that Rachel Carson, a woman, basically started the ecology movement and Margaret Mead helped revolutionize anthropological research. Anyhow, publicity would be sought *after* an idea was discovered, definitely not before."

"And you don't think they'd leak it to the press?"

"The kind of women I'm talking about wouldn't last five minutes in this game if they couldn't keep their mouths shut."

But it wasn't so much the publicity I worried about, it was the women themselves. "How many of them have studied several disciplines? Most of them are lucky if they have a Ph.D. in one subject. How could they do systems analysis? And they'd hate being beholden to me."

"But think, Janet, of the impact a group of women could have. And many of them do have degrees in different subjects and all of them work twice as hard as men. Imagine the havoc they could create if they came up with a really innovative idea."

"I grant you that it would be wonderful if we could find the right women and they were willing to think of nothing but the bomb. But would they?"

"I, Hal Palmer, a man, have faith that they would and might just come up with a truly creative answer to the nuclear impasse. And if you fail, who is the wiser? Also there's less chance the government will be interested. No one follows female personnel changes in think tanks that closely. Twenty women could fade out of the scene and no one would notice."

"What difference? This isn't a secret operation. I have nothing to hide from the CIA or the KGB. We won't be dealing in weapons and destruction, but in ideas that we would share with both sides."

He took a cigarette out, lit it without removing his eyes from mine and said nothing. Clearly the only idea that interested him at the moment was his own.

"It would certainly simplify your recruiting problem," I said at last.

"True, but that isn't the point, is it?"

"No, the point is: will it do any good? Will it work? Do I like it?"

I left the table, walked over to the window and looked at the women rushing to work along Park Avenue, clutching their pocketbooks, waving and running in their high-heeled boots. Their tiredness concealed with makeup. Their fear hidden under leather. But anxiety blatant in every movement.

All that effort to function and succeed in a world they hadn't made, that world they worked twice as hard in, that mighty male world which made history and could destroy us before the century ended.

But isn't history all we have to go on? Hal had asked.

Maybe not. Maybe women could offer the world something different to "go on". Had I in misjudging and underestimating myself, misjudged and underestimated them? Was Hal's idea a good idea?

Of course it was.

Not because it made his recruiting easier. Not because it had potential publicity value and was "different" but because, given a chance, women – practical, hormone-jostled, life-giving, temperamental, non-violent, *history-less* women – just might find the new idea the world so desperately sought.

Men had failed and God had disappeared. Who else was left but women?

I went back to the table, sat down and stirred my coffee. His eyes were lowered, but every muscle in his body was alert to my movements. "Congratulations," I said.

He looked up quickly. "Then you agree?"

"Yes. It's brilliant."

He leaned back, almost blushed.

"Go through your files again and pick out the best female names you can find. Then look into women writers and academics. I don't think we should limit ourselves to think tank people. Tell the ones you trust the whole strategy, but don't tell them who is behind it. They'll find that out when I see them for the final interview." He grabbed a pencil and started writing down names.

"Do you think they'll be willing to be segregated in Little Middletowne to work on a project organized by an unknown millionairess who just turned thirty-two?"

"Not *all* of them. But enough. I'm sure, Janet, that we can put together a group of prestigious, qualified women." He slapped down the notepad, threw the pencil over his shoulder and walked around the table to embrace me.

Odd, pleasant feelings were flipping around in my chest. "Something strange is happening to me at this very moment." I was grinning and couldn't stop. "I think I'm beginning to feel *happy*. Maybe this isn't only an experiment. Maybe with only women, oh my God, Hal, it might actually work!"

I was laughing. So was he. I nearly spilled my coffee. If he hadn't been there, I would have leapt in the air.

Which is why Wylie Cavanaugh did not receive his lost inheritance.

I was back on track. Hope and magnanimity were carrying the day. And there was the smallest possibility that my 250 million glorious dollars might find a place and a function after all.

And Wylie, poor Wylie, would just have to go it alone, playing his lute in Goa, Washington DC or wherever he had chosen to endure the lowest grade of life on the human spectrum.

7

"So you would give six months of your life living in the company of women?" I asked Padma Sarup, putting down my glass of white wine on the coffee table. It was six o'clock in the evening, the middle of August and the temperature in the Regency Hotel suite was 80° Fahrenheit. Gray vaporous August air rising from the pavement below was suspended outside the windows. When I wasn't interviewing, I walked through the city, which was like strolling around inside a radiator.

Padma was the sixty-first woman Hal had screened and sent to me for the final sizing up. "If the subject of the research was the woman problem," she made quotation marks in the air with her fingers, "I would refuse. But the nuclear threat interests me greatly."

Her eyes had that luminous, knowing look peculiar to many Indians, but she wore no sari and did not paint a red spot in the middle of her forehead. She also smoked mentholated cigarettes.

I looked down at the card Hal's secretary had typed up and sent to me before the interview. She was a Brahmin from New Delhi who had earned her Ph.D. in astrophysics at MIT in 1953, then gone back to India where she lasted ten years as a housewife and mother. Since 1963, she had been leaving her husband (a successful retail merchant in India) to teach every year in the United States, first at Wellesley, then at MIT, where she was currently a professor emeritus.

Her second discipline was Hindu philosophy, which explained the eyes. In the summer, the card said, she returned to India to be with her family. She had just gotten back.

I couldn't help smiling at the thought of this large, middle-aged woman, plunging back into Indian domesticity once a year, haranguing servants, ousting her husband's concubines and directing the lives of her two sons. They were now married,

91

she had told me earlier, to Indian girls whom they (the sons) dominated. And so the pendulum swings. For certainly no man ever dominated Padma.

I leaned closer and caught the scent of Elizabeth Arden's Blue Grass cologne. "Do you think feminism has failed?" I asked. In each ear, she wore a huge solitaire diamond.

"Good question." She raised a chubby linen-covered arm and cradled her chin in her palm. Her skin was golden and shining; her pores wide and generous. "If by feminism you mean that mixture of wishfulness and rage tied into the notion that women can share equally in men's privileges and still maintain control of the home, yes, I would say it is a failed idea." Dimples appeared in her cheeks. "But research and feminism have nothing to do with each other. Women's minds are not inferior. Only their position is."

She had written several books. Her best known was *Gravitational Forces Within the Solar System*. Hal Palmer said he had leafed through it and found it respectable. Nothing in her background indicated any special interest in nuclear weapons, but then, neither did anything in mine.

I took off my glasses and studied her majestic form. My legs were encased in stiff new jeans I'd bought the day before out of nostalgia for the poor old days when life was simple.

What was it that I had thought about being rich enough to delegate everything? That I would never again have to submit to tedious detail and bureaucratic formalities? Back in London, I had said: "Cyrus Cavanaugh Institute", and, abracadabra, it was supposed to be there.

"I am a religious woman," Padma was saying. "I once spent six months meditating on the mysteries of the *Bhagavadgita* in an Ashram. When Mr Palmer told me of your plan, I thought: 'Now is perhaps the time to meditate on man's nature and the weapons he has created.'"

"But this is not a meditation group we are assembling," I said. "The purpose is to look for one concrete, easily communicable idea."

"First, we will meditate. If a solution comes, it will come."

The thought of her as a large silent meditative presence among the quick thinking, immensely practical women I had already recruited was worrisome. "Is that what you do before you write your books?" I asked.

She nodded serenely. "And the books have come. That is my method of work. I cannot change it."

"And you think an answer might come."

"How can I be sure? I am only one small mind among many great ones. I am willing to try. That is all I can promise."

Hers was the women's usual response. Cautious and neutral, bordering on pessimistic. Nevertheless, I wanted her with us. There was something of the high priestess about her with that long neck and those glinting earrings. She could contribute a vitality and eccentricity that the group needed.

"Your background definitely qualifies you and I'd be very happy if you'd join us," I said crossing my legs with effort in the new jeans. "I'll have Mr Palmer show you the contract. Unfortunately, I can't give you the exact date the group will convene. Up until two weeks ago, I thought we could get into Little Middletowne by early October, but the latest report from the contractor is that it won't be ready for another six months."

We had started work late. Negotiating the price down to a figure Moriarty approved of took months. After the closing, we discovered that in addition to replacing all the electrical wiring and bathrooms and remodeling the dormitories – repairs we had anticipated – new water pipes had to be laid and all the auxiliary buildings needed new roofs. Not surprising. I had never bought an eighty-year-old boys' school before. How was I to know its precise state of decay? How could I guess that the building inspectors whom Tom O'Riley had so prudently hired to inspect the estate were in the pay of the seller?

The building delays, the interviews with the women and the long, frustrating hours spent with lawyers and accountants to work out the formalities entailed in creating a non-profit, tax-exempt foundation had eaten up ten months.

"Half the Northern Hemisphere could be blown up before the women even sit down at a conference table," I moaned to O'Riley after a four-hour session with the accountants. (I had finally told him of the think tank's real purpose. He took it well. Undoubtedly because he thought no solution to the nuclear crisis was possible and therefore, "Cy's money" was safe.)

"So don't plan on getting into Little Middletowne right away," he said. "Inaugurate your think tank with a preliminary conference in some meeting center or hotel and move to Connecticut later."

Mabel, who had seen Little Middletowne once and come back saying we should burn it down, collect the insurance and relocate to some nice modern place in Arizona, ecstatically endorsed O'Riley's suggestion. "You can call it the Cavanaugh Conference," she said. She had been lobbying to get rid of the Cyrus in the name ever since I had decided to recruit only women.

I liked the name but flatly refused to hold a conference in one of those steel and chrome hotels that catered to sales meetings and conventions.

"If we were to hold a preliminary meeting somewhere other than Connecticut," I asked Padma, "would you be willing to go there?"

"It depends. Where were you thinking of going?"

"I've been thinking of somewhere in the Third World."

"Really?" Her eyes snapped and her left hand rolled into a round, tidy fist.

I hadn't told anyone this new thought except Hal, who said it was brilliant. "Just think how it will strengthen your future publicity value," he said. "A group of women stashed away monastically in the Third World would make a fantastic news item when you're ready to publish. It would give the women a better perspective too. They'd be seeing the nuclear threat from below, as it were."

Since perspective and publicity were the two pillars on which Hal had built his not unsuccessful career, his approval was important to me. Although our affair had long since run its little course, we still talked to each other almost every day. Of all my "advisors", he was the smartest and most helpful and his continued support and friendship mattered.

"I'd like to leave the United States because its propaganda for the bomb is so insidious," I said to Padma. "If we were in a neutral country, everyone's mind would be liberated. I was thinking of somewhere in Africa." She cocked her head and looked at me attentively. "Africa's in such a state of flux and

94

so uncertain of itself, it couldn't have much influence on the group's thinking. Then too, it's where man is supposed to have begun. What better place to contemplate the end of man?"

She sipped her white wine. "Many of my country's people are in Africa." Then, turning her perpetually inspired eyes on me: "What role do you envision for yourself at the conference?"

"I am only a catalyst," I said hastily. This section of the interview was even harder than the beginning when I gave them the unpleasant news that I, a woman younger than all of them, was the Institute's sole benefactor. "My ignorance is appalling and I would never burden any of you with it. I have not specialized in any discipline."

"But you are a journalist? Mr Palmer said . . ."

"I am, but it's no more than a craft. My only real discipline, and I believe it is a difficult one, is being a very, very rich woman."

She had the grace not to smile at that. "What will you do during the conference?"

"Just be there. See that the assignment is being fulfilled, that everyone is working as hard as they can to find a solution to the nuclear problem. You will all have to answer for that."

"Answer how?"

"By showing you are doing the assignment."

"And if we can't?"

"You may be asked to try again."

She sent me a long, measuring look as she inhaled her cigarette.

"You see, Mrs Sarup, what I lack in mental discipline, I want to make up in will. When I say I am a catalyst, what I mean is that I'd like to be a real force, willing all the women to concentrate their enormous mental powers on nothing but the fact of nuclear destruction. I have this idea that the human mind is as strong as the energy locked inside the atoms around us. That the battle is maybe not between Russia and America, but between our minds and that energy."

"Nuclear energy is a physical force."

"So is the human brain."

She fingered an antique ivory bracelet on her wrist. "I'm committed to teach at MIT this winter."

95

"Almost everyone I've spoken to is committed to be somewhere else."

"What sort of women have you found?"

"Good women. Your peers. I wish some were from Communist countries, but Hal says that to invite them is to invite the KGB and the CIA. But at least they aren't all Americans. Most are scientists, but we've also recruited a writer and Shakespearean actress. I wanted to mix creative people with scientists and scholars, in itself an unusual idea for a think tank."

"Different, certainly." She sighed lightly. Art was not high on her list of priorities. Something else was preoccupying her. "I deserve an adventure, if only an intellectual one. I've been a professor for twenty years. That's a long time."

"The salary was quoted to you? $20,000 for three months and $80,000 for the year if you choose to join us permanently at Little Middletowne when it's ready."

She raised her chin. She was a Brahmin. By the old laws, she wasn't supposed to earn money, think of it or even need it. "That is a very generous salary," she said distantly.

"Not when you realize that what we're seeking is priceless."

She looked at me pensively, then at the gray swamp clinging to the window behind me. I fanned myself with a file folder and waited. The phone rang at my elbow. I leaned down and unplugged it. She sent me a look of gratitude for prolonging the silence.

At last she spoke: "All right. I'll do it." She rose in one grand sweep and held out her hand. Her large linen back was as straight as a military officer's. "It's a deal, Mrs Cavanaugh." An awkward Americanized Indian had unaccountably surfaced.

I stood up quickly and we had a big Texas-style handshake over it.

8

What I did not tell Padma – or anyone – was that, not only did I want to go to Africa, I wanted to hold the conference in a game park.

I don't know how the idea came to me. Perhaps in a dream. Or maybe it took root the day I heard the man from the Pentagon say that Africa was the asshole of the earth. Any place he hated so much had to have a lot to recommend it.

Whatever its source, once the vision of a group of women thinking, studying and conferring in a game park was implanted in my imagination, I couldn't let it go. All I could think about was the bush.

I had only caught a glimpse of that orderly, savage universe during my brief stay at Treetops in Kenya five years before, along with fifty other awestruck tourists. But as the days passed and I listened to Tom O'Riley drone on about the wonderful meeting centers in Florida and Hal describing a forty-two story hotel in Singapore he had once stayed in, my head swam with memories of chattering monkeys, water holes and fig trees. The thought of returning there filled me with unreasoned, irresponsible joy.

True, when I had first thought about organizing a gathering of intellectuals, I had imagined modeling it on the great salons of the eighteenth century. But the more I talked to the women, the clearer it became that my fantasies of elegance held no interest for them. They had spent their careers blinking at computers in cold institutional rooms and presenting their ideas, not to kings, but to television-wary men with fearful, wandering eyes.

What they needed was not only to get away from western thought and technology, but a radical change of climate and environment: to be surrounded by sunlight, clean winds, a place where the world was still awake, where life, not death, dominated the air they breathed.

The idea took a while to gestate, but by the time I announced it to Tom, Hal, Mrs Obie and Mabel during a working dinner in the Regency suite, I had made up my mind. If an idea were to be found that would save us from nuclear destruction, I was convinced we'd discover it in Africa.

Tom and Hal were horrified: malaria, cholera, not to mention tsetse fly, revolution, communism, starvation, general filth, corruption and occasionally cannibalism. On and on. But to no avail. They knew that many safari camps were comfortable and well-maintained. What was irritating them most was the originality of the idea.

Mabel was uncharacteristically silent, but Mrs Obie, who was suffering from a cold caught tramping around Little Middletowne during a windstorm, was the first to come around. She was tired of fighting the contractor at Little Middletowne and Connecticut's thirty-mile winds and wanted to go where it was warm and the natives still had some respect.

I was not surprised. From the beginning Little Middletowne had over-stimulated her. Perhaps because she was the first to see it with me, she felt responsible for it. Almost every day, she would call up the hotel chauffeuring service, get herself driven out to Western Connecticut and come back to the Regency late at night reporting nervously on the incompetence, profligacy and truculence of the New England construction worker. Without her close surveillance, I would be spending another million, that is, if the workers didn't sabotage it, she said darkly one evening after three Scotches.

She was drinking more. How much I didn't know. I wasn't up to counting the empties in her room and didn't want to think about it. I needed her around. She was my link to Cy and more.

Tom and Hal were amazed when they heard her backing my idea, but it made an impression on them. By the time dessert was wheeled in, Tom was remembering that various multinational companies often held executive meetings in game lodges in South Africa. "South Africa is the only place to consider, of course," he said. "At least their game parks have paved roads and the government is stable."

Hal was so upset by the mention of South Africa, he lit two

cigarettes at once and said he was ready to resign if I even considered going to a fascist country. "You'd lose all credibility with the press," he roared.

"Then it has to be Kenya," Mrs Obie said. "It's accustomed to tourists and not at war with anyone."

I immediately seconded this suggestion since I had already decided on Kenya. Not only was it one of the most beautiful African countries, it was also more or less a free nation, despite its tough, pro-Western, one-party system.

"Which I guess makes it safer for a millionairess," Hal said, leaping with his usual agility to another set of principles, then added grumpily: "Not that I believe for one minute that Janet can get a middle-aged woman like Annabelle LeLeu to go to a game park." Since Annabelle was our only Nobel Prize candidate, he knew he was touching a sore spot.

Ignoring him, I asked Tom questions about currency exchange, insurance and other tiresome details which Tom, being Tom, couldn't stop himself from answering.

After the men left, shaking their heads and clamping their jaws together, Mabel took me aside and quietly resigned. Her daughters (both married) needed her and would never let her go to the jungle.

I barely paid attention to her. There wasn't the slightest doubt in my mind that her curiosity would get the better of her and she would be down at Macy's buying safari suits before the month was out.

I took her with me when I went to see a Miss Maitland, one of the most knowledgeable safari organizers outside East Africa, whom Mrs Obie had heard about.

Miss Maitland told us that a small group of women studying animal behavior (for security reasons, Hal and O'Riley had advised me to refer to the think tank thus) could easily find accommodation in the Masai Mara, the most beautiful of the game reserves.

If we went in February, we would have two months before the rainy season began which was difficult, but not too insurmountably awful.

She recommended Camp Urudu, a first class safari camp in the Mara, and showed me pictures of its solid stone administrative buildings and roomy, fully equipped tents on the banks of a yellow, meandering, billion-year-old river.

Two weeks later, Mr Zareda, an elderly dark gentleman with a youthful face and old Hindu hands, who was Camp Urudu's owner, came all the way to New York to clinch the deal. He met Mabel and me in my suite. In his briefcase was the camp's guest book, studded with the names of various Prime Ministers, show business celebrities and English aristocrats as well as two dozen letters of thanks from former guests, going on and on about the camp's beauty, amenities and superb service. I passed them to Mabel and told her to get them xeroxed.

Zareda was delighted to turn his whole camp over to me and my group of harmless, non-shooting, white women. The effects of the recession were being felt in Kenya as much as anywhere else in the world and a full house for three months was a windfall.

The list of celebrities and the guarantee of electricity and plumbing in all the tents, broke the back of Mabel's devotion to Arizona motels and presumably silenced her daughters. She would like to retract her resignation, she announced in front of Mr Zareda. If it was all right with me, she would sign up right away for a course at the YMCA to learn how to set up a small library. The archives could wait, but a library was still essential to the undertaking. It could be in the little stone building that housed the gift boutique, she decided, after studying the photos. Typing and xeroxing could be done in the reception building.

Could a new generator for our electrical office equipment be installed? I asked Mr Zareda. "No problem," he assured me. No problem for anything with this affable man.

When Moriarty heard I was making plans to hold the conference in the Masai Mara, he called from Chicago and raved. He had gone on safari there with his wife for their thirtieth anniversary. "Are you aware that wild animals wander around those camps at night?" he bawled.

I laughed. "I'm sure the animals don't come near a bustling active camp. We're just outside the game park's borders."

"What about doctors? I hear most of the women you've been interviewing are in their seventies."

"Don't be ridiculous. They range from thirty-five years old to sixty. Anyhow, there are flying doctors in the area and one missionary hospital thirty kilometers away."

"But no phone," he growled. "You can't tell me they've put up any telephone poles since I was there."

"There's an excellent two-way radio system and a telex machine. The whole idea is to get away from phones and modern civilization. I'm only sorry that the Masai Mara isn't wilder than it is. If it was at all safe, I'd rather go to the Serengeti in Tanzania."

"Don't worry, there are plenty of buffalo in Kenya to gore you if you get in their way."

"Kenya depends on its wild life to attract tourists. They don't let people go into the bush and get killed."

"You'll never find enough women crazy enough to go with you to Africa."

Wrong, wrong, wrong.

Armed with the camp photographs and my xeroxes of Mr Zareda's fan letters, I was able to convince the majority of the women to go. Mabel helped with remarks like: "With Mrs Cavanaugh's kind of money, what's to worry? She could hire an army to protect us if we ever got into trouble." Or: "Look, I was afraid, too. But for the rest of my life I'd wonder about what I missed."

Six of the women who refused to go had legitimate reasons like lecture engagements and obligations to their families which they could have handled from Connecticut, but not from Kenya. Only two objected on the grounds that the whole idea was insane.

Hal was stunned when I told him that Annabelle Leleu was among those who were going.

I never doubted that most of them would. Somehow I had always known that geniuses are first of all adventurers, and secondly brilliant.

9

I was grateful there were so few of us. The hoped-for twenty would have been unmanageable. Yet the quality of the group had not suffered. Every day, I read and reread my final list of participants in the Cavanaugh Conference.

CAVANAUGH CONFERENCE

Members' List

(In alphabetical order)

FARAH BEZHAD. An Iranian telecommunications expert. Author of *The Microchip Comes of Age*. Staunch feminist. Divorced from her Iranian husband who joined the Ayatollah's revolution in 1978. Bluff hearty laugh. Practical experience in the labs of ITT. Twelve years at the Rand Corporation. All degrees from the California State University system. Unhappy. 52 years old.

THERESA CRATER. American novelist. Overweight, opinionated, fun. Books swarming with characters and big, original science fiction ideas. Called the C. P. Snow of American literature, but less precise. A television "personality" seen frequently on talk shows. 54 years old.

ELSA HEINZELMANN. German physicist and chemical engineer. Worked in industry in Germany and the US. A two-year stint at the Institute for Defense Analysis in the late 'sixties. When I asked her to explain isotopes, she had the grace not to be condescending. A chubby, short-legged woman who combs her dark brown hair straight up in the air, perhaps to give the illusion of height. Divorced. Odd. 53 years old.

ANNABELLE LELEU. Cheerful, hardworking, peasant-like French anthropologist and linguist. Our only Nobel Prize candidate. Accompanied Lévi-Strauss on expedition to South America. Single. Lives with her secretary/housekeeper in Paris, commutes to the Université de Lille, where she teaches two days a week. Puts out two or three monographs a year in learned French journals. Author of three tomes on tribalism in South America and Africa. 49 years old.

CLAIRE MONTMORENCY. English, RADA-trained actress and stage director. The most exquisite Portia in the history of the Royal Shakespeare Company. Five film credits, but not a celebrity in the US. Stubborn and independent. Could be one of the most creative persons in the group. Quite beautiful. Hal Palmer's personal friend. Says she is 35. I say 39.

DOROTHEA MOWBRIE. Mathematician and economist, born in Harlem. On leave of absence from Yale. Two and a half years at the Hoover Institute in the mid-'seventies. Six years at the Heritage Foundation. Divorced, no children, probably lonely. Quite frank about undergoing extensive psychotherapy. Thick bi-focals on shining brown skin. Long neck. Afro haircut. Very sharp. 42 years old.

ANN PEABODY. American microbiologist and geneticist. Unmarried. Four years at the Institute of Society, Ethics and Life Sciences. IPS before that. Young looking. Pale blonde hair, eyelashes and clothes. Very still waters. 44 years old.

PADMA SARUP. An Indian Brahmin, astrophysicist and student of Eastern philosophy. A prolific writer. Six books. A natural leader. An air about her. As if just barely suppressing the power within her. 54 years old.

CAROL SCHUMACHER. Canadian biologist and chemist. Frizzy gray hair, intelligent, poodle-ish face. Influenced by Edward O. Wilson while at Harvard and a sociobiologist of sorts. Two grown sons, both in scientific research. Worked with Hal Palmer at the Rand Corporation as a young woman. Most recently at Princeton. Married to a professor of philosophy at Rutgers. 48 years old.

HITSAI SOEDA. Japanese physicist educated in California and Tokyo. Expert on electromagnetic effects. Married to Dr Alfred Soeda, a renowned archaeologist. She broke her contract at the Institute for Contemporary Studies to join us. Had been overlooked for promotion. Tiny, geometrically perfect figure. 38 years old.

JEAN WEINSTEIN. Ph.D.s in psychology and philosophy. As tough as Theresa Crater. A stint with Hutchins in Santa Barbara in the late 'sixties but primarily an academic. Politically conservative, but a closet feminist. On leave of absence from Columbia University. Husband at New York University. 57 years old.

SUSAN WU. Chinese-American economist who is also a noted China watcher, employed by the State Department under various Democratic administrations. Definitely a liberal. Worked on and off at the Brookings Institute. About to go to IPS when Hal approached her. Intrigued enough to try us instead. Several books on China. The best known: *The Scientific Establishment in the People's Republic*. 61 years old.

There were no Marxes or Freuds among us, but I hadn't hoped to find one. From the beginning, I had believed that a group effort would accomplish more than a solitary genius. The nuclear problem was too vast and our quest too arrogant for anyone to tackle it alone. A group would provide strength, companionship and, if the need arose, consolation.

When I sent the list (a more formal version, with degrees, honorific titles, awards and publications carefully recorded) to Tom O'Riley, he said I should be proud. He had never thought it possible to recruit twelve such talented women so quickly. Maybe something will come of it, he conceded.

With that "maybe" pounding in my brain, Mabel and I set about preparing for the conference. We were scheduled to arrive in Kenya on February 8th and there was much to do. All supplies had to be sent ahead. I helped Mabel pack twenty cartons of paper, pencils, pens, staple guns, scissors, rulers, erasers and pocket computers – all our loaves and fishes which, if the dream went according to plan, would soon be multiplying into a thousand billion beams of light and enlightenment.

Kenya

1

"We're outnumbered," was my first thought when our Cessna landed on Camp Urudu's airfield and a herd of gazelles grazing on the runway thundered off to join dozens of similar creatures with Giacometti legs. To the left and right of them: assorted wart hogs, wild dogs and many more small scampering, unidentifiable beasts. Less than a hundred yards away: a legion of brown-black hairy hulks that were buffalo. They watched in silence as Mrs Obie, Mabel and I stepped cautiously out of the plane with binoculars, cameras and pocketbooks thudding against our chests and hips.

Waiting beside two parked trucks were Ron Watkins, the camp's manager whose picture I had seen, and three natives in immaculate khaki shorts and starched shirts. All four men waved at us enthusiastically. The ratio of humans to animals was about 10,000 to one.

"Welcome, welcome, Mrs Cavanaugh," Watkins shouted, walking up to Mrs Obie with his hand extended. He was a stout, muscular man in his mid-forties with a wide grin, marred only by the absence of one of his upper front teeth. "I'm Ron Watkins, the manager of Urudu." His accent was that of an English-speaking South African.

"This is Mrs Cavanaugh. I'm Madeleine Obie," Mrs Obie said as I struggled forward, trying to balance all the gear hanging from my shoulders.

He turned to me. "Sorry, sorry, well, good trip? Smooth ride?" As he spoke, he glanced at the buffalo with a quick, street-smart look that reminded me of a New Yorker on the alert for muggers. It was a look we would all adopt in a very short time.

His voice and manner indicated only amiability, tolerance and total acceptance of the utter peculiarity of caring for a group of women for three months in the middle of the bush.

Mabel smiled faintly as he pumped her hand. I knew that missing tooth was going to bother her a lot more than it did me.

We quickly got in the back of one of the waiting vehicles while our luggage was piled into the other. Ron sat in the front beside the driver, a solemn, immensely lean African.

Opening the overhead hatch of the car, Ron invited us to stand and view the game while we rode to camp. Joyfully realizing that, of course, this was a safari truck, I stood, looked up at the high, wide, cloudless, equatorial sky, then at the immense, five-foot termite mounds and dry yellowing grass under it. Raising my binoculars, I tried to focus on the abundant wild-life as we bumped across the savanna. Everywhere there were little territorial enclaves, soft hooves, watchfulness, and hunger.

There is no eighteenth century here, I thought, feeling another rush of self-doubt and panic. No universal ideas, no clockmaker God. In this savage place, the hand of God is green and furred. What truths can our puny, abstracting intellects possibly grasp with that furred green hand in the background of our thoughts?

I reminded myself that God, if he existed, had disappeared, and adjusted the lens of the binoculars, but we had already left the wildest part of the game park. Trees were appearing, then a winding, hard mud road. We were in a sun-dappled riverine forest beside a sluggish yellow river with ancient, caressing mud on its banks. A small wooden sign informed us that we had entered Camp Urudu. On the northern side of the camp, but in full view, was a dark marshy area of high grass and spindly trees. In its center: a family of elephants, lolling, honking and spraying their young.

Everything was as green and beautiful as I had wanted it to be. I felt tears in my eyes. I had seen it all in the camp pictures, but now it was real and here and mine for three months. Whether we achieve our goal or not, I thought, some good has to come of this venture. I have not made a mistake. Brilliance could flower here.

We stopped at my tent, which was on the outskirts of camp, as I had requested. I knew instantly that it was going to make me happier than any home I ever had. It was a sturdy green canvas affair mounted on a concrete plinth. Overhead was a thatched roof covering. Opening the roaring steel zippers, Ron showed us the inside: a comfortable bed, chest of drawers, desk, two chairs and small lamp. A smaller tent with a private shower and toilet was behind it. Everything was clean and nicely worn. Hemingway neat. Conrad simple.

"Are the elephants in the swamp any danger?" Mabel asked Ron in a strange, cramped little voice as we continued our tour of the grounds.

"Not really. Unpredictable though. You've got to be careful of the solitary males. Those over there are females," he said, still beaming with the innkeeper's automatic affability.

We followed him to the center of the camp where four stout, stone buildings were clustered. "This is the main house," he said, waving at the largest which opened out to a wide, concrete terrace where several round tables were set up. Their white table cloths flapped in the warm wind. Inside the main house, two young black men were setting up the wooden partitions which would divide the building into lounge, indoor dining-room and conference room.

Down a small incline was a dark, one-room structure filled with African carvings, postcards and guide books which would be the library. Mabel entered and craned her neck to see into its somber corners. She expected to spend several hours there setting up her newly-learned, simplified Dewey Decimal system. "This is it?" she asked disconsolately.

"We'll get all those boutique items out tonight," Ron assured her.

"Each woman is bringing a maximum of two book cartons," I said. "There should be enough shelf space here, but we'll have to discuss lighting later."

Ron nodded and his eyes slid away from mine. "The generator is, well, we'll talk about it later."

The next building was Ron's office in which he had crammed two desks, a couple of file cabinets, the radio system that linked us to Narok county and a huge silent telex machine. At a smaller table in the corner, a black girl was laboriously typing on a manual typewriter. She looked up and said: "Jambo."

"Jambo," Mabel, Mrs Obie and I replied in unison. It was the first word on our list of fifteen essential Swahili words we'd read on the plane.

The last building was Reception. "Here's where guests check in, talk about their bills and so on. This is Bill Spears," Ron said as a tall, bearded, white man behind the reception counter stood to greet us. His tan, sun-lined face was handsome, but then, the pilot of the Cessna had been handsome and almost all the other white men we had seen in Nairobi. Stewart Granger seemed to have set some kind of standard in Kenya. Or maybe only handsome men had been able to survive in this land of Mrs Macombers.

"Bill is our resident naturalist. In his free time, he takes photographs of animals that sell to the *National Geographic* and the Audubon Society."

"What I really am is a nature guide who takes pictures," Bill said, looking not at us, but at the counter and almost blushing. "I also supervise the drivers, make sure the vehicles are in good condition, that kind of thing." He had the same soft, swiveling, South African accent as Ron.

Mrs Obie looked apprehensively at Bill Spears, then at me. She perceived a problem at once. Mabel, who knew nothing of my weaknesses, was delighted to see another white on the premises. (In Africa, the polite term for whites is "Europeans", but since we all thought in terms of color, especially in the beginning, I am foregoing that nicety.)

"Would you care for tea?" Bill asked, leading us toward a grassy slope where additional tables had been set up under a wide spreading tree. He had the awkward, loping gait of a confirmed bachelor. His desert boots were immaculate, no doubt because his eyes never left his feet.

As soon as we sat down, an extended family of baboons emerged from the thicket of bushes that bordered the lawn. A mother with a baby clinging to her breast strode towards us with insolent eyes. A quick grunt from one of the waiters stopped her in her tracks.

"Our baboons aren't as aggressive as the ones in Amboseli because we never feed them. Once baboons know humans have the ability to give them food, they become terrible pests,"

Spears said. His words and posture were stilted in contrast to Ron's muscular affability.

"Do they come into the camp at night?" Mabel asked, still in that cramped, uncomfortable voice.

"After sundown they vanish completely, but other animals might stray in."

"Lions?" I asked softly.

"Sometimes. But you're more likely to run into elephants, zebra or water buffalo. Though schools of hippos can be a problem, too. Every night the average hippo must eat about three hundred pounds of herbage. On occasion, they come looking for it here." He smiled brightly. "That's why no one must leave their tents alone at night. For obvious reasons, we can't patrol every corner of the camp."

"We can't leave our tents at night?" gasped Mrs Obie who loved wandering about before she settled down with a couple of Scotches.

"Not unless you signal for a guard with your flashlight. That's a serious rule." His manner was maddeningly, unattractively officious. Mrs Obie had nothing to fear.

"A friend told us that animals wander around at night, but I thought he was exaggerating," I murmured.

"Don't worry about it," Ron said. "All the tourists, even the Japs, get used to it. Ah, here's Driscoll." He stood up and beckoned to a stocky, gray-haired African gentleman with gleaming brown corduroy skin.

"This is Isaac Driscoll, my personal assistant and camp major-domo."

"Very pleased to meet you," Driscoll said in precise tones. His smile was radiant but in his eyes was that African look that half pleads for affection, half readies itself for rejection that I remembered from my first visit to Kenya.

"Driscoll is a Kikuyu. Same tribe as Kenyatta. The best, right?" Ron said, in a tone that teetered unpleasantly between condescension and camaraderie.

"I want your stay to be agreeable. I am in charge of that," Driscoll announced with a short bow. "How is the banana cake? I supervised its cooking this morning." He lifted a knife from the tray, cut himself a slice and popped it into his mouth.

"Everyday, we have a different sort of cake at tea-time," Ron said, pouring strong tea into cracked white crockery cups. I glanced at Mabel who was probably born knowing that hepatitis is carried between the cracks of cups. She smiled bravely as she brought her cup to her lips.

We chatted about food and menus. Claire Montmorency, the actress, was a vegetarian. Could we find vegetables for her? No problem, Driscoll said. They were flown in fresh from Nairobi every other day along with the meat and fish. No produce was grown in the Mara because the animals would, of course, eat it. No, there were no fences in Camp Urudu. Why bother? Almost anything could leap over them.

A warm, puffy breeze passed through the trees and fluttered about the sleeves of our safari jackets as we enjoyed the green afternoon light. Our three hosts fell silent. No doubt they were used to guests arriving in a stupor. My body ached from the hours of travel, excitement and apprehension. Two giant buffalo lumbered into the outskirts of the swamp where they were joined by a few stumpy, bristly wart hogs whom they ignored.

"Do you love the animals as much as the tourists do?" I asked Driscoll lazily who was still standing stiffly to the side of us.

"They are very good for Kenya and business."

"Love the animals?" Ron roared slapping Driscoll's forearm. "All he thinks about is eating 'em."

"Hippo meat when cooked properly is an excellent cuisine," the major-domo replied solemnly, sadly.

As soon as we had finished tea, the men suggested we take a siesta before dinner. We needed it. Although we had slept twelve hours in Nairobi, we were still in a state of geographic shock.

"David has already taken your luggage to your tents," Ron said.

A very tall boy, with inch-wide holes gouged in his ear lobes, appeared from somewhere behind us. "This is David," Ron said, then pointing to a stockier fellow whose ears had not been tampered with, "and Ephraim."

We followed them down a grass path to Mabel's tent. She had asked to be as close as possible to the main building. Her daughters had insisted.

"Shabby elegance," Mrs Obie said, nudging the graying lambskin rug on the floor of Mabel's tent with her foot.

Mabel said nothing. Her eyes were fixed with terror on a five-inch rip at the bottom of the zippered tent door through which any small beast might enter.

I thought of what Mabel's apartment in Queens must be like, with everything "nice", a kitchen floor so hygienic you could deliver a baby on it and germicidal sprays in all the bathrooms. "Can we get the hole in the zipper fixed?" I asked David.

"Hole?" He looked straight at it and shook his head as if denying its existence.

"Can it be mended?"

"Oh yes. No problem. You 'fraid of animals? They don't bother you. Never."

"We'd like it sewn up anyhow," I said. Mabel sent me a look of dumb gratitude.

Saying goodbye to Mrs Obie who went off with Ephraim to her tent, I followed David to the end of the camp, loving the feeling of old-new land under my feet, knowing it contained the fossils of those earliest, wordless primates, who might yet have something to teach us.

"You're a Masai, aren't you?" I asked David, remembering the pictures I had seen in Miss Maitland's office of the Masai's gouged ear-lobes weighed down with colorful earrings.

"Yes. Am only Masai hired here." He frowned, then quickly smiled. His two lower incisors had been removed, another Masai custom.

"Your tribe owns the whole Mara, doesn't it?"

"All here is ours." He waved his arm to indicate everything in sight, including the spot where I was standing.

As we approached my tent, I realized that the tan-colored tree I had seen ahead of us was actually a giraffe. He glided regally away, pretending to be leaving on a whim, not because he was afraid of David.

David proudly turned on the shower to verify that it had hot water and opened my Thermos of drinking water on the nightstand. Its lining was covered with brown stains.

"Chemicals?" I asked inanely. "The stains are from chemicals they use to purify the water?"

His answering smile was resplendent with innocence and respect. "Yes, Mama, yes."

Mama, I had learned in my Swahili book, was a term of affection, meaning "lady".

He left and I sank into bed listening to the chorus of birds. insects and skittering crawling things outside my tent. Perhaps, I thought, this music of the ecosystem is as refined and mathematically correct as a composition of Mozart's. If there is an order in cells, why not in the sounds the cells produce? Why assume they are random? I smiled cheerfully to myself in the dark. It was the kind of insight Cy used to have about things.

I fell asleep realizing that never before had I felt so happy, expectant and blessed.

In truth, the opposite of those emotions would have been appropriate. But I am an American, a child of the Enlightenment, an optimist, sometimes a fool. Danger and failure were not things I thought about. Tragedy never.

2

This letter I wrote to Hal during our first week at camp was in his file on the Cavanaugh Institute that I made him send me when I returned to London.

Dear Hal,

I am sitting on the slab of concrete in front of my tent, which is more or less a veranda, and looking at the camp's private swamp in which three large and two small elephants are now relaxing like fat ladies in early Picasso paintings. In the trees are vervet monkeys, but very few birds, since most have migrated in advance of the rainy season. The sun is hot; the grass parched. We all long for rain and relief.

Am I boring you with my nature descriptions? Can't stop. Like the birds and the dry ground, I am in the grip of the Serengeti ecosystem. Every day I look up in the sky and search for gray clouds. For with the rain will come the women's brilliance and a great gush of magnanimous ideas. Isn't that how we programmed it?

All the scholars have arrived. Without exception they have been good sports about the small physical difficulties of camp life that none of us had foreseen.

I have been doing my best to improve conditions. Have already sent to Nairobi for new water Thermoses, crockery and extra blankets. (No heat in the tents at night, just hot water bottles.) Mrs Obie is in charge of complaints but this responsibility has shifted to Mabel.

Something has happened to Mrs Obie. She isn't happy, yet she was the one who most wanted to come here and leave New York. She is out of kilter with things, almost sullen at times. The natives scare her. She told me she keeps a small switch-blade under her pillow that she bought from a bell-hop at the Regency. I'd like to take it away from her, but how can I when Nancy Reagan sleeps with a little gun?

117

Oddly, Padma is the only genius here that Mrs Obie can relate to. The only thing they have in common is that the staff doesn't like either of them. Mrs Obie because she's autocratic, English and demanding. Padma because she is Indian. Feeling against Asiatics is still running high in Kenya, Ron told me, when I remarked upon one of the waiter's rudeness toward Padma.

During the Rebellion, a lot of Indian stores were looted and Indian girls raped. The problem hasn't reached Ugandan proportions, but some of the same ugliness exists in Nairobi.

In general, the women are being extremely well coddled. Their only serious complaint has been over insufficient lighting in the tents and no comfortable place to sit and read. After some thought, Mabel and I decided the best place to read is in bed . . . like pampered housewives. Have ordered five dozen extra pillows to be used as backrests. Since the extra electric generator I asked for never materialized (endless excuses about this, too frustrating and boring to describe here), I have also bought five dozen battery-operated lamps and sixty cases of batteries. Even geniuses can't use up more electricity than that in three months.

So far, no difficulties in my relationship with the women. They are intent on ignoring their dependence on me and proving that I deserve no extra homage. They are here out of the goodness of their hearts. Period.

One fortunate thing: they are enamored of the beauty here. They are taking a week off to view the animals and get used to the altitude (5,200 feet) before the conference begins.

The buffalo, zebras, elephants, etc. who come into camp at night to graze and occasionally push against their tents frightened a few in the beginning, but most of the time, the wild-life charms them. After years of treading library corridors, waking up and finding a mound of hippo dung on the grass path in front of your tent may well be a cheerful morning sight.

I'm glad I didn't go along with Tom's suggestion to have a team of bodyguards with us. They would have been hideously out of place and ruined the mood of the conference. The native guards are alert and sublimely unafraid of the animals.

None of them carries a gun, just metal spears or long sticks they poke the animals with. We are in no danger at all. The Air Force Rebellion that took place mainly in Nairobi last August was completely squelched and President Moi is very much in control of the government. In the Mara, the only serious crime is poaching. A lot of rhinos and elephants disappear every year. But it's obviously in the poachers' interest to stay as far from an inhabited camp as they can. The only person here who has a rifle is Ron Watkins, the manager, a tough, energetic, bullying sort of man, but perfect for the job which can't be easy. The natives respect him.

The staff's wondrous courtesy and eagerness to please have enchanted the women. When I remarked on this to Ron, he shrugged and said: "You grow to hate them as much as you love them."

Africa and Africans are a revelation to Theresa Crater. She hasn't stopped scribbling notes since she arrived. If nothing else comes out of this conference, a new sprawling, Craterian novel will. She wears nylon hose under her size eighteen slacks and sort of rocks when she walks.

Since almost all the women are overweight, climbing into the safari trucks and trudging up and down the short hills in camp does not come easily to them. Watching them troop down the paths, puffing ever so slightly, smiling bravely, wearing four layers of clothes (necessary, you peel clothes on and off all day), and turning their gray heads every time a baboon does something interesting, I want to weep for them. How ever did humanity progress from crawling, babbling primates to upright, middle-aged quiz kids like these?

Hitsai Soeda and Claire Montmorency are the exceptions of course. Hitsai, who can't weigh more than ninety pounds, looks very smart in her impeccably tailored slacks and tiny designer T-shirts. She has gone mad for photography and shoots any beast she can get her telephoto lens on.

Being an actress, Claire is more of an outsider than Hitsai. Her only real ally is Theresa Crater who saw her perform at the Aldwych in London and respects her creativity.

Of all the women in the group, Claire is the only one who would be remotely at home in the Paris salons I used to dream

119

about. Her mind is so elegant and quick. That such a rare, Ariel-like creature would consider joining our unglamorous think tank still amazes me. Unfortunately the scholars have given her a terrible inferiority complex. The other day she announced that she couldn't possibly come up with an idea that would pass muster with the group and accused me of hiring her only to promote whatever idea the women came up with.

Not that there have been any ideas to promote. They're all too busy going out on game rides. "There won't be many good days left," Bill Spears told them when they arrived.

Spears is the camp "nature guide", a young old-boy who can be annoyingly rigid about regulations and wild-life protocol. Mabel says he has the hots for Claire. Saw him mooning around her after dinner the other night. Nothing goes unnoticed in a community this size. He's on salary to Camp Urudu, but my guess is he lives mostly off tourists' tips. He stays at the research station seven kilometers away. Apparently the Kenyan government built this inefficient (electricity, but no plumbing) building on the outskirts of the bush, which has been vacant for years except when rented out to former Peace Corp idealists and strays like Bill who are willing to pump their own water.

He and Ron are both English-speaking South Africans: claim to be anti-apartheid, dedicated conservationists, love Kenya and Kenyans, etc., etc. Both boring, but competent and deferential towards me. Even if the women don't perceive me as the boss, they do. I was the only one they told about the lions.

Last night while we were eating dinner, we heard a blood-curdling scream from somewhere in the back of the camp. The guard in the dining-room shouted, "Simba!" and bolted into the woods with his spear. Ten minutes later, he came back grinning sheepishly, assuring all the women (who were naturally petrified) that it had been a false alarm. There was no lion. Later, Ron and Bill told me there had been not one, but two young nomadic male lions hanging around the camp for two days, one of whom had terrified the cook's assistant whose scream we had heard. But not to worry. There was plenty of game in the bush to satisfy the lions' appetites. I believe them. It is ridiculous to be afraid when no one who lives here is.

Padma certainly isn't afraid of them. You should see her in her baggy blue jeans and sweat shirt strolling nonchalantly around the swamp where the elephants bathe.

Unfortunately, Mabel is still scared of the animals, even the monkeys, and almost never leaves the library. Though she gets on well with the women, she's seriously annoyed with them because they haven't claimed the weighty tomes they had shipped to the camp. All they want to read are picture books on wild life and skimpy adulatory studies on the Masai, the pastoralist tribe that owns the land the camp is on and controls all of the Masai Mara (1120 square kilometers).

She has also been besieged by requests for Swahili grammars. They found out how easy Swahili is to learn and can't resist adding it to the list of languages they already speak and write.

I am no better. We could all forget why we're here. One glance at the purple escarpment against the horizon at dawn and you find yourself thinking that missiles could never rip through that sky and destroy this serene and beautiful place. It is unthinkable. *Unthinkable!* Have I brought myself and these women half way around the world only to fall into the unthinkable trap?

The other distraction is God.

Last night, Theresa Crater said: "The more I read about the Serengeti ecosystem, the more I'm tempted to believe that there is a mind governing us all."

"What is an ecosystem really?" asked Mabel, who is too busy executing the women's orders, organizing laundry (hand-washed by the staff's wives, who live on the outskirts of the camp) and trying to get the Xerox machine to work to do any nature reading.

"It's what's going on around us," Theresa said, immediately launching into an explanation of the interdependence of soil, drainage, rainfall patterns and animal migrations, tilting her head just-so, in the manner of gray-haired, middle-aged celebrities accustomed to appearing on television. (My late husband would have been very amused by Theresa's act.) No one except Mabel bothered to listen. Doubtless because they have all whipped through the same books Theresa had read, absorbed the data, neatly separating fact from theory and fixing it in their brains in clear outline form as geniuses are prone to do. Nevertheless I was glad she got off God.

At this conference, God is the enemy. He has forsaken humanity and I want no part of him here. At night, my only prayer, if I must pray, is: "Oh God, get out of the women's minds and mine. I don't know what your plan is. Perhaps to create a new experiment after we have blown ourselves up. Whatever it is, my plan is to outwit you. To stay on earth, even though, quite possibly, you may want us to go."

No, I wouldn't even give him that many words. If I prayed, it would be to Astarte or Isis or Eurynome, the Goddess of All Things, who divided the sea from the sky "dancing lonely on its waves". (Robert Graves.) In between game rides, am reading about pre-Hellenic cultures and other lovely things. I still think about Crete. Flowers and chariots and trade, but no war. Goddesses, but no gods.

Was the world matriarchal when people still believed in the Mother Goddess? Was it more peaceful then?

Enough of that. Am impatient for the conference to start before the sweet power and innocence of this land smothers us all with questions we can't answer.

Am also getting a bit edgy. A small thing happened yesterday that puzzled me. You remember that I brought a miniature Sony TV in the event there was a television aerial in the vicinity? (There isn't.) Yesterday, I found that someone had taken it out of my trunk and plugged it in. I turned it on, got nothing but a blank screen and static, put it away and went to dinner. When I came back to my tent, someone had plugged it in again. Not good. Ron has assured us that except for cash, nothing in our tents will be taken or tampered with.

I asked David, my sweet Masai tent attendant with soft vulnerable eyes, if he had been playing with it. "No, Mama, don't know, don't understand." I believe him. He looked too enchanted by the little 7″×7″ screen to have been the culprit.

It's late. Tomorrow, I must give my speech which will formally open the conference. I have rewritten it twenty times and hope it doesn't sound horridly stilted.

Much love, dear Hal. I won't say I miss you yet, but the time when I will may be drawing near. Please don't tell me you miss me until you actually do.

J.

3

I looked at them sitting around the newly built conference table, waiting for me to speak. If my face wasn't blushing, my soul was. Who was I to lead this group? Why weren't we all standing behind our respective stoves, nurturing our men, inspiring and serving humanity in the old indirect ways?

Trying not to tremble, I plunged into the first speech I'd ever given in my life: "There is probably nothing more implausible than a group of women who think that they can effect a change in the world's destiny. And yet, that is what you are here for. At no time, must we consider our goal to be any less magnanimous than that.

"The nuclear problem has defied man for thirty-eight years, but is not insoluble. It is the result of human, not divine, will. Human beings chose to create nuclear weapons. They can choose to abolish them. But in order to make that decision, they must have an idea that will motivate them. Your task is to find that idea."

I looked up. Their lined, academic faces were stony. No one was going to comment or react until I had finished my piece and possibly hung myself with the inordinate amount of rope that had been allocated to me ever since Cy died.

I passed over three paragraphs I had written imploring them to try to think on that grand, lonely scale philosophers used to risk and speeded on to a more practical vein. "There are just three points I want to make. First, I do not intend to participate in your discussions, though I may sit in and listen and, with your permission, Mabel will take notes.

"Second, if no solution is found, nothing in our lives will be changed. We will be the same frightened people living under the nuclear threat that we always were and, since our goals have not been publicized, failure will never be attached to your records.

124

"Third, you should know that I have inherited a little more than a quarter of a billion dollars from my late husband. Except for meeting some obligations to the people who work for me, I am free to spend it on whatever I wish. If one of you comes up with an idea that has a chance of success, $250 million could go a long way toward disseminating or implementing it.

"That's all I have to say for now, except to thank you for being here. You are among the bravest and noblest women in the world. Whether you succeed or fail, you must never forget that."

I sat down, placed my hands over my notes and waited. The only sound was Padma's Dunhill lighter clicking in front of her broad golden face.

Dorothea was the first to speak. "What you say is very surprising, Janet. We had no idea you planned to put all your money behind the project. Was there any reason you didn't tell us before?"

"It was the best way I knew to separate the truly creative candidates from the non-creative ones. Only creative people would be willing to search for an idea even if they thought they'd never be able to implement it."

"It would have made my decision much easier if I'd known," Hitsai said, her black eyes searching the faces around her for confirmation of her feelings.

"But, you see, you came anyhow," I said. Carol Schumacher sent me one of her tense, hasty smiles which meant, I guess, that she saw my point and agreed.

"Were you afraid we'd want to work on an anti-missile system like pop-up deformable mirrors or some other Star Wars project too costly for this group?" Elsa Heinzelmann asked, giving her stiff black hair a quick upward tug.

"Perhaps," I replied. "But then I would never back any anti-missile system that gave one side technological superiority."

"What kind of pop-up mirrors?" Theresa Crater barked, her writer's imagination already at work.

Hitsai shrugged her trim little shoulders. "Plans for making them have been kicking around the Pentagon for years. They're large mirrors that would be sent into space at the moment of attack to gather and point energy from ground-based lasers."

"What do you mean by 'implement'?" Claire Montmorency asked, twisting gracefully in her chair to get away from the sound of the scientists' voices.

"I'm not sure exactly," I replied. "It depends on the idea."

4

"Congratulations Janet Cavanaugh! You much brave determined woman."

Those were its first words. I will never forget them.

It was eleven o'clock at night, the evening after I gave my speech. I had returned to my tent after dinner and there was my little Sony television on my desk. Someone had taken it out of my suitcase again, plugged it in and turned it on.

On the screen was a round light, translucent at its borders, fiery in the center. And this strange, screeching, hermaphroditic voice. Not a woman's. Not a man's. No accent, no rhythm. Nothing identifiable.

"I've had enough of this. I'm reporting it to Ron right now," I said, knowing it was imperative that I get whatever it was on the defensive immediately.

"Just want give a compliment. Don't be angry and go thundering out tent without guard."

"I don't need to. All I have to do is unplug this television and throw it out."

"Not going ask who I am?"

"I don't care who you are. As far as I'm concerned you're first and foremost an intruder on my privacy." My hand was shaking as I lifted it to yank out the plug.

"Don't. Please, give five minutes and I will explain."

The voice sounded so distressed, I relented. "Okay. Five minutes. But first tell me who is hooking up this television? Is it David? One of the women?" My tent was fifteen feet away from anyone else's, but I was whispering.

"No one. I do it. But no one can catch me, see me." Its squeaking voice was exultant and full of mischief.

"Okay, I'll bite. Who are you?"

It didn't reply, just flickered silently on the screen. "You've only got five minutes," I said. "You're using up valuable time."

"Am trying phrase my response so it not you scare."

"Look, I'm already terrified, so why don't you just spill it out." I wasn't lying. I was indeed frightened. My vulnerability there on the other side of the world in the middle of the bush with no weapons to protect me, no knowledge of how to use a weapon even if I had one, and the ease with which I could be kidnapped were coming home to me in an ice-cold wave of terror.

"Thought if I just voice, would not frighten you."

"It's not your voice I'm afraid of. It's where you're coming from. What you want. I can disband the whole conference tomorrow, you know. Just forget the project completely. The women are too valuable to risk their lives."

"Would never harm you. Am total peaceful. Am on your side."

"I don't care whose side you're on. You're all equally evil. What does it matter if you're with the CIA, the KGB or a terrorist group? This is a group of innocent women engaged in an intellectual experiment. All they're doing is thinking. Why can't you leave us alone?"

"Would hate living in world where I feared my own species so much."

I managed a brave snicker. "Because you are not of this world, of course."

"Correct. Am not. Considering condition of world you in that should relieve you."

"Not of my world!" I tried valiantly to laugh. "Well, maybe some day we'll meet on the other side." I started turning the volume towards off.

"Please, up the volume." Its voice had been reduced to the tiniest of shrieks. "If you turn me off, find other way you contact."

"Good, write me a letter."

"All want is open dialogue with you and get know human being."

I looked at the image on the screen. The white light had grown, as if with emotion. In spite of myself, I was intrigued and turned up the sound again. Since we had already been infiltrated and betrayed, why not find out what it wanted?

"I've never spoken with human directly before. Could learn much each other."

"Okay. Talk. Where are you from? Mars?"

"No, not Mars. *Never*. Another place. Can't tell everything this night. Will speak again me soon?"

"Do you have antennae on your head and a little steel body like outer space creatures in comic strips?"

"Words that come closest to describe me are 'mind energy'. Have no body, no body at all."

"Which is why you talk through televisions?"

"Yes, light on screen not me. It's visualization I create to relate to you better."

"Because I'm limited by my abominable five senses, right?"

"Yes, without electronic device, you never understand I, me."

"Where did you learn your awful English?"

"Am studying human language many century."

"Are there many of you mind energies around?"

"No answer there."

"Aren't you disobeying orders coming to earth and disrupting all the mystery shrouding life in outer space?"

"Am a rebel. Always." This was followed by a wheezing, metallic sound, presumably a sigh.

"I know who you'd like. Theresa Crater, she writes philosophical science fiction books."

"Not want speak with your hirelings about problem."

"Which is?"

"The earth's bombs. Subject of conference."

"And you say you don't represent any espionage branch of any government? You're just this bodiless, disinterested observer from outer space come to have a dialogue with me?"

"Precise that."

"Well, I don't want a goddamn dialogue with you," I screech-whispered, lunging forward and yanking out the plug.

Ten minutes later, I was under the covers hugging my tepid hot water bottle and shaking. Every ten seconds I imagined a different way the camp could be attacked: a silent parachuting in of Green Berets, an invasion of spear-throwing Masai warriors, an orderly rounding-up of the group by uniformed Nairobi policemen who stuff us into paddy wagons.

Who was the voice? It didn't matter. It was an alien presence listening, recording and reporting. To whom? Which side?

What if – the most unthinkable of all the unthinkable things the women had to think – someone did come up with a solution which would lead the world to disarm? What if this intruder, this grotesque comedian with its hermaphroditic voice, stole or somehow destroyed the idea? Destroyed us?

I woke up just before sunrise and heard the rain, a gentle, slow-falling downpour, almost Londonish in its steadiness, hushing all the usual animal, dawn sounds. My bedclothes were clammy, possibly from the humidity, but more likely from the several cold sweats I had endured through the night.

Throwing off my covers and rubbing myself with a terry cloth towel, I decided not to tell anyone about the voice except Ron. If there was going to be fear in the camp, he and I would have to absorb it.

I would ask Ron to launch a discreet search for wires and any odd equipment in the camp right away. Chances were we would find the source of the voice without creating any undue fuss. It could well be one of the women operating some sort of radio system out of her tent. They were all geniuses and eccentrics. One could already have gone around the bend without Hal or I realizing it when we hired her.

I looked outside at the leaves on the trees bending submissively under the downpour. There wasn't an animal in sight. Even the elephants had left the swamp, which seemed greener in the gray rainy light.

David was walking gingerly down the path, now glossy with mud, carrying a large black umbrella over his head and a tray with coffee and hot milk. The television was still on my desk. I quickly buried it in the bedclothes.

"Six o'clock. Coffee, Mama," David crooned as he knocked lightly against the wall of my tent. His lean Masai body stooped as he entered. He was young, no more than twenty years old and his eyes, even at that hour, blazed with life-loving African joy. I watched him closely. If he looked just once at the desk where the TV had been, I was willing to believe he was the voice's accomplice.

"Rain today," he said placing the tray on the night table without looking at the desk.

"Yes, rain." I waited for him to notice the lump in the bed where the television was hidden. He didn't.

With lowered eyes and a little air of disappointment that I did not want to exchange our usual four or five sentences of morning conversation, he left the tent. Unfurling his black umbrella, he walked slowly back to the center of the camp through the gray, silencing rain.

5

After breakfast, I went immediately to Ron's cluttered office and told him in as few words as possible about the voice. He listened attentively; head bent over his desk, fist covering his unfortunate mouth.

The whole thing sounded so absurd and awkwardly feminine. Who but a group of women would have some crazed electronic intruder claiming to be from outer space, show up in camp ten days after their arrival?

"Did he give any hint of who he was?" Ron asked.

"He says he's from outer space," I said in the flattest, most virile voice I could muster.

His eyebrows shot up and his mouth puckered to a whistling position, but naturally no whistle resulted. "Outer space?"

"Yes. He said he'd like to open a dialogue with me."

He shook his head and sighed. I looked at the disorderly papers on his desk. Both of us listened to the rain.

"The first thing to do is search all the women's tents and the staff's quarters for any electronic equipment," I said, breaking the silence. "Do you have anyone you trust to do that discreetly?"

"Only Driscoll and myself."

"I think you should start today."

"During lunch?"

"Yes and after lunch. The women have a meeting scheduled for this afternoon. Carry plumbing equipment with you in case anyone asks why you're going in and out of the tents. I also want someone to sweep my tent for a microphone. If this . . . this person can hear my voice, there has to be some sort of bug around. I've already looked everywhere but another pair of eyes might do better . . . even with my lenses in, my vision isn't good."

"I'll do it myself. I've had a little experience with that kind of thing."

132

"In South Africa?"

"I was with Army Intelligence. It's a long story." He smiled broadly. The missing tooth gave him an idiot look that was unfair. I sensed that he was an extremely clever man.

"You had better get someone to dig up the ground near my tent. If he's using a closed circuit TV system, he'd need a cable, wouldn't he?"

"Yes. If it is a closed circuit TV system."

"It *has* to be."

"Strange."

"Very."

"How did the voice sound?"

"Peculiar."

That afternoon, armed with wrenches and other plumbers' tools, Driscoll and Ron tip-toed in and out of the tents while the women were gathered in the main house. Mrs Obie and Mabel, who would be the first to spot something fishy, were kept busy rearranging all the books in the library to accommodate two table counters which I insisted on having built that afternoon.

By nightfall, every tent had been inspected and a small moat had been dug around my tent. Nothing had been found.

"I don't get it. We've been through every tent and the entire staff's quarters and not a trace of anything suspicious," Ron said when he came to see me that evening in my tent. "What beats me is how he can talk through the bloody TV without a cable?" He shifted his weight in the camp chair. "We'll just have to look some more. They could be hiding something in their mattresses or burying equipment in the ground under their tents. I'll have the whole camp dug up if you like."

"And all the mattresses split open? No. If you do that, I may just as well pack up and go home to America now. If the women find out what you're searching for, they'd leave anyhow."

"You could just throw the TV out and hope for the best."

"You're right, only . . ."

"What?"

"He said he'd find another way to contact me if I did."

"Do you think he will?"

"I don't know. But the thought gives me the willies."

"Then you've only got three other choices. One: let me dig up every electric wire in this place. Two: leave Urudu altogether – Zareda would fire me if he heard me suggesting that. Or three: keep talking to him."

"Keep talking to him?"

"Why not? Pretend you believe he is what he says he is. Ask questions but tell him nothing. He hasn't threatened you, has he?"

"No."

"So play along with him."

"If I only knew what he wanted. Why he cares about us."

"The only way you'll find that out is by communicating with him. And you never know, he might really be . . ." His brown eyes wandered apprehensively around my tent. Was Ron, with his cropped hair and choppy walk, being tempted, if only for a second, to believe that the voice was actually from outer space? "What did he look like on the screen? I mean, do you think it's possible that . . ."

"No, it is not possible. After millions of years of silence, someone from another planet is not going to come to talk to a thirty-three-year-old woman in her tent in Kenya."

"Right." He rose from the chair and unzipped the tent door. Then, just before he turned to go: "Why *not* talk to you? And why not in Africa?"

Long after he left, those soft, swiveling, "Why nots?" kept turning in my mind.

No, it was absurd, egocentric, silly, and romantic.

So why not keep talking to him and find out where he really was from? He had said he wouldn't harm me and I tended to believe that. If he wanted to kidnap me, wouldn't it be simpler to come into camp and nab me rather than go through this elaborate television charade?

And if he were a political spy, did it matter? Our goal was to come up with an idea that would persuade *both* sides to disarm. Or if the voice belonged to someone from the media, a much more likely theory, why not buy his silence by promising him a much better story later?

Then too, he could be nothing but some lonely, eccentric ex-colonial in the bush who knew something about electronics

and had an idea or two about nuclear weapons to communicate.
Was that so bad?

And if he were really a creature from outer space, a mind
energy as he had said . . .

We were, after all, conducting a highly unusual conference
on a subject that could well be of interest to other forces in the
universe. And wasn't it likely that a nuclear holocaust would
upset the balance of the entire galaxy? In ways we didn't
understand?

And wouldn't it be wonderful if he were truly from another
star? Should I cynically ignore that remote, minuscule possibility
and miss what could be the greatest opportunity of my life?

No. Childish, stupid, self-deluding.

Interesting though, that he (or she, of course) had chosen to
pose as a creature from outer space. For didn't our dream that
there were intelligent beings in space, who would "carry on"
the business of consciousness, secretly console us when we
thought about our eventual extinction? Didn't it insidiously
encourage our resignation to the idea of a nuclear holocaust?

The next day, the conference began in earnest. Hitsai abandoned
her cameras, Farah sent telexes around the world for more
books and Jean Weinstein xeroxed so many sheets of paper that
Mabel accused her of writing a new history of philosophy.

At the meeting I'd missed the day before, the women had
decided that in one week's time, each would present her first
seedling ideas. Naturally everyone wanted to come up with the
idea that would set the pace for the rest of the conference.

Talk at meals was limited to light subjects. They were all
keeping their cards to their chests and saving their insights for
the day they would present them. One could feel the ambition
in the air.

No one was phased by the rain which unseasonably,
unpleasantly continued to fall for several days. Donning their
rubber boots and hoisting the camp's black umbrellas over
their heads, they adapted. Watching them plod through the
mud, their cotton slacks flapping wetly around their ankles,
their hair lank or uncontrollably curly, I liked them more than
ever, especially the older ones.

How can I tell them we have been infiltrated? I asked myself as rainy day followed rainy day and still I did nothing about the television. It would be destructive to interrupt their thought processes so early on. Their enthusiasm and determination would never be as intense again.

"We knew it was going to be like thees, n'est-ce pas?" Annabelle Leleu would say in her semi-grunt whenever I ran into her. "But is *luxe* compare to what we *souffert* in South America."

She had a cough and runny nose, but when I asked if she'd like me to contact the flying doctor, she said: "*Non*. Hot tea and honey and am *en forme* in two days." Hearty laugh and a big show of yellow teeth, but her eyes were watering and she looked as if she could use a week in bed.

All of them rebuffed my inquiries about their well-being with an incredible show of stoicism. When I commented on this to Jean Weinstein, she replied with her usual eloquence: "We're living a romantic dream here. To complain would mean we were inadequate to that dream. In Santa Barbara with Hutchins, where conditions were relatively comfortable, we never stopped bitching about something. There was no fantasy to console us for the leaky toilets."

Not only leaky, but smelly. It was typical of the spirit of the camp for Jean not to mention this unpleasant new phenomenon which had arrived with the rains.

Mabel reported that when Elsa Heinzelmann slipped in the mud in front of the library and all 175 pounds of her fell directly on her coccyx, she adamantly refused to be helped up. Yanking herself to her feet without wincing, she briskly told Mabel to find her a chair. "I've fallen on that spot before and it usually rights itself after a few hours."

She then asked Mabel to bring her the Bible; she wanted to check something in Revelations.

"If Revelations was good enough for Isaac Newton, it's good enough for me," she said, explaining that Newton – to the dismay of his colleagues – had also explored this ancient, peculiar data for answers to the universe's enigmas.

I, myself, refused to do any serious creative thinking. My ambition, which was to organize and finance a think tank, had been fulfilled and not for a minute did I think that a great idea was inside me waiting to be born. My secret, most depressing worry was that underneath their repeated declarations of enthusiasm, the women felt the same.

Every day, I tried to spend a little time with Mrs Obie who had burrowed even deeper into her neurosis. Not only was she paranoid about the natives, she made mistakes in the minimal accounting I asked her to do, and stumbled when she walked any distance. Something was coming apart inside her and she had lost the will to snap it back into place.

She was sixty-four. Too old, perhaps, to be in the bush. When I asked her if she would like to go back to London, she insisted that she was quite all right and would not dream of leaving me. Again I was grateful to Padma. Of all the women, she was the only one who was aware of poor Mrs Obie's confused existence.

I spent hours reading alone or, occasionally, I would go out into the bush with one of the drivers, but it wasn't the same as being with the group. I hadn't counted on being quite so solitary.

My feelings of isolation were reinforced by Hal's first and only letter to me, which arrived on the late plane just before tea one gloomy afternoon. It totalled twelve lines, including the signature. Writing in a brisk, chilly prose, he informed me that he had signed a new contract "of a confidential nature" with the government and would be much busier than he had foreseen.

A polite, but definitive kiss-off. I wondered if the contract was with the Defense Department. No matter which department, none would approve of Hal continuing his association with his anti-nuclear millionaire client and her female satellites in the jungle. He would expect me to understand.

And I did. But I still felt abandoned. I had trusted him to hang in there and continue to care about the project. His smart, pragmatic mind not only gave us ballast, it was our link – no matter how tenuous – to the world of power.

Overcome by a depression which Hal's rejection didn't merit – but provoked all the same – I returned to my tent and took out the television set.

Hoping I wouldn't regret it later, I decided to do as Ron had suggested and find out what the intruder wanted and who he or she was. Though it was probably foolish, possibly dangerous, to communicate with him, it was better than worrying about him contacting me in some other way. It was also something to do.

When I turned on the set, nothing happened. No sound on any of the channels. I sat on the bed, propped three pillows behind my back and waited. Apparently he had not outfitted himself with a beeper alerting him to my interest. He would come to me when he chose to. I picked up my Robert Graves book and tried to lose myself in tales of the Medusa.

After about forty-five minutes, he appeared, heralded by electronic beeps and random flashes of light.

"Amazing," he said in his weird, warbling way. "Just turned on controls to test them and saw you ready to receive."

"We're having a little slump in excitement so I thought I'd see what you were up to out there in space." The white light sauntered gaily about the screen as I spoke. "One of the things I wanted to ask you is your name."

"Don't really use names. We know who we are without them."

"Well, if you're going to talk to someone lower down on the evolutionary scale, you've got to have a name. How about Toto?"

"Toto? Not sure like."

"It happens to be the name of the only dog I ever had. Kind of a beagle. I named him after the dog in *The Wizard of Oz*. It means 'all'. My mother gave him away."

"Sad. Why?"

"Too much trouble, not house-trainable enough, ugly. Who knows why mothers give away kids' animals? I've never forgotten him though. He was an ideal only child's dog."

"What is only child?"

"An only child is one who grows up without brothers and sisters in a human family. God, I wish you'd stop playing this charade and admit that you're human."

"Must have dog's name?"

"Yes. Toto is a wonderful name. I've decided who you are by the way. You're either Bill Spears or Farah."

"Who are they?"

"Farah is our expert in telecommunications and Bill is our

resident naturalist. He's the tall man running around camp giving everyone orders. And he's you. Tell me, Bill, are you as interested in Claire Montmorency as you look?"

"What talking about?"

"You follow her around like a lost lion cub. Can't you see that she's too beautiful and famous for a naturalist who makes $10,000 a year tops and lives in the bush?"

Not for a minute did I think an emotionally stunted creature like Bill Spears could ever assemble a masquerade as elaborate as this one, but if I accused him of being Bill, it might provoke him to reveal who he really was.

"Am a mind energy. Sooner or later you will believe."

"Great. Then tell me more about yourself, how you live, what you eat. . . . No, of course, minds don't eat or have sex, do they?"

"We *do* eat. Consume knowledge. More we consume, more mobile we become."

"Not bigger?"

"Have no size. Size is human condition."

"Stars have sizes. Galaxies have sizes. Why can't you have a size?"

"Because don't. Have mobility. Have lots of mobility, otherwise wouldn't be here. And no, don't reproduce or have sex differences. Also don't die. We just are."

"I'm surprised you don't bore yourselves to death."

He made a sound like a tire deflating. "Maybe that's why am here. Need stimulation."

"Me too. The fright you gave me the other night was the best antidote for boredom I can think of."

"Am sorry frightened you."

"Later, I realized, of course, there's nothing to be afraid of at all. We're not subversives. All we're doing is looking for an idea which we will one day make public. In fact, we're less dangerous to the system than a priest in Dubuque, Iowa, organizing a protest march."

"Glad you see it that way. Thus we speak freely. Nice I contact you, not other Russian groups who much work on same problem."

"We're not unique?" I didn't care if he heard the disappointment in my voice.

"You only all-female and only one in Africa."

"It's about time the Russians did something. Whenever I think of them, I see this great fatalistic mass of bent backs waiting to be clubbed."

"Will help if I say they no nearer to idea than you?"

"Why? We're not competing with anybody. We don't care which side comes up with an idea as long as someone does. But tell me, do the Russians have any wonderful Slavic insights into the problem that we should know about?"

"Not truly. It all illusion anyhow. None of you believe can really succeed."

"Bullshit. All the women do. That's what makes this experiment so remarkable. They're all pledged to believing the mind has the power to overcome the problem."

"We see. Price of maturity is resignation."

"I don't know what you're talking about."

"First lesson human child learn is resign himself to not getting what he wants: power over everything in his environment. Before nuclear bomb, resignation was fine, useful tool for building human society. Now not."

"Ah, but when I got Cy's money, I learned differently. Now I am *never* resigned to anything. Do you know who Cy is?"

"Know almost everything about you."

"You're beginning to give me the creeps again."

"You want talk again in three days? Have more much to say. If you turn on television around ten, am contact in with you."

"If you promise to tell me about what's going on in Russia."

"First you prove worthy of my confidence."

"Okay, that's enough," I said rudely. "I'll talk to you in three days."

I lifted my hand to turn off the television, but he had already disappeared. I wondered if I had hurt his feelings.

6

Arching her long brown neck, Dorothea Mowbrie looked arrogantly through her triple-thick bifocals at the women filing into the conference room. She had an idea. That was obvious, but watching her drum her sharpened pencil on the table, I sensed that her idea had not pounced into her mind with the full, sparkling resonance of genius. It was tentative and smacked of the also-ran.

Dorothea, like everyone, was nervous. I had not realized until then how competitive the women were. Nothing wrong with competition except that when things fall apart – and they did – it turns too quickly to suspicion and fear.

A week had passed since the women had met and resolved to present their initial ideas.

I had claimed the right to sit in. Mabel was beside me. Both of us were near the plywood partition that separated the conference room from the dining-room and seated on those ubiquitous low-slung camp chairs that are among the most uncomfortable reminders of Kenya's colonial past.

Mabel eyed the women warily and slunk back in her chair. Her awe of the geniuses had not been diminished by her proximity to them. Though she did have her favorites. Elsa Heinzelmann was highest on the list.

The room was clean and the conference table smelled of fresh new wood. It was a beautiful day filled with soft, sweeping mountain breezes. The sun had returned and the myriad, tiny, talkative beasts that inhabited the camp were feasting in the lush new grass that had grown two inches during the four days of rain. By the end of the rainy season the grass in the Mara would be four feet high. Whereupon a million wildebeeste would chomp it down to lawn length.

When everyone was seated, I realized that Claire Montmorency wasn't there. I looked at Theresa Crater and

141

mouthed the word, "Claire". The author answered with a shrug of indifference. No one else bothered to mention her absence. For an actress to evade the first, most challenging meeting of the conference was to be expected.

As had been agreed earlier, lots were drawn to determine who would be chairwoman. Theresa, whose deep, beautifully modulated television voice had already gained her respect among the scholars – in spite of her fictional pursuits – drew the winning slip. I was delighted. For surely, the author of such sprawling, quasi-metaphysical scientific novels had the scope and creative tolerance to preside over this brilliant, multi-racial gathering.

Wasting no time, Theresa called the meeting to order with a sharp rap of an ashtray. "Let's start with a brief progress report from everyone. Just a statement of your idea, whether you want help at this stage and an estimate of how much time you need to develop it. We'll start with Padma on my left."

She turned to Padma, who, for some reason, had decided to wear a sari. On her arms were ancient, ivory bracelets with gold fittings; in her ears the gleaming solitaire diamonds she had worn the first day I met her.

She rose with a dreadful solemnity and began what, we soon realized, was a carefully prepared and memorized speech.

"After one week of thought, I have chosen to focus on the darker side of my nature and my fascination with aggression. I came to this decision after going on only one game ride.

"I asked Moses, the best driver here, to take me out into the bush alone at dawn." She smiled apologetically. "I didn't want to share my first experience of this paradise with anyone else. That is my nature.

"Before we'd gone two miles, I realized the whole bush was alive with fear and scuttling. Zebra, alert to some dread scent, were darting to and fro. Topi, standing on termite mounds, were poised for flight and hyenas, ignoring the vulnerable prey around them, were intent only on fleeing from whatever was ahead in the east.

"Moses, who knew what was happening, slowed the vehicle. Turning to me, he motioned me to stand. I quickly reached for my binoculars, opened the hatch and peered into the rising sun.

And then I saw them: a pride of lions, lying in the dry grass like sultans after a picnic, sublimely heedless of us, our noisy vehicle and the timorous beasts around us."

The women stirred impatiently. They didn't really need this dramatic rehash of what they had all seen, but Padma was not to be deterred, not even by Theresa's tightened chin line.

"Moses turned off the motor," Padma went on, "and we watched in silence as two of the lionesses rose and ambled off to a small pool of water under an acacia tree. And what did I want? *I wanted to hear them roar and witness a kill.* See a zebra strangled. Watch the lionesses rip apart its entrails and carry bloody mouthfuls to their young. I wanted violence, cruelty, a *show*."

She lowered her voice. "I am a student of religion, an intellectual with soft hands, a mother who can weep with love for her children and yet, above all . . ." She paused and looked down at us with fierce, luminous eyes. "I am a predator," she shouted. It was a full, round bellow of rage and self-realization that put a stop to all fiddling with pencils and movements of feet under the table.

Large, dark-skinned, dominant, she repeated the words: "I am a predator."

"*Ich bin ein Berliner*," I thought suddenly, for no reason. It just came into my head.

Knuckles grazing the table, bosom heaving under soft silk, she continued in a harsh, shouting voice. "Who am I – and you and you, all of you – but the offspring of thousands of generations of predatory animals who have killed and feasted their way to civilization? What affinity do we have with those shy herbivores: the zebra and the monkey? They have nothing to do with us. We are, will be, our egos say, over and over, dominant over all, predators like *them*. And our deepest identification has always, will always be, not with peace, but with our brother, the lion, our father, the warrior, his weapon, the bomb.

"For what is the nuclear bomb, but a bigger, deadlier roar? The most glorious of all killer human inventions that has made us masters, not just over this or that nation, but over the destiny of the entire planet.

143

"How can we stop the killing now? How can we adopt the pacifist ways of those timid, hooved beasts trembling before a pride of lions? A *pride*, not a herd, not a pack, but a *pride*. I tell you cruelty is the price of man's domination on earth and the nuclear bomb is the natural outcome of that destiny. And not all the thought in the world can change that terrible reality."

All eyes were fixed upon her. Yes indeed, a predator. Not a woman a rapist or thief would want to meet in a dark alley. Bowing her head, she sank into her chair.

Mabel's hands gripped the arms of her chair. She had not written a word. I nudged her and pointed to her notepad. She looked at me with unfocused eyes. She had just seen herself being eaten alive.

I assumed everyone had been equally flattened by the speech, but I was underestimating the resilience of these intellectuals. Throw them an idea and they might be temporarily taken off guard by its force, but within moments, their critical powers rose like a pack of wild dogs, stripping the idea of fat and gristle, until they were down to pure bone, or no bone, which seemed to be the case here. Apparently Padma had not presented an idea at all.

Theresa was icy. "Thank you, Padma. Your observation should be helpful."

Ann Peabody, who was next, brushed a strand of gray-blonde hair from her face. "Could I comment on Padma's words?" she asked in a treacherous, lilting tone.

Theresa's scalp shone pinkly under the overhead light as she nodded, yes. "If you keep your comments brief."

"I would like to say that man's predatory nature has been well-documented by all the world's major religions. Although Padma's identification with a pride of lions may have come as a surprise to her, it would be no great shock to any of the architects of the doctrine of original sin."

She paused for breath and would have gone on, if Hitsai hadn't headed her off. "This can only lead to depressive, non-productive discussions. We are all aware of the so-called territorial imperative and other negative aspects of the hunter-primate. Our task is to work with the non-violent traits of man."

Farah yawned agreement. "It will just carry us back to some tedious utopian dream of changing man's nature. Was it B. F. Skinner or Arthur Koestler who wanted to devise a non-aggression pill for mankind?"

"Well, it was better than putting the spirit of Woodstock into the water supply," Jean Weinstein chuckled.

The air filled with mild laughs and chair adjustments.

"I think now we can go on to Ann," Theresa said in loud, chairwomanly tones.

Ann leaned her chair back and looked up at the rafters possibly searching for fruit bats who were known to spend the day there. "Through analysis of the rise and fall of civilizations, could we not identify what specific evils incite the lower orders to overthrow a cruel, expansionist ruling class and somehow recreate the same climate that . . ."

My mind drifted. Her monotone voice and blonde eyelashes closing over her colorless eyes told us all that a new idea was not forthcoming. Only a vague dream of revolution which Farah, fresh from the pain in Iran, dissected and threw back at her like so much chewed meat.

Farah's proposal wasn't much better. According to her, the disparity between the Eastern bloc's economic development and its military strength was the real reason to fear Russian aggression.

We should therefore convince western industrial leaders to teach the Soviet Union how to increase its productivity. There was no question the Russians wanted to learn. Their industrial spies were all over the West.

"If the Russian people's standard of living were improved, their leaders would be less paranoid and start giving the people more political freedom. Once the Russian people were free to express themselves, an orderly, popular anti-nuclear movement would be inevitable," Farah stated in a voice of impressive authority.

For a moment, I was agog with the vision of ordinary people from Kiev to Indianapolis storming the citadels of power and crying for peace while leaders of Russia, the US, China and Europe huddled together in a bunker wondering what had happened. Had humanity gotten out of control?

145

Susan Wu swiftly demolished that happy projection. "The Soviet Union's defense system, like ours, is based on fear, not gain. Increasing Russia's wealth or political freedom will not decrease its fear. In the West we have freedom and wealth and what does the majority vote for? More bombs."

Susan's wrinkled yellow hands plied the air, like a child trying to catch snowflakes, only in this case, it was truth. "Peace requires leadership and leadership must come from the heads of state in the Soviet Union, the us, Europe and China. People follow leaders, not mobs."

She spoke with such conviction, I thought for sure she had a counter-proposal. But like Hitsai, Jean Weinstein and Annabelle, she regretfully informed us that her ideas still needed further development.

Carol Schumacher was a bit further along. Gripping her notebook with her usual unreleased tension, she said she was studying the nuclear problem from a feminist angle and that she would present her ideas after she had re-evaluated them in the light of Padma's excellent, very relevant comments.

My hopes rose. Feminism was not a favored topic among these women, but I was heartened to hear that at least one person in the group was mindful of it.

Nodding wearily at the mention of feminism, Theresa said no one was under any pressure to have her ideas formulated after only one week of study. She, herself, had not got very far, but wondered if anyone would like to discuss the role art could play in the peacemaking process.

"Art," Jean scoffed. "Almost every great work of art in the twentieth century from *Guernica* to *The Tin Drum* has been a cry of rage against war. And where have these masterpieces led us? Into an even greater proliferation of nuclear arms. Art has no power. It is the great disappointment of this century. Give me back the religion James Joyce threw away when he said he would forge the conscience of his race in the smithy of his soul. What soul? What conscience? I tell you art can never replace the restraining power of religion."

"Perhaps religion is not so dead," said Elsa Heinzelmann who was next. Giving her hair a little tug, she told the group of her search through Revelations for the mathematical secrets that might be encoded there. They found her research so frivolous, no one bothered to comment on it except Padma.

"Revelations," the Indian woman intoned, "is one of the most vicious, war-like documents to come out of Christianity. You will not find peace there, Dr Heinzelmann, only a lunatic's fantasy of total annihilation of the non-Christian world."

Mabel, who had had her money on Elsa, glowered at Padma.

I stretched my legs and tried to stay interested. The smell of fried pork and delicious African seasonings drifted in from the kitchen. I was starved. Only Dorothea Mowbrie had not spoken.

"I have no concrete solution yet, but a direction which I think all of you have ignored," she said, her mouth set in the prim attitude of someone heavily encased in the laws of reality. "If Padma was made aware of her predatory nature by the bush, I have become aware of my practical nature by Janet's remarkable generosity.

"Ladies, remember while you're chasing after ideas, that we have $250 million at our disposal. With that money, we can turn the best of our ideas into action. Instead of theorizing, ask yourselves: what terror can we create? What seed can we sow?"

She flung her hands out in a pleading, preacherly way. "Do any of you realize the dynamics of genius and money acting together? Bring your minds out of the clouds. Think like Harlem. Think tough. Plan. Create that one deed."

Theresa was kind. "Thank you, Dorothea. Money is indeed a vital factor here. I think now, it's time to adjourn for lunch."

We filed out of the conference room and strolled around the lawn that skirted the main house. Hitsai and Elsa ordered drinks. The rest of us hovered aimlessly about in the sort of stupor people fall into during the intermission of a play they don't want to return to.

Padma moved off to the side of the building and stood alone. A deposed Aquinas in brilliant Indian silks. Her words had rung true, had been true, but more was steaming in that subcontinental brain. I went up to her.

"I hope this doesn't mean you will leave us," I said.

"Why do you ask?"

"Because you seemed to see no hope for us at all."

"True. But perhaps in despair is a beginning."

"How?"

"I will speak again when I have something to say." She smiled, but her eyes were hard. I asked her if she had a copy of her speech, explaining that Mabel had taken no notes. She pulled a copy from the sheaf of papers she was carrying and gave it to me. Hearing the lunch bell, we joined the others and went into the main house.

Just as the second course was being served, Claire came sauntering down the grass path that led to her tent. Her cheeks were flushed, her hair askew and damp. She didn't look embarrassed by her failure to attend the last meeting. She looked like a woman who had just had an orgasm.

Her walk had an obscene little bounce to it as she moved across the room to sit between Mrs Obie and Theresa. She poured herself some sparkling water. "I'm on to something," she said, raising her glass and toasting herself.

Mrs Obie, who loathed her beautiful Thespian countrywoman, ignored her. She was looking at Ron who was walking across the concrete floor with a calm, tinny look in his eyes. She liked and leaned on him as she had with Dempster and was given to asking him for small extra favors.

"I have fixed the lamp in your tent. There won't be any more problems with it," he said gruffly. If it had been just a little more paranoid, I would have thought a message had passed between them.

Claire reached for the bread basket, put two thick slices on her plate and smeared them with butter. She ate voraciously, heedless of the lock of hair falling in her eyes, smiling to herself between bites.

I thought about joining Claire and Theresa, but decided to forego the rest of lunch and have my coffee sent to my tent. If Claire had an idea, I would hear of it later. Or never hear of it. I was sick of the abstract and wanted to make love.

7

"Odd, when Padma bellowed out those words: 'I am a predator,' all I could think of was Kennedy shouting *'Ich bin ein Berliner,'*" I said to Toto.

True to his word, he had appeared when he said he would, which also happened to be the night following Padma's speech. There seemed no harm in telling him about it. Even the most vicious paparazzi could not make much of her insight into man's predatory nature. Yet by confiding this much, I figured I might get him to open up and reveal more about himself. "Maybe because it had the same number of syllables," I mused.

"Or was same message."

"How?"

"Maybe what he telling West Berliners was simply that: I am a predator. Will kill to save you. I, the hunter, I, the savage."

"And how they cheered."

"He was most dangerous man alive with biggest arsenal on globe, promising to protect them. Naturally they cheer."

"I don't think of Kennedy as a predator."

"He ordered one thousand ICBMS made. He sent sixteen thousand men to Vietnam. He threatened whole world with nuclear annihilation when he faced Russians in Cuban water."

"And he won, little Toto," I replied, noticing that his grammar had improved somewhat.

"He accomplished what he set out do. But his days numbered after that."

"So you think his assassination was a conspiracy?"

"No, think Oswald acted alone, but saw Kennedy from Russian point of view and decide to kill him before he got any more big ideas."

"So Oswald is a hero? Is that how you see him on your star?"

"No. Don't know. Can't read human minds. Guess that Oswald more than anything was victim."

"Victim of what?"

"The life-force. Will to Live. *Elan vital*. There many names for that force that animates your globe. Some say it is only necessity of DNA to create more DNA. Whatever it is, it make sure life never stop. If human gene pool accidentally produce a Kennedy, it also produce an Oswald to get rid of him. Otherwise, possible you and none of beasts grazing outside would be here. And earth would be restless as the wind."

"I'd hoped you'd be objective and not a Communist."

"Am *not* Communist. Am objective always. You know you being ridiculous. When will you liberate your mind and let it roam as freely as mine?"

"When you tell me who you are."

Nevertheless, after I turned off the television, I did as he suggested and let my mind wander among lovely, swoony thoughts about the life-force. Or rather *élan vital*, clearly one of the most beautiful phrases to caress the human tongue and one of the most romantic views of the universe there was.

Mankind, like the lilies of the field. God, a kindly horticulturist, with calloused hands. Gently prodding the world towards more life with a loving, mudcaked thumb.

But deep in the bush, lions dreamt of the morning's kill, maribou storks waited for the carrion that would come and everywhere, the smooth, white bones of yesterday's carcasses lay gleaming under the moon.

Would we never escape the cruelty and gore from which we sprang?

So why not forget life and be done with it? That treacherous suicidal whisper again. Why not die now, before the holocaust, the predator's final, inevitable act?

Peace finally. Rest. End of confusion, money, power, *doing something*. End of Mrs Cyrus Cavanaugh.

The spears the guards carried. How gruesome, but easy to imagine that sharp, dirty-gray spear plunged into my lily-of-the-field heart.

Death isn't what we really fear, is it? Aren't we all, under our noisy individualism, secretly resigned to it?

150

Isn't the real dread for that cruel morning when we look up in the sky, see the fireball and hear the whirr of sirens no one answers?

Ich bin ein Berliner.

Of what use the predator's cry then?

8

The weeks slid by like the mud under our feet and life took on a terrible sameness. Because it was raining almost every other day, we were completely sedentary, yet consuming the same number of calories as when we were going out on twice-daily game runs. Sluggish muscles and stultified minds – modern man's twin disabilities – were in full force. Were the twilight years of the dinosaurs any different?

Dorothea's practical insight that we consider my quarter of a billion dollars as a starting point yielded few creative explosions.

Hitsai came up with a complex, technical scheme for fouling up the red alert systems of all the nuclear powers which Farah, calling upon her vast knowledge of telecommunications, demolished in less than fifteen minutes.

Meanwhile Theresa persevered with her notion that only through art could fear and suspicion between the Eastern and Western blocs be diminished. Everyone agreed that art could indeed be helpful, but not even Claire could support spending $250 million on it.

Susan Wu suggested that we devote the money to proving the "nuclear winter" theory. "According to new studies by Birks in America, a 10,000 megaton nuclear exchange could cause so many fires and so much soot, the sun would be blotted out for months and the earth's temperatures so drastically lowered that all life would perish. If we could substantiate this theory, we'd be proving that winning a nuclear war is impossible and therefore nuclear weapons are useless."

"And the neutron bomb would be brought back and more money poured into outer space weapons," Carol Schumacher rasped. "Don't you see, no new dimension of terror can undercut these men's murderous policies?"

We reached our nadir the day Farah and Jean simultaneously came up with the idea to use my $250 million on an enormous anti-nuclear advertising and public relations campaign in America.

"How can you hope to make a dent on the American psyche with a quarter of a billion dollars' worth of publicity?" Theresa asked derisively. "No paid-for political announcements can ever have the media impact of Reagan meeting the Russians in a locked room to discuss the bombs they are never going to get rid of. If he so much as wears a plaid suit, he makes headlines around the world."

"It isn't that he controls public relations in the US," Padma said. "He is that through which half the American public relates to the other half."

None of us quite understood this last, but it had the ring of truth and I was glad Padma had more or less rejoined the group.

Her mood had changed remarkably. The despair which had followed her "predator" speech had lifted. Walking through camp in her blue jeans, her eyes fierce with inspiration, her heavy head tilted towards heaven, she looked as though she were in direct communication with Krishna.

Has she, I wondered, found solace and refuge in the idea of the life-force as Toto has? Did Hindu philosophy embrace similar misty views? But it didn't seem in character for her to be taken in by them.

The other scholars also sensed something important growing inside Padma. I noticed that Theresa Crater had taken a liking to her. Claire, who was still simmering with an idea she refused to divulge, was also friendlier towards Padma. One night, watching her light Padma's cigarette, I got the uncomfortable feeling she was buttering her up.

The women had more or less divided into two groups. Theresa headed the smaller one which I thought of as the "Creatives" since Claire and Dorothea, our outspoken, high strung mathematician, and the philosophical Jean Weinstein were part of it. They tended to congregate in the main house around five o'clock to discuss everyone from Aeschylus to Heidegger in loud, dissonant voices while consuming amazing amounts of vodka and rum.

The rest fell into a larger group whom I privately dubbed the

"Drudges". They were more withdrawn than the Creatives and generally busier. Most were maintaining some sort of fitness program and were working on an outside project. Susan Wu was translating a Chinese text that she'd been given by a colleague from Brookings before she left Washington. Others were composing future lecture notes or completing some scholarly article unrelated to the conference.

Almost every other evening, I talked to Toto. In retrospect, it seems absurd that I indulged myself in this dangerous pastime and accepted his presence with such equanimity. But I was extremely alone during those weeks and a conversation with him was very appealing.

His simple declarative sentences and succinct views on say, jogging and dieting (gives western man the illusion that he is in control of his fate) or the Mother Goddess (yes, the world was matriarchal eons ago) were a relief after hours of listening to the geniuses' turgid, convoluted discussions.

He also didn't *act* dangerous. He seemed perfectly content simply to converse and, as he said, "get know human being." He never asked me to do anything that would endanger me, nor did he betray any interest in the women's knowledge of weaponry or ask about their ideas. He assumed – rightly – that they hadn't got anywhere.

"Takes so long for human minds to turn over ideas," he said with disdain. Or maybe pity. "Plow through thought process like wooly mammoths."

"Well, we can't all be as brilliant and evolved as mind energies," I retorted.

"Brilliance not needed to rid world of bomb. Life-force will provide."

"If the Mother Goddess still ruled and women were dominant, the life-force wouldn't have to trouble itself with solving this problem. There'd be no war. No bombs."

"Mother Goddess will never return. World never go backwards in evolution."

"You think men's domination of the world is a step up the evolutionary ladder?"

"Much progress since then. Life better than before, no?"

"Only technologically, not morally."

"Story not over yet."

He was at his best when discussing such generalities. I enjoyed and saw no harm in listening to them. And there was always the chance he would give himself away. To this end, I often did most of the questioning.

"Do you people believe in God?" I asked him one night.

"Of course," he laughed-croaked.

"Can you see him?"

"No, but we are aware of his movements."

"Movements?"

A steely wheeze that was laughter. "I forgot, your intellectuals who still believe in a God see him as some sort of Unmoved Mover, not right?"

"In a way, yes."

"Well, assure you, He quite active. Would thought humans guess that when they discover theory of relativity."

"Do you love him?" I asked, hoping to find at least one area where he was vulnerable.

"Course not."

"Do you love anyone?"

"No, love not something we have. Have everything else: immortality, freedom from pain, ever-increasing knowledge, but no, no love."

One afternoon when only a few of the scholars were in the conference room, Carol Schumacher introduced the feminist idea I had been waiting for. I took my own notes. Mabel, who had long since begged permission to stop attending the meetings, was in the library reading thrillers.

"Padma's views on man's predatory nature were correct," Carol began. "Her only error lay in her identification with men, male weapons and destruction. These are *borrowed* projects that have nothing to do with women."

Padma, who was sitting at the end of the table, filling the air with cigarette smoke, grimaced, but said nothing.

"Women have never had anything to do with the predatory enterprise. As nurturers and gatherers, we have never needed to develop that sense of aggression and obedience crucial to men who hunt in groups. We are made to obey different laws than men, to serve life, not destroy it. To love and give, not kill.

"Whereas men, trained to hunt in teams, have been locked into a system based on obedience and aggression since the beginning of time. When their leader points to the prey and says 'hate', they hate. When he says 'kill', they kill. And now, when he says 'build a better bomb', they build it. Like packs of well-trained dogs.

"Since pre-history, the two systems functioned together perfectly. Men killed. We loved. And the species thrived. Four and a half billion people now inhabit the planet, which is perhaps why women, who must serve life, have never meaningfully withheld their consent to the predatory enterprise. But now, because of the nuclear threat, I believe they can and will.

"Because we are freer than men. Free to love as they cannot. Free because we have been mercifully locked out of that system of obedience and aggression that stunts men's minds."

Before anyone could challenge these statements, Carol quickly outlined her proposal to use my money to form an international movement dedicated to achieving female political supremacy in all the nuclear states by the end of the century. Not in the name of "women's rights", but in the name of life.

Her narrow shoulders were trembling under her Brooks Brothers shirt when she finished speaking. Since I had never felt comfortable with Padma's lumping us all together with the lion's roar, I liked Carol's speech. It also seemed to answer Hal Palmer's theory that men were women's weapons. The scholars disagreed.

Hitsai was the first to respond. "The suffragettes dreamed that when women got the vote, we would have universal peace. But what followed? World War Two, nuclear weapons and Mrs Thatcher, one of the most war-like, pro-nuclear leaders in the world."

Theresa attacked from another angle: "You will never be able to convince women that they are not aggressive," she barked. "Look at this group. Each of us has clawed her way to the top of her field with an aggression that far exceeds most men's."

Susan Wu doubted women's ability to organize themselves. "Women can never create a powerful political movement, precisely because, as Carol rightly stated, women lack the gift of obedience." She smiled at the group serenely. Her small, wrinkled hands, poised on each side of her papers, looked like two delicately carved, ivory book-ends. "Because women were nurturers and gatherers, they never had to learn to work in teams. Even today, they have no respect for female authority and despise things like pecking orders and chains of command – all the ingredients required to create a cohesive and effective political force. This is the real reason men have always controlled society."

"Women are extremely good team players," Carol said, her head swiveling on her neck as she turned left to right to meet these attacks. "A whole new generation of young women in business have proven they are."

I smiled at this, remembering the many articles I had been assigned to write on "playing the game at the office" and grabbed a fresh notebook. At last the women were having the feminist debate I had been hoping for.

"We also got the vote through organized demonstrations and other forms of pressure," Carol continued, glaring at Susan Wu.

"Indeed you did. Some sixty years after your Negro male slaves did," Padma boomed from the end of the table, smashing her cigarette into the overflowing glass ashtray in front of her. Happily Dorothea was not present.

"Men didn't always control society," Carol declaimed hoarsely. "Countless anthropologists believe most human societies were matriarchal in pre-Bronze Age cultures."

"*Feminist* anthropologists," Theresa snorted.

Carol's fist came down on the table. "The myths of a supreme Mother Goddess demonstrate clearly that at one time the female sex was the more powerful one. The Sumerians, the ancient Greeks, the Druids – all had myths pointing to –"

"Myths. That's just what they are," Susan Wu replied frowning at Carol's clenched fist. "How can these oral legends prove anything scientifically?"

Padma turned to Carol. "I give some credence to the theory

that the world might have been matriarchal before men discovered that women were not the only ones responsible for procreation and that semen also had something to do with it. However, once men made this great discovery and, more importantly, once they realized that the species would thrive and grow if women spent less time ruling and more time breeding, women were deposed, the patriarchal system came into being and humanity made a great leap forward. And although women suffered a great injustice, no one can deny that humanity has enjoyed unimaginable progress since then."

Carol tried to interrupt, but Padma ignored her and swept on. "In any case, all this talk of male or female supremacy is not, let me remind you, the question here."

"But it proves the power of ideas," I said, breaking my rule never to interrupt during the women's meetings. Surprised, they all turned to look at me in my camp chair shoved against the plywood wall. "If men became dominant when they realized that the more babies they could force women to have, the faster society would grow, it shows how ideas can change the world."

Padma nodded to me regally. "Your point is well-taken, Mrs Cavanaugh. Nevertheless, I think we would do better to return to the subject of the conference, which is war. Feminism is irrelevant. We have no proof that these matriarchies were peaceful. We know only that war is an established institution in almost every society on earth and that women have never seriously tried to thwart it."

"That's because women are suppressed," Carol protested, clenching her hair at the roots.

"Women are suppressed because it serves their interests to be suppressed," Padma retorted. "For if I am dominated, I am free of the guilt of war. If I grow fat on the kill, it is because he made me eat. If I mourn my son slain in battle, I can say his father, not I, made him die. I am free to hate the killer and not myself even though I have always been men's accomplice in the evil that is war. The *original* evil."

She paused to look directly at me with her great, black, mystical eyes. "For make no mistake, war – the killing of one's own species for gain – is the original evil which, from the beginning of time, has been directed towards only one end: the final evil, the destruction of us all."

No one challenged her. Her last sentence had clobbered all thought.

Finally, Elsa Heinzelmann's sorrowful, German-accented voice filled the little plywood room: "Padma is right, Carol. It doesn't matter which sex is more or less responsible for war." She was sitting near the middle of the table, so short, it was a strain for her to keep her plump little elbows on the table. "The real mystery is why has this predatory enterprise, which seemed to serve life for so long, culminated in the deployment of 50,000 nuclear warheads? Why did God sow the seeds of its own destruction into human nature? Why did He play this cruel joke on us, who were made in His own likeness?"

The silence that greeted these questions was as dry and cold as the air in the room. Through the window, I could see the last impersonal rays of the setting sun.

"It's already getting dark," Jean said at last, pointing listlessly to the window. Without further comment, the scholars gathered their papers together and donned their numerous sweaters.

Carol was the first to leave. I wanted to run after her but did not move. There is no consolation for the eternal, constantly renewable defeat of the feminist dream that women are morally superior to their rulers.

Although the sun shone intermittently, the sky was mostly bleak and the nights cold. The staff were unhappy. At times, overtly rude. They were bored with these heavy-hipped women with their library eyes and strange product, ideas. The same high standard of service was maintained, but gone were the shy smiles and approval-seeking conversations. The padlocks on the bar where the liquor was kept were broken one otherwise uneventful afternoon. Ten bottles of whiskey were stolen. Nothing to get excited about, but still, it was theft.

"It's nothing," Ron said when I expressed concern. "They always get like this when the rains go on too long."

Added to this: Clothes that never were fully dry, the yellow mud caked on our shoes, papers that stuck together, and Mrs

Obie's repeated, incendiary remarks and quarrels with almost everyone.

She had broken off her friendship with Padma. Impossible to know why. "Indians aren't really Caucasians," she said one night at dinner in an inexcusably loud whisper. "I don't know what I ever saw in that woman."

But the worst was the silence in the camp.

The women had retreated into their minds and found nothing. I know the pain that comes from that emptiness. It spreads through the creative classes like a cancer and can attack anyone from an underpaid editor on *Woman's Work* all the way up to Nobel Prize candidate, Annabelle Leleu.

The project looked so feasible. They saw the problem, opted to tackle it, bravely lowered their buckets down into the well, and there it was: the most frightening truth about themselves. The well was dry. Nothing. After all those years of faith and sacrifice.

While other women lay spread-eagled on beds reaping diamonds, they had labored on campuses, backs bent with the weight of books, skin sucked of color by overhead fluorescent lights, driving the brain, swatting the heart, lowering the gas on emotion . . . for what?

For love. For creativity, that unusual gift that set them apart from most of humanity which must never dry up, because they knew, beneath the rivalry, the greed for recognition and bitter knowledge of what they as women had missed, they were put on earth to give, not take, not because they wanted to, but because they had to.

And this brash millionairess comes along and unleashes long-repressed hopes with the clarion call of giving the world the ultimate gift of all.

And they think: there in the bush, surrounded by the innocence and cruelty of animals and grass that grows visibly in the night, genius may flower. But nothing.

Except for Claire. Bouncing down the grass paths, grinning mischievously, swinging her silken hair, sowing resentment, but still not willing to reveal her idea or plot or whatever it was.

9

"Ha! Ha! HEEEEEEE!" His laugh was something between the sound of a diesel engine's combustive process and a primal scream. Was Toto drunk or had he gone mad?

I turned on the light near my bed and reached for my travel alarm. It was 3 a.m. I had fallen asleep with the television on, waiting for him to come in. Perspiration from the center of my breast bone trickled down my body. Another night of chills and sweats, and now this laughter.

"Just occurred to me, Janet, that you're after final orgasmic delight. You want to be God."

"Doesn't everyone want to be God?" I answered quickly. Glib was the only defense at that hour. The screen was blazing with light. I glanced in the mirror: swollen eyes, damp hair, skin as smooth and greasy as floor wax.

"You want to stand outside world, look at your creation and move little chess pieces about."

"If I want to be God, it is an impotent one. I believe in free will, you see."

"Ridiculous. No your modern philosophers believe that. Men are pawns. Freedom an illusion."

"Wrong. Our freedom is God's cruelest gift. I want to speak to him about that. I wish you could arrange that."

"Came here only to tell you your search for ultimate thrill to save world is doomed. You been blown up by riches and ego. Your hubris beyond blasphemy."

"Look, let's get this clear. I don't think I personally am going to save the world, nor that I am God. All I've done is finance a conference of brilliant women so they can think about one problem that has been bugging the world for almost forty years. Since it's a new problem, it may have a solution."

I threw back the covers and searched for my slippers and

161

sweater. I was not going to lie in bed and discuss such matters looking like an invalid.

"Little American believing in solutions," he screeched.

I raised my voice. I was almost shouting. "All we need is ONE idea. There have been great ideas before like all men are created equal or the earth is round or men are instrumental in making babies. Another idea could come to the women. Humanity *does* evolve. There is progress and we *can* find solutions."

"Ho-heeeeeee. Ha!" And other grotesque screeches. By comparison, a hyena's cries were soft and limpid. "Those aren't solutions, but discoveries. Don't you know, there are no solutions to the way things are? Only discoveries."

10

The next day, the wind, blowing through the grass, now over two feet tall, was soft, sighing and warm. When David brought my morning coffee, I told him I would not be getting up and would have breakfast in bed.

Maybe Toto is right, I thought, as I buttered my toast. Maybe I do have God-envy. Maybe the women do too. According to Mabel, they were beginning to invent bugs in their soup. But surely anyone who thought about the nuclear problem long enough would start wanting to be God.

The sun shone through the net windows of my tent. Typical that nature would defy me and fill the camp with sunlight the day I had decided to be sick in bed. Praying for rain, I closed all the window flaps and turned on the television set. A half hour elapsed before he came on.

"Hi there!" he said in a ghastly new wind-up voice.

For whatever reason, he was back to his normal, non-belligerent self. So was I in a way. The conversation of the night before had been a kind of cleansing operation. Violent as his words had been, they were mostly true.

"I thought about what you said, Toto, and I concede that many great truths are discoveries. However, solutions do exist. Revolution is a solution for an implacable class system. Sex is a solution for loneliness. No, that's not right. Oh Christ, Toto, I don't know where I am. Why do you take the trouble to argue with me? Don't you see I'm just a woman who got very rich by accident?"

"Quite, yes. In some ways you very dear."

Encouraged by this unexpected compliment and overcome with what was clearly self-pity, I babbled on. "We started out with such great hopes and not one real idea has surfaced. We're exactly where we were two months ago. The women are sick of failing and bored. Even the staff's changed. I'm beginning to realize what a dangerous place this is. Hah! Listen to me. I'm telling you I'm afraid when you're the most dangerous thing of all."

"Am least dangerous."

"In May, we will be a normal think tank in Connecticut. Or I can dissolve the whole thing and turn Little Middletowne into an old people's home so it will be waiting for me when I die. I don't want the earth to blow up and I don't want to die alone. Those are my two wishes."

"Wish could say something to cheer you up."

"It seems no matter what I do, I end up sounding like some hyped-up American on a phone-in talk show who thinks there's a solution for everything."

"You not only one. Look at geniuses. And most aren't American. Trouble is you and none of your hirelings have discovered that only illusions will motivate man to save your world. Not truth."

"But truth is what they and all great thinkers are dedicated to finding."

"The truth is too unbearable to get people to do anything. The truth is that you don't know why you are here or why you should stay or if there is a God. You know only that your life is full of pain. But what saves humans from suicide when they confront such terrible facts, are illusions which give reasons for living."

"Such as?"

"An angry God. A merciful God. One for all, all for one. The good of the people. They all illusions and all serve the life-force because they give hope. Purpose. And unlike truth they are comforting and convincing and explain the whys of things. Otherwise no one would believe them. Greatest illusions are those with touch of mumbo-jumbo added to make them seem like truth. Like Trinity. Three persons, one God. So mysterious that people believe it true for almost 2,000 years."

"Or like the Categorical Moral Imperative," I said, wondering at what point during the conference I had lost faith in the eighteenth century.

"Excellent sonorous example. Twelve syllables. All great illusions like humanitarianism, thesis, antithesis, synthesis rest on backs of long words. The more syllables, farther idea travels. See syllables as little feet, trotting out on world stage, bowing to life-force."

"Is Nirvana a lie?"

"Less of a lie. But then, fewer syllables."

I liked that. Right or wrong, he was intelligent and one of the most stimulating beings I'd ever known. I hugged my pillow, realizing that I was somehow hugging Toto, too.

"You know I love talking to you," I felt an urgent need to tell him that.

"Like talking you too," he said softly, humanly. His voice had real warmth in it.

I felt goose flesh rising on my arms. Tread carefully, a voice inside me commanded. Quietly, with no change of pace, no pause, I asked: "Do mind energies have emotions?"

"No," was the too quick reply. "Though probably have acquired some human responses after years studying man. Like ethologists working with animals may acquire superior sense smell. But no emotions. Only views. My view is that you probably nice person who is in over her head."

"Won't you tell me who you are?"

"Have told you. Am a mind energy."

"Then why don't your people come down to earth and give us the new illusion that will make us disarm?"

"You think world listen to mind energies?"

"Maybe. If they were real and not journalists."

Some fruit falling on the roof of my tent thudded above me, then a dry scratching sound near my zippered door. Was someone listening to me talk aloud to my television? "Don't go away," I whispered. "I want to see what's going on outside."

I stole over to the window flap, lifted one corner, and saw a pair of knobby, brown spotted knees.

"It's that damn giraffe again. His knees are practically at eye level," I said, turning back to the TV, trying not to sound nervous. If he began to kick, he could knock my teeth out. But did giraffes kick? I had never seen them do anything but run away.

"Sit on floor with bed between you and him. Attendant shoo

him away when sees him." His voice was sure of itself, calm, protective.

"I'm building a barricade," I said as I piled all my pillows around me, laughing, acting as though Toto were a real person, a friend.

"Listen now. Have talked so much today because must leave you. Must go back to my star."

"Leave?" I couldn't believe what he was saying. Couldn't believe the feeling of desolation that was coming over me. "But you *can't* go away without telling me who you really are."

"Am here much too long."

Stay Toto, I wanted to say. *Just stay and talk with me*. It was unthinkable that I cared so much about this strange teasing creature's departure, but I did. I could hear the caring in my voice.

"Came here out of curiosity. Am ashamed now," he said.

"I don't care why you came, the fact is you did. Do you have any idea how isolated I feel at the head of this group?" I blurted out. "Do you know what it is to be one of the richest women in the world?"

"In a week, you convince yourself I interlude in overwrought imagination."

"You hope. Let me tell you that if I ever pick up a newspaper one day and see anything written about this group, your publishers will never recover from what I'll do to them. Tell them that, will you? Tell them they should prepare themselves for bankruptcy, harassment and so many well-publicized law-suits that they'll never know what hit them."

"I am not with media."

"Fine. You're from a star. You're one of the women in this group with a sick sense of humor. Or some crackpot in the bush. I don't care who you are. All I know is I've enjoyed you and we were getting somewhere in our conversations. It's too soon to leave."

"Don't say that. Don't want . . . I regret . . ." His voice faded out under a roar of static.

There was a scuttle of hooves outside, then an African voice shouting harshly in Swahili.

A muffled knock on my door. "You all right, Mama?"

I rose and peered through the side of the window flap. David's face – large, brown and huge-pored – glowed back at me. His big eyes twitched towards the television. I quickly turned round. The screen was dark.

11

By eleven o'clock, I was desperate for human company. Dressing quickly, I went outside. The sun had disappeared and gray gummy clouds hung over the camp. The wind had stopped blowing and the tall grass on the edge of the paths was standing straight up, greedily waiting for its next meal from the sky.

I still couldn't accept that Toto had left without telling me why he had come. Yet, somehow, I'd always known from the beginning that he planned to involve me, then disappear. Like Cy, like my mother, even like Hal. Everyone has a karma. Maybe mine was dealing with loss.

As I was making my way towards the main house, I saw Theresa by the door of her tent eagerly beckoning to me.

"We want to talk to you," she whispered, all smiles and triumph. "Claire has finally told us her idea."

My hands prickled with excitement. I had never seen Theresa looking so positive or radiant. Maybe we had not been defeated after all. Hadn't I always said that Claire was the most creative of all the women?

Feeling some of my old confidence pushing me forward, I followed Theresa into her tent. Books and papers were piled on every available surface, except the bed where Dorothea Mowbrie was sitting.

"I claim some credit Theresa," Dorothea said, gleeful behind her bifocals. "My idea of using the money was what sparked Claire's idea."

"Yes, indeed," Theresa said with her usual benevolence.

"*Tell me*," I pleaded.

"To stage an invasion from outer space and threaten the world with annihilation unless all nuclear weapons are dismantled," Theresa said lifting a pile of books off a camp chair so I could sit down.

"To stage what?" I asked helplessly.

"The whole thing top secret, of course," Dorothea said. "A vast conspiracy would have to be formed. No one here knows about it except Claire, Theresa, Mabel and me."

"And Padma," Theresa muttered.

Claire stuck her head through the zippered tent door. "Can I come in?" Her pony tail bobbed happily against her long swan neck as she sauntered in and sat down on the sheepskin rug.

"You told her?" she asked softly. Theresa and Dorothea nodded. She turned to me, sapphire eyes mellow with self-appreciation. Portia after she had won her case. "It's interesting, don't you think?"

Mabel, wearing a red pantsuit, puffing and strutting with excitement, entered next. "I've got all the notes here. Isn't it wonderful, Janet? Finally an idea." She looked like an agitated fire hydrant.

"*Please* say it again slowly," I pleaded.

Claire took a deep breath. "Quite simply: to terrify the world into disarmament by means of a simulated threat from outer space."

"To create a hoax like Orson Welles did on the radio years ago?" I asked, wishing the air in the tent did not smell so strongly of insecticide.

"Yes, but better. A world-wide hoax that would really convince them."

"How?"

"Through non-violent means. With nothing but light effects, we could create world hysteria in forty-eight hours."

"During which time, voices that seemingly belong to people from outer space would order the earth to get rid of its nuclear weapons or be annihilated."

"Where would these lights be coming from?"

Theresa lowered her voice. "Technology exists to light up the sky for 800 miles with projectile beams. It was developed by a group that broke away from the Raman Institute in Bangalore."

"Listen, Janet, you got to sit down and hear how they've worked it out," Mabel said.

"I've been thinking about staging a hoax since the second week of the conference," Claire said, "but I couldn't think of a way to make it credible until Padma told me about these light experiments going on in India.''

"And now Padma's furious she told her," Theresa said.

Dorothea nodded. "Because she has another idea of her own.''

"She has? What is it?" I asked, perhaps a little too eagerly.

Claire frowned. "She's angry for another reason. I get the feeling this scientific center is somehow illegal or involved in another sort of conspiracy.''

Theresa glanced at her watch. "Mabel, would you go and stall Padma? We're not ready for her to come in yet.''

Mabel left unwillingly.

'Why would these outer space people want the world to get rid of its nuclear weapons?" I asked.

"Because a nuclear explosion would disrupt the ecosphere,'' Theresa replied smoothly.

"What kind of threat would they make?"

"They could say they were going to divert the course of the sun or blast the earth off its axis." Claire's voice was gay with triumph. "It doesn't matter what the threat is as long as it's consistent with current scientific knowledge. Anyhow, we have plenty of time to work out those details.''

"How could you get the heads of the nuclear states to believe it?" I asked.

"We'll have agents planted in scientific communities throughout the world who will say it's a real invasion and add to the terror already created by the inexplicable lights.''

"But won't other scientists figure out where these lights are coming from?" I tried to sound objective and calm, but all I could think of was Toto. Toto and outer space. And that this was an illusion and not a discovery.

"No," Claire said excitedly. "The source point is no bigger than a small computer and impervious to radar. None of the technology has been leaked to anyone, which is why we should think about buying the center in Bangalore right away and either persuading the scientists to join us or silencing them.''

Theresa shook her head at Claire as Padma, wearing her baggy blue jeans and no diamonds in her ears, pushed aside the tent flaps and entered, nodding briskly to all of us. Mabel followed, rolling her eyes apologetically for not having been able to detain the astrophysicist.

"The best thing about Claire's idea," Theresa said diplomatically, "is that it works *with* man's nature. Warring nations have always united when faced with an outside threat."

"Hello Padma," I said.

"They've told you?"

"Yes."

"You're willing to put your money behind this thing?"

"I have to hear more about it. Right now, it sounds like it's going to cost a lot more than $250 million dollars."

"Raising money would be no problem," said Dorothea. "If every person who marched in last year's anti-nuclear demonstrations gave $10.00 we'd have billions."

"We wouldn't need to go to the marchers for money," Theresa said. "Do you think Janet is the only millionaire in the world willing to give money to save the earth?"

"Yes, probably," Padma said. "But assuming she isn't, how are you going to raise so much money and still keep the matter a secret? And how are you going to fool the scientific community? If I know about these experiments in India, you can be sure some brilliant young scientist in Finland is working on the same phenomenon right now."

"That's why we must act right away," Claire said excitedly.

Padma raised her eyebrows. "You are a brilliant woman, Claire, and a great actress, but you must beware of fanaticism."

Theresa studied Padma for a long time. "It doesn't matter if we use their technology or not," she said at last. "Claire's idea of using terror to bring the world to its knees and thus enforce disarmament is still valid. Your negativity is appalling, Padma."

Hands folded in front of her, mystical eyes at half mast, Padma said: "Your hoax is impossible because all scientists share the same body of knowledge. This is not a negative but a positive observation. Human science, like our capacity for love and trust, is shared by all of us."

"But of course, Padma. No one argues that," Claire crooned, as if speaking to a child.

Padma jerked her head to remove Claire from her line of

vision. "Our task today is to make trust, not suspicion, the dominant force on this earth. Trust, not fear of an attack from outer space that you can never successfully simulate, will save us and nothing else."

"But highly unrealistic," Theresa's voice flowed into the silence that followed Padma's embarrassingly simple pronouncement. "I refer you to 'flower power' in the 'sixties." She sent Padma a swift dismissive smile. "To get back to the hypothesis at hand. In 1974, the Institute for Scientific Strategies did an in-depth study on the Nazi Holocaust called *The Flight From Truth.*"

Sensing that whatever Theresa was going to say would be vital input, Mabel pulled her pen from her pocket and sat down on a corner of the bed with her spiral notebook on her knees.

"The question the Institute asked was: Why didn't knowledge of the systematic slaughter of the Jews leak to the most interested party: the Jewish people? How were enormous enterprises like Dachau and Auschwitz kept secret when thousands of ordinary Germans worked in the death camps, wrote home and had leave? How was the truth so distorted that millions of Jews *walked* to the boxcars believing that they were going to desert work camps?

"The Institute's answer was that terror paralyzes the mind. In a panic, human beings will believe anything that gives them hope for survival. The Nazis understood this human weakness and used the panic they intentionally created to manipulate the truth as they saw fit.

"In addition, the Institute concluded that conspiracies work. Padma is wrong when she says scientists can't keep silent. Thousands of them did in Germany and thousands more will do so in the cause of nuclear disarmament."

"I submit Janet, that we can form as great a conspiracy as the Nazis did. It would take years, all your money and billions more, but it could be done.

"Looking at us, five women sitting in a tent in Africa, it may seem ridiculous. But was a lonely, deranged, Austrian housepainter any less ridiculous when he decided to rid Germany of its Jews?"

Padma glowered at Theresa: "Hitler decided on the final solution when he was a head of state with iron control over the minds of his people."

"What difference?" Dorothea asked. "Even if some scientists suspect that it's a hoax, they will be swept into believing it's real because no matter how brilliant they are, their minds can be overwhelmed and subdued by terror."

"Questionable terror," Padma hissed.

Theresa glared at her: "I tell you that if the extermination of six million Jews worked, this will work."

Padma hunched forward in a bull-like attitude of resistance. "For the sake of argument, let's assume you are successful. How do you propose to maintain disarmament once the hoax is eventually exposed? Won't nuclear weapons simply be reconstructed?"

"We can't know," Claire said. Her voice was low, passionate and resonant. "But the longer the world is disarmed, the more hope there is that political leaders will see the insanity of a new arms buildup."

Sweat poured beneath Mabel's comma curls as her pen darted across her steno pad.

"Then the purpose of this 'invasion'," I said slowly, "is to get the world back into a non-nuclear situation so that when the hoax is finally exposed, world leaders will look like such fools they will never rearm."

"Exactly," Dorothea said with a dark, Harlem chuckle. "The Age of Universal Embarrassment."

"What do you say, Padma?" I asked. "If there is the slightest chance that we could buy the earth a few more years' existence, isn't Claire's idea worth some study?"

Actress, writer and mathematician turned their heads to face the Brahmin impediment to their idea.

She ignored them and directed her answer to me: "I do not believe that terror will ever be an instrument of peace. I also think the risk of being found out is too great. What if one of the great powers is not fooled and does not abandon its weapons? So far, the policy of deterrence has worked because there is a balance of power. A hoax risks upsetting that balance and creating a worse evil than that which already exists."

173

She unzipped the tent door and departed without another word.

The women looked at me expectantly. Money, the casting vote *par excellence*, should now speak.

"This is going to require a lot of thought. You may be on to something enormous," I said indecisively. "But I do know this: until you convince Padma that it can work, your conspiracy doesn't have a prayer."

After leaving Theresa's tent, I walked disconsolately through the camp, pushing aside the moist, overgrown branches reaching across the footpath.

The absurdity of Claire's idea kept colliding in my mind with its stubborn plausibility. In its way, it was as feminine a concept as Carol Schumacher's dream of female supremacy. The other side of the woman coin. Fruit of ancient slave knowledge and artifice. The temple prostitutes in ancient Babylon would have understood such guile perfectly.

Fair-minded Theresa, waddling across the grassy knolls, would be outraged when it dawned upon her that she was supporting that most female of strategies, a trick. On men.

But why not? If woman, the servant, had learned nothing else, she had learned that men can be fooled.

Ten minutes later, I was standing in front of Padma's tent which, like mine, was isolated from the others, but on the opposite side of camp. A sari was hanging limply on a camp chair on the veranda.

I had been as startled by her mention of trust as anyone else. Didn't she see that it, like love and beauty, was a fleeting, elusive idea, a mere flicker of light in the human cave and not at all the conference's concern, which was the survival of humanity, with all its ugliness and violence intact? How could she betray the iron-assed intelligence and adherence to provable fact the group stood for?

She bowed as she opened the door of her tent and invited me in. The air inside was a pleasant blend of mentholated cigarettes and incense. Bright silks were strewn carelessly about and hand-painted papier mâché boxes were perched amid her small collection of books. It looked like the inside of an Indian boutique, except that on the desk was a slender sheaf of neatly typed pages.

"They told me you have an idea," I said.

"Did they?"

"Do you?"

"Yes, but this nonsense about a space invasion is upsetting."

"You shouldn't have told Claire about the light experiments in Bangalore."

"Artists!" she snorted. "How was I to know it was going to spark such an insane conspiratorial idea? I hope you told them it was out of the question."

"It's too early to make a decision, but you must admit the idea has its merits," I said, still hoping that, somehow, the idea could be made to work. "If the God we invented didn't save us from our predatory natures, perhaps it's time we invented space men who will."

She sent me one of her long, measuring looks.

And that was it. My fantasy that Claire's idea could ever succeed was gone. We had failed again. Failed and failed again.

She put her hand on my arm and her large brown eyes filled with something like kindness. "Don't be disheartened, Mrs Cavanaugh. The conference is not yet over." She tapped the papers on her desk. "I have another dream for you. A better one. I wanted to present it sooner, but it will have to wait until next week. With those three against me, my argument must be as tight and convincing as possible."

"You were talking about trust in Theresa's tent . . ."

She smiled elusively and turned to her desk. "When I am ready, I will speak."

Leaving her tent and walking around the wooded outskirts of camp to avoid meeting Theresa or Claire, I heard the swish-swosh sound of elephants before I saw them.

There were five of them, trotting leisurely toward the parking area. When the heavy rains started, they had deserted the swamp and gone to play in the open, wet savannas. I loved the thought of those happy, hefty herbivores galumphing under the cool, soothing rain. I was glad they were back. In truth, I wished I were one of them.

Still, it was better not to get too close. I headed toward the center of camp. The door to the library was open. I could see

Mabel's bright red suit, a hundred feet away. She was sitting behind what used to be the display counter for carved wood animals from Zaire.

"Anything the matter?" she asked as I entered.

"Do I look that bad?"

"Yes." She patted her curls and sighed. "I thought you'd like Claire's idea. I know there are a lot of complications, but at least it's *doing* something."

"Yes, but not the right thing. There's too much risk of someone betraying us. You know that as well as I do. Our only hope, our last hope, really, is Padma's idea."

"I'll believe it when I see it."

"It might be good. We'll see when she presents it."

She looked at me hesitantly. "I don't know if I should tell you or simply forget about it."

"What? You've got to tell me anything I don't know."

She sent me a fast nod of agreement. "Right. But let's talk outside." She walked around the counter and guided me gently out of the library. Aside from the usual scampering and twittering of the animals, the only sound in camp was some plate-banging from the kitchen. Where was everyone? Reading novels quietly in their tents? Composing their letters of resignation?

We strolled a few yards down the path. "It sounds ridiculous and probably is," Mabel said softly, looking up at the gray pulpy sky, "but there's a rumor going around that Padma is an agent."

"Padma a spy? You're right. It is ridiculous. Where did it come from?"

"Ann Peabody told Jean Weinstein who told me."

"Did they mention which side she was working for?"

"Communist I think, but no one will tell me outright. It's all very vague. I'm lucky to know what I know."

"Communists don't wear diamonds," I said, but thought that, of course, if one were a Communist, what better red herring than a pair of fabulous solitaire diamonds in one's ears? "Have you told Claire yet?"

"No. I thought I'd wait for some kind of hard proof."

"Good. I loathe rumors. Next thing, they'll start saying that Mrs Obie is a witch."

A smile flickered on Mabel's face which she instantly suppressed. "The thought has crossed a few minds."

"She's worse than ever, isn't she?"

"Yes, but it's not booze. I think she's having some form of nervous breakdown. But if you try to talk to her she insists she's fine."

"I can't get through to her either. She won't even talk to Padma any more. Oh damn. Why did I make this a three-month conference when two months would have been more than enough? We could be in Connecticut right now eating hamburgers."

"No, we can't. They haven't even painted the inside of the building because the electrical problems haven't been solved. I got the letter yesterday from the contractors."

"How long before we're scheduled to go home?"

"Seventeen days from now. April 21st. Anything else?"

"Yes, where did Ann get her information about Padma being a spy?"

"From Ron, via Mr Zareda, the camp's owner, who got it from the Indian Embassy."

"Ron told Ann and not me? I just won't buy that."

"I think she overheard it or something."

"Where's Ron? I'll get to the bottom of this right away."

"In Narok. He went for supplies." Narok, the Masai-controlled county seat, was some twenty miles away. She brushed her tennis shoe lightly over the thick grass that bordered the path. Her red suit reminded me of a children's devil costume for Hallowe'en.

"Then I'll see him tonight. I wonder if Ann is trying to set Padma up for something. If anyone is working for the CIA, Ann could be. With that watery voice and those no-color eyes, she'd make a perfect undercover agent. And she hates Padma, too. I noticed it at the first meeting."

"I think Ann and Jean are straight, but I wouldn't know a CIA agent if I stepped on one."

She looked over my shoulder and grimaced. I turned. About thirty yards away, Susan Wu was jogging down the path toward the main house with an elderly stoicism that made me want to weep. We waved nonchalantly.

The bell for lunch sounded. Without missing a beat, Susan switched course and jogged back to her tent. Like most of the women, she had started eating lunch alone.

Mabel and I strolled toward the main house. Driscoll was standing on the threshold of the dining-room. Hands held stiffly against his body, he scanned our faces, took in our furtive expressions, noted Susan's retreating back, and looked troubled, like a stocky zebra poised on a termite mound, sensing, if not danger, change.

12

Ron did not return from Narok that evening. He would probably spend the night there, David had told me in a mournful, lost-child voice. Even the best of the camp's four-wheel drive vehicles were outdone by the clay-like mud on the roads.

Since there was no chance of talking to Ron about Padma, I had my dinner sent to me on a tray. I did not want to sit in that dining-room wondering who might or might not be a spy.

By ten-thirty, the rain we had been expecting all day finally came. Great, deafening, black quantities of it poured over the roof of my tent, interrupted only by claps of terrible thunder and the desperate honking of animals. It was a night bulging with noise, a night for King Lear to come stumbling through, bellowing with madness and despair.

Just as I was ready to crawl into bed, I saw a fist punching the front of my tent.

"Mrs Cavanaugh, are you there? Let me in." It was Mrs Obie screeching hysterically over the hard, steady drumming of the rain.

I quickly unzipped my door and saw her standing motionless on the veranda. She looked like a mad prophet. Damp white hair shot out from the sides of her head in spokes and the muscles of her face had collapsed. Her mouth was a trembling black hole. Behind her, nothing but great, silk charcoal sheets of rain. The kerosene lamps that bordered the grass path in front had not been lit.

"What's happened to you?" I asked, pulling her into the tent. She was curiously weightless, as if fear had relieved her of the solace of gravity. Leaving long, watery tracks from her tennis shoes in her wake, she let me gently push her into a chair.

"Shut the zipper. Listen." She put her finger to her mouth. Far away, there was a dull rumble of thunder, then, under the bludgeoning sound of the rain, something like a moan, or a chorus of moans. "It's the staff. They think we'll accuse them of killing her. They want to terrify us."

"Killed who? What are you talking about?"

"Padma. Padma Sarup is dead."

"It can't be. You're crazy."

Her pale eyes glinted with tears and rage. "It's true. Just outside her tent. A spear right through her."

"I don't believe it. Why didn't someone come and get me?" I threw my raincoat over my nightgown, tripping over her feet to get to the door. Her strong red hand came down on my shoulder.

"Don't go out there. The staff has gone mad."

"Where's Driscoll? He'll talk to them."

"He was there. He left. I think he's as afraid as we are. He's waiting for Ron and Bill to show up. But those Mau Maus out there could rape and murder us before dawn."

A low, fulsome howl from a single African voice swept through the night.

"When did you find out about Padma?"

"I was sitting at the dining-room table after dinner when Hitsai came in and shouted that Padma was lying dead on the path with a spear next to her. Some of the women ran outside. I guess to look at the body. I didn't. I believed Hitsai. Then the waiters began that awful howling and turned into savages before my eyes. Claire pulled out a horrible little black pistol from her purse and said not to worry, we were safe because she was armed. I was almost as afraid of her as I was of the staff. So I came here alone. There weren't any guides and my flashlight wouldn't work. Look." She pushed the switch of the flashlight back and forth with her thumb to prove her point. "Any animal could have charged me. Oh God, why are we here? Why did you want to come to this awful place?"

I struggled to put my canvas shoes over my bare feet. "We've got to get a doctor. What if Padma is still alive? We can't leave her lying there in the rain. If the staff won't move her, we'll have to do it ourselves." I went through the door, stood on the veranda, and turned on my flashlight. Its small beam of light dissolved into a mist before it was four feet long.

While I stood there, pondering how to negotiate the path

with so little light and so much darkness, I heard the loud crackle of breaking branches in the patch of woods behind me. Then a crash. The sound a medium-size tree makes when it falls, followed by startled, heavy grunts.

The sky flickered with lightning, illuminating the woodsy area. Standing not more than twenty feet away was a huge bull elephant with his ears spread wide. Behind him, several smaller members of the species. Then, thunder, delayed by at least five seconds. The lightning was far away. It had not struck down the tree. The elephants had. I stepped back into the tent and pulled the zipper closed.

Mrs Obie's eyes were dull with relief when she saw me come back inside. "Elephants?" she asked.

I nodded. "About five of them. The biggest one is flapping his ears. We'll have to stay inside as long as they're out there."

"Oh, God, I told you and told you that you should have a rifle. What are we going to do?"

I didn't know what to answer. It was unthinkable to do nothing, but with no guns, no spears, nothing to protect us from five of the most unpredictable mammals in the world, what choice did I have?

I threw on a pair of slacks and two sweaters. At least I would be dressed and ready before the elephants stampeded us, the murderer forced his way into the tent or the staff decided to massacre us.

No, not possible, I told myself. Law, order, fat, happy President Moi. Kenya was the jolly democracy of Africa, the West's proof to the East that capitalism and a modicum of civilization could survive and succeed in black Africa.

As if mindful of my desperate, well-wishing thoughts for Kenya, the shouting of the staff lessened. Something – another family of beasts in the camp? – had quieted them down. I lifted the window flap to check on the elephants. Without lightning, I could see only the outline of trees and, in my mind's eye, Padma's mountainous body pierced by a spear on the path near her tent, the rain washing the wound, blood running down through the roots of the high grass, her luminous, mystical, dark-ringed eyes open. Murdered before she was able to present her idea.

"Who do you think killed her?" I asked Mrs Obie.

"How do I know? I can't imagine a woman doing it. Certainly not with a spear. Who would use a spear except a native?"

"Anyone. They're light. I've held one." Had even thought of one rammed through my own heart. Strange. But not the strangest thing that would happen that night.

She shivered and grabbed the quilt at the foot of my bed. "Can I use this?"

"Of course. Take off your coat. I've got an extra one in my closet."

She plucked at the front of her coat, but her fingers were unable to bend around the buttons. Her lips were as white as her face. Stabbing uselessly at her chest, she began to shake pitiably with hopeless, animal-like spasms.

I put my arm around her. "We're okay here. Just try to stay quiet. No one will dare come near us with the elephants right outside." Leaning across her, I switched off the lamp. "We're sitting ducks with that light on."

"Oh no, we can't be here in the dark." Her back tightened and her arms, hard with fear, cramped around her as raw, harsh wails coursed from her old-woman throat.

Some branches, sounding like guns, cracked outside the tent. Close, inches from the canvas wall. Were the elephants coming or going?

Then far away, deep out of the dark, an African voice shouted something in Swahili. Then another. Not moans. Directives.

"They're coming to get us. Oh God, where's . . ." her garbled whisper ended in a word that was incomprehensible.

Or not incomprehensible. It hung in the air like a suddenly remembered nightmare. Two syllables.

"Did you say Wylie?" I shouted at her, grabbing her wrist, partly to frighten her, partly to calm my own terror.

She wrenched herself free and wrapped her arms around herself, refusing to reply. She was like a hard rocking ball. Impenetrable, tough, rubbery stuff.

"Why did you say Wylie?" I wanted to pummel her, bounce her against the floor, punch the truth out of her.

Wylie, of course, Wylie. A murder in the camp, my camp. My think tank, my project, ruined. The slender hope that Padma

182

would give us a worthwhile idea, destroyed. Who else hated me? Who else wanted to see me fail? "Tell me, Madeleine Obie, who killed Padma? Did Wylie kill Padma?"

"No, no, I didn't say anything about Wylie," she wailed. "You're hearing things." Rocking her body, she retreated behind a wall of moans.

There was another clap of thunder and more commotion in the trees. Then: "Get those goddamn lights on."

A mean, hard, white, male voice bellowing over the storm. It was Ron. Ron was back! I opened the window flap and saw two flashlights dancing in the rain, then Ron's stocky, sure-footed form behind one of the beams of light.

Mrs Obie darted off the bed. There was a sharp clicking noise. I turned and saw her pressed against the closet in the back of the tent. In her hand was her small, but lethal switch-blade.

"Put that away. Help is coming." I turned on the lamp and went back to the window. "Watch out for elephants," I shouted to Ron and whomever else was with him.

The zipper of my tent opened and Ron plunged in. He saw Mrs Obie's knife before he saw me. "I'll take that, please." In seconds, he had disarmed her. He swung around to me; his thick neck glistened with rain. "Did she kill the Indian?"

"No, she was having dinner with the others when the body was discovered. She came here alone to tell me. I wanted to go outside, but then, the elephants – have you seen Padma's body?"

"No, but Driscoll did. I had to quiet the staff. They're okay now." Ephraim shyly entered the tent and stood behind Ron, looking ashamed. Of his people or of his loyalty to Ron?

"Did Driscoll take Padma's body into her tent?"

"Says he did."

"And there's no hope that a doctor . . . ?"

"None. She's been dead for hours."

"Did you and Spears just get back? They said you were staying the night in Narok."

"I finished up earlier than I'd expected and decided to drive back tonight, but I got stuck in the mud. It took me two hours to get out. Spears wasn't with me, but he's here now, helping me calm down these idiots. Driscoll and Ephraim were the only two that didn't go berserk."

"Do they think we'll accuse them of killing Padma?"

"Seems to be the problem. We're telling them we don't think they did it."

"If they didn't, who did?"

"I don't know. Any ideas?" His clever eyes darted from me to Mrs Obie. She shrank back against the pillow of my bed. Her terror was gone. Something crafty and stubborn had replaced it. Her eyes were moving so fast they were invisible.

"She says Claire has a gun," I said.

"Really? Where'd she get it?" he asked skeptically.

"I have no idea. Have you radioed the police? Are they coming?"

"In this storm? Best thing is to stay put until morning. Ephraim can guard your tent all night if you like."

"He can't," Mrs Obie cried, rising from the bed with remarkable speed and planting herself between Ron and me. "He'll attack us when you leave. Don't let anyone stay here. The elephants are enough."

"Don't be ridiculous. He's just a kid," Ron muttered angrily. Ephraim lowered his eyes. His face was a mask.

She raised her thick, red hands as though to beat them against his chest. "Give me back my knife. I won't spend the night here unarmed," she shrieked with fear, but also fury.

"You'll get your knife back when I'm ready to give it to you." He sent her a look so full of disgust she lowered her arms and stepped back a pace.

"Maybe we shouldn't stay here," I said hastily. "If we were all grouped together in the main house tonight, it would be safer, better for everyone's morale. And warmer. I'm freezing in this tent."

"I'm telling you the camp's calm, but suit yourself. Get your umbrella and we'll escort you back."

I held out my raincoat for Mrs Obie to put on. Somehow my gesture gave her the confidence she needed to renew the struggle with Ron. "Tell Bill Spears I want to see him," she said in an autocratic tone that she usually reserved for chambermaids and natives. "He will let me have my knife."

"No knives," he grunted. "Get that? No knives." He pulled the door flap open for us. "We ready? Let's get you both up to the main house."

I slipped on another raincoat, grabbed my umbrella and pushed Mrs Obie ahead of me.

Huddled together under the umbrella, we waded and stumbled down the flooded path toward the main house where Padma's killer would undoubtedly be joining us.

13

Moths and other harder-backed bugs batted their wings and heads against the bright overhead lights in the lounge of the main house. The room, abandoned by the staff, was filthy; the air, fetid with smoke and humidity. Ashtrays were overflowing and the floor, streaked with rain and mud, was hazardous to cross.

Dorothea and Jean were seated on one of the sofas, talking together in whispers, nodding occasionally at Claire who sat on the damp, dirty floor with her back against the wall and her knees up. Theresa, looking like a competent nurse with a dangerous patient, stood beside her.

Mabel was by the fire, still in her red pantsuit, now spattered with rain. She looked as familiar and reassuring as a tea kettle steaming on a stove.

She came up to me immediately. "They killed Padma. It's got to be them."

"Who? The natives?"

"No, the other side. There's another agent here who found out about Padma and got rid of her."

"You don't know that for sure."

"Then why was she murdered? What had she done?"

"I don't know. If I knew why, I'd know what to do next. Has Claire got a gun?"

"Theresa's trying to talk her into giving it up. But it's there, under those blankets. She won't let go of it."

"Well, at least she's not pointing it at anyone. Are there any extra blankets around? If we're going to spend the night here, we've got to be warm. Mrs Obie is soaked through."

Mabel looked without interest at Mrs Obie, who was walking hesitantly towards the fire. "She could get seriously ill if she stays in those wet clothes," I said. "She's an old woman."

186

"Right, only there aren't any extra blankets. They were all distributed weeks ago. There aren't even extra pillows. If we went to get them out of the tents, they'd get soaked."

"How many hours till dawn?"

"Five, five and a half? But that's no guarantee the rain will stop."

"It will," I said. "It has to."

Someone was pounding on the door. "Door's locked," Mabel said and moved quickly to open it. Farah Bezhad and Elsa Heinzelmann, looking disoriented and terrified, entered the room accompanied by Ron.

Farah stared dully at us, then at Ron and shuddered. "You think we're safe?" she asked. "They could surround us in here. Maybe we were better off in our tents."

"No one is going to surround anyone. Just stay here until I get everyone together," he said curtly and disappeared through the door before Farah could answer him.

She approached the center of the room warily. Clearly we were all suspects in her mind. Pulling out one of the canvas chairs near a coffee table, she sat down. Elsa joined her. The table was covered with dirty coffee cups and saucers. As if in a trance, Elsa began to stack the dishes in front of her.

The air was electric with panic. I felt powerless and uncertain and hated this menacing limbo that the storm, the dark, and the ferocity of animals had thrown us into. I should be questioning the women, tending to Padma, I thought nervously, but like the rest, I did nothing, as immobilized by dread as they were. I didn't even attempt to talk Claire into giving up her gun. Perhaps I was glad someone on the female side was armed. Though it did occur to me, even then, that if I were going to kill someone with a spear, to reveal later that I had a gun would be good thinking.

Soon the rest of the group arrived, bundled in blankets and raincoats: hair wet, faces anxious, angry and accusing. Bill Spears, who had escorted them, was the last to appear at the door. He looked more confident than usual. Less lanky and uncoordinated. Perhaps it was the rifle he was carrying that made him seem bolder. Perhaps it was . . . but I never finished the thought.

At the sight of Bill, Mrs Obie, who had not moved from the fire, hobbled forward. Relief, something like joy, radiated from her pale, old-woman eyes as her lips moved slowly to form the word, "Wylie".

Bill ignored her. Turning to speak to the women at large and pulling at his beard, he said, "Driscoll is getting the keys to the bar and pretty soon we'll have brandy for everyone. There isn't any more dry wood, but we're bringing in some kerosene heaters."

That voice. The air in the room – or perhaps my connection to it – moved into a different, tenser register.

"And the staff?" I asked, knowing my own voice was shaking.

He didn't look at me, but at Theresa. "The staff's fine. They didn't murder anyone."

The pitch was lower, the accent, still cultivated English South African, but the timbre and the soft slur across the "r" sounds was unmistakably Toto's.

So Toto was Bill Spears.

Bill Spears was Toto.

And Wylie.

Wylie was Toto was Bill Spears.

Wylie Goddamn Cavanaugh had made a fool of me.

It was not the moment to pause and consider the twisted humor and baroque ramifications of this strange, ungainly joke, but already, in spite of Padma's murder, in spite of the black Learean storm outside, the elephants with flapping ears and the maddened staff, a smile was appearing in the backwaters of my soul. And I knew that if I was lucky – very lucky – that smile could remain with me for the rest of my life.

I started towards him. His eyes – dark, moody, not Cy's – shifted away from mine. I kept walking until I was a foot in front of him. Finally our eyes met. There was no defiance, no hate, no heroin-induced glassiness, only resignation in the look that he sent me.

Then, unforgivably, he grinned. It was the same grin hidden in between the lines of his neat little Christmas notes, the same grin under that piercing, computer-simulating voice.

"Hi, Janet," was what he said.

I opened my mouth to reply, perhaps scream, but Mabel was

already standing near us. "Did anyone get a doctor?" she wanted to know.

"I'm afraid it was too late for a doctor," he replied, turning away from me to give Mabel his full attention.

"Are there any suspects?" Mabel asked.

"Do you have any clues?" Elsa inquired, leaving her cups and saucers to join Mabel. Soon the women were crowding around him and bombarding him with questions: Are you calling the police? Will we be safe in this godforsaken place? Where the hell are the natives? Do they have rifles?

He held up his hand for silence and got it. They turned to him with frightened, imploring eyes, hoping and wishing that he'd say Padma wasn't dead, that she had only tripped, that her great arrogant face would soon be peering down at us again, and that by morning, we would all be grappling with the familiar combination of awe and resentment she inspired.

He spoke in low, controlled tones. "The staff has calmed down. We've ordered them to stay in their quarters for the rest of the night. They've been told that we think she committed suicide and that no one is to blame. Or they think we think that. The fact is Mrs Sarup has been dead for several hours and we have no idea who did it and no clues. Because of the rain, there are no fingerprints or footprints. The authorities in Narok won't be able to get here until tomorrow, provided the roads are better."

"Whose spear was it?" Jean Weinstein barked.

"A tent attendant's. It's been in the laundry shed leaning against a wall, mixed with the brooms and mops, for months. Anyone, including Mrs Sarup, could have taken it."

"No woman would kill herself with a spear," Jean bellowed.

"It was the best story we could come up with," Bill replied. "The objective was to get the staff under control immediately. Tomorrow when there's a formal investigation, we'll know more."

Seeing the sickening reasonableness of this ploy, the women's protests subsided, but their faces were tense with worry and suspicion. The lie to the staff had not allayed their fears *vis-à-vis* each other. If anything, it increased their panic.

"Driscoll and Ephraim are going to stay with you here in the main house," Bill went on. "There's nothing more to be afraid of, but it's better someone's on guard. If any of you want to return to your tent, be sure they accompany you. There are elephants roaming around Mrs Cavanaugh's area who don't sound very friendly tonight." Making one of his "nature guide" salutes, he turned to leave. "Above all, stay calm. Nothing more is going to happen tonight."

Before more questions could be asked, he was gone. I followed him as he knew I would. Sheltered by the canopy over the door, we stood facing each other. Light from the lounge shone on his face. His eyes were dancing. Maybe mine were too.

"I've got to see Ron, but I'll meet you in your tent at sunrise. If you want me to."

"I want you to. But tell me . . ."

"Let's not talk yet. Please wait."

He took a step backwards and vanished into the dark before I could tell him how furious I was. And fascinated. Definitely. But he already knew that.

14

"Even if Padma were working for the KGB, that still doesn't tell us who murdered her or why," I said, truculent from fatigue and the stress of the night before.

"When the answer comes, I guarantee that it will be political and obscure."

"And no help to Padma."

Bill-Wylie and I were sitting on the veranda in front of my tent. Damp, but not shivering. The air was dry, the sky, pink and clean as a baby's skin. Light and the kindness of God had returned to earth after all. Even the elephants, who had terrorized me the night before, were munching peacefully in their old habitat, the swamp.

"It's terrible and heartless, but I want desperately to stop thinking about what happened," I said. "I hate the idea that someone in the group killed her. If I had the legal power, I would have Padma buried this morning."

"It's tempting."

"You have no sympathy for her, do you?"

"I didn't like the way she deceived you, by seeming to be apolitical."

"Was it any worse than your deception? I mean toward me, personally." I glanced at the TV set I had made him disembowel to show me where he had hidden the receiver that had carried Toto's squawks and sighs. It hung on a wire from the picture tube, like a tooth on a string. In the palm of my hand was the minuscule voice-activated transmitter that had been wedged into the primitively carved swirls of my closet door that I'd been looking at for two months. Both had been linked to the Research Station through a transceiver with a powerful amplifier concealed in Ron's office. The light on the screen had been created by activating a video component.

191

"My deception, little mother, was amusing. Padma's was immoral."

"So Toto, the fatalist, is a moralist after all."

"I'm decent. It's a minimum precaution. Padma wasn't."

"Wrong. She believed in trust. At least in the end."

The inert, lifeless, powerless end. Before meeting Wylie, I had insisted that Ron take me to her tent to see her.

Someone had laid her on the bed, combed her hair and put coins on her eyelids. Her cold, ashen face held no answers or clues. Her death, perhaps like the death of the world, was going to be no more than opaque, uncompromising, unanswerable *fact*.

Hoping to find out what her last idea had been, I searched frantically for the manuscript I had seen on her desk the morning before. Her diamonds and ivory jewelry were neatly packed in silk-lined boxes, her saris carefully folded, but the manuscript had disappeared. And been burned? Had she been killed because of her idea? She'd called it a better dream. Had it only been that or had she come up with a truly original concept about trust that someone had killed her to suppress?

"All that hot air," Wylie was saying. "That piousness and those false belladonna eyes." His eyes seemed to darken to the color of Padma's as he did a fair imitation of her mystical, glinting look that had so enchanted me. By making it theatrical, he was lessening its power over me.

He was a devastating mimic. No wonder he had wanted to be an actor as a child. But also a man with a secret. Perhaps most of the secrets in the universe. The fool in the tarot pack. Looking at his pleasant face, at Cy's forehead (I now saw), the slim body, I fantasized that written in his soul, with the precision and grace of notes on a harpsichord, was all the meaning I needed to continue my life. That through him, the puzzle would assume a shape.

"Oh Wylie, you know, we could get along," I said, because one never says the first thought, only its distant cousin.

"You won't turn into a wicked stepmother?"

"You're so much better than I thought you'd be. I was so sure you were an emaciated heroin addict with track marks on your arms."

192

"You're prettier than your pictures. You're not photogenic at all, you know. Probably because your expression changes so fast. It's very appealing."

"I realize now that a day didn't go by that I didn't think of you."

"After my first Christmas card, I thought for sure you'd force a confrontation. But then Mrs Obie told me you'd throw me out if I set a foot near your door."

"Did I say that? I suppose I did. I was so afraid of you. I was certain you hated me and wanted to kill me or rob me."

"She never told me that, only that you hated me."

"I never told her I was afraid. I was too busy convincing her that I was strong. I had some vague idea that she needed my protection. It never, never occurred to me that she was plotting to bring us together."

It had taken almost an hour to unravel all the deceptions that had been effected by him and Mrs Obie, starting with the day she told him about the think tank to her support for going to Kenya to Ron's consenting to hire him as a nature guide.

Ron, who had known Wylie since 1968 and "owed" him, had helped him install the bugging system. It had been an afterthought. Two weeks before the conference started, Wylie had met a former Peace Corps worker who was trafficking in arms and espionage equipment in Nairobi. He was selling this high class, but out-dated transceiver rig at a price Wylie could not resist.

Mrs Obie, who had suggested I bring the Sony (after Wylie called her from Nairobi and told her to), had plugged in the set the first two times. Both she and Ron had thought the TV caper was a terrible idea and had tried to talk him out of it, but he had persisted.

"Wasn't it more effective and intimate to speak to you directly in your tent, rather than as a mere servant?" he had asked, cocking his head Bill Spearsishly.

There was a lot of Bill Spears in him and Toto too, but his actual personality was somewhere between the two and included yet another dimension, that of film producer. Tom O'Riley's information that Wylie was making movies had been correct. Since his father's death, he had produced and directed two documentaries in India. Wylie, whom I had always pictured in a loin cloth and playing a lute, had sat in a director's chair and made Asian camera men jump at the sound of his voice. Which explained his officiousness as Bill Spears. The boss dimension would be the hardest to shed.

When he had met Mrs Obie in Dublin, he had been trying to raise money (unsuccessfully, which is why he had written to Tom to ask for $50,000) to make a documentary on missionaries in India. But then, when he heard about my think tank, he decided to come and investigate it and me rather than start the film project which was running into trouble with the church authorities anyhow.

I had listened in silence, no longer shocked, not even angry. Maybe flattered that I had been the center of so many people's lives for so long.

But there were still too many mysteries. Why had Cy said he was a drug addict? When I had questioned Wylie about it, he denied he ever was addicted, but "to a guilty man like my father, dope was the only explanation for the way I felt about him." The terrible calm he imposed on his voice was chilling.

I didn't probe further. Neither of us was ready for a discussion about his relationship with his father. I had loved Cy. Wylie had not. There had been lies and misunderstandings. Maybe on both sides. But why and how they had begun was something we could excavate later. If there was going to be a later. Already I was hoping there would be.

"The crusade in Mrs Obie's life since I got out of the Army was to reconcile my father and me," he was saying. "When that failed, she shifted her attention to bringing you and me together. She saw it as her duty."

"She looked horrible last night when she realized that she had given you away."

After I had seen Bill-Wylie out of the main house, I'd returned to the lounge and tried to offer her some brandy.

Hair clamped wetly to her head, her back taut with rage, she had pushed my hand away, refused to talk to me and gone off to huddle alone by the kerosene stove.

"Nothing went right for her. Her first mistake was telling Padma about me and the transceiver rig. She literally went mad with worry that Padma would tell you." He shook his head wearily. Mrs Obie would be a trying accomplice at the best of times. "She didn't want to give me away last night, but with Padma dying, she lost control."

"Anyone would have lost control," I said, feeling the full horror of Padma's murder welling up inside me again. "Why such a cruel weapon? What reason would anyone have?"

He sighed. "Perhaps no reason."

Something cawed plaintively in the tree above us. "Go on," I said at last. "Finish about Mrs Obie."

He smiled glumly. "Her dream was very clear. After the conference, she was going to invite us to a beautiful dinner at the Norfolk in Nairobi. Some time during the meal, she'd raise her wine glass and say: 'Mrs Cavanaugh, I have an announcement to make. This is not Bill Spears, a contemptible nature guide, but Wylie, your loving, decent stepson.' We would embrace first her, then each other, and somehow we'd divide up Dad's money and install her as the dowager queen in an upstairs suite of the palace we'd build together. Then, not too long afterwards, there'd be a little Cavanaugh princeling and heir who'd adore her and all four of us would live happily ever after."

"And the world would be out $250 million."

"Yes, I'm afraid her dream did not include giving anything to the world. It never occurred to her, or me, that you would find a solution worthy of a quarter of a billion dollars."

"Do you still want half?"

"No. I never did. But I don't expect you to believe that for a long, long time."

He was right. It would take a long time.

"Claire had an idea that would have used up all the money and much more," I said.

"She's a nice girl," he said evasively, teasingly.

"Wylie, you didn't . . . please tell me that wasn't your idea."

"Yes and no. It kind of grew out of our conversations."

"You and Claire discussed it before she told Theresa?"

"It just came to me. I was in this outer-space space, if you'll

195

excuse the pun, and she was so desperate for an idea and so lovely."

"Did you sleep with her?"

"Me? A mere staff member?"

"You."

"I'm not promiscuous, dear mother. You are."

There being nothing to say to this, I turned away from him and looked out once again at the world – this vale of tears – I was going to save and turn into a mountain of delight. Two thousand years of Christianity had taught me only how to defy it. Not its pessimism.

A small, simian hand darted through the bushes, felt the earth for fallen fruit, disappeared and emerged again. Moments later, a whole gang of monkey youths swarmed through the grass, searching for the booty the rain had driven from the trees.

"Nevertheless, the conference was worth the try. There was joy in just making the effort. At least in the beginning. But nothing at all was accomplished, was it?" I was dismayed at my matter of fact tone. I sounded like a child reporting failure after having spent a whole afternoon digging a hole in the ground to reach China. "Maybe I would have been better off joining the anti-nuclear demonstrators."

"You still can. If the world lasts, the demonstrations will last. Everything is still the same."

"Except that Padma is dead."

"Padma had to die. She courted danger every minute of her life. She might have been killed by any number of people: another agent in the group who was working for the us, any of the three women involved in the space hoax or even by poor, confused Mrs Obie."

"Or you."

His neck snapped as he turned to face me. "First, you think I want to rob and kill you, now you think I'm Padma's murderer." Hard tarot pack eyes. "Why?"

"Because you court mystery and love deception more than truth," I said gently, appeasingly. I was enormously attracted to him.

His face relaxed. "That's part of my charm. I understand the value of illusion. Truth doesn't work. That was the discovery your intellectuals couldn't make."

"The truth is that man has never built a weapon that has not eventually been used."

"Deterrence could mean the end of all wars. Look on the bright side."

"So you're an optimist after all. The true face of Wylie Cavanaugh revealed at last." But of course I still knew nothing, had no idea what his true face was, assuming there was one.

He smiled. Straight white teeth against taut, tan skin. Slender cheekbones, nicely arched eyebrows. Better looking than Cy. His mother must have been a beautiful woman.

Whenever I thought of her, I saw a head on a pillow and wandering, piteous eyes, a gray memory breaking through Cy's long, reminiscing monologues. Dead of a broken heart. Could that be true? Hadn't doctors with their ghostly masks and blood-cleansing techniques put an end to all that?

"Tell me, little stepson, under that beard, do you have Cy's chin or your mother's?"

"My father's. Including the dimple. Mrs Obie said that if you saw the dimple, you'd recognize me instantly."

"I don't like beards. Will you be shaving it off?"

"And lose my strength?" He smiled again. His hand reached out, paused in mid-air between us. One second only. Then both hands, his left, my right, came together. Sun warming them both. He squeezed my fingers, then quickly, nervously, returned his hand to the safety of the camp chair.

"We need some breakfast," he said.

"Yes and I want to take a shower and change my clothes." I stood up, took a deep breath of the sparkling, rain-cleaned air, then coughed. "Oh Christ, every time I start feeling better, I think of Padma and something collapses inside me. It's so awful. Awful."

He looked at me with concern. "I've got to talk to Ron. Do you mind being alone?"

"No, I'm fine."

He walked to the edge of the veranda.

I looked at his legs, the same strong Bill Spears' legs I had been eyeing for weeks, without knowing I'd been eyeing them. The same narrow rear end. But now those legs, that body were Wylie's, and oh yes, I was glad they didn't belong to Claire Montmorency. Nor to anyone else, it seemed.

"If you see David, could you please tell him to bring me some coffee?"

Smoke was rising from the outdoor grill in the center of camp. Tent flaps were open. Showers were running. A murderer was among us, but the rain had stopped, the breakfast fires were burning and all was somewhat well with the world, at least for the moment.

I brushed the hair out of my eyes and took off my glasses. "I must look terrible."

"For someone who has been up all night, you look wonderful. You're the most beautiful stepmother I've ever seen." The desire in his eyes was unmistakable. Lust, but with other nuances too. I stopped breathing. So did he, I believe. Then, making a quick salute from some other comedy he had played on some other stage, he left.

After I had taken a shower, I went outside and felt briefly, mindlessly happy. In spite of Padma's terrible death, because I had found Wylie, no longer feared him, was maybe already in love with him, I was suddenly confident that hope was still applicable, that the glass was half full, and that a pot of coffee would be waiting for me on the veranda.

Instead of this, I found Mrs Obie. She had changed into dry clothes, but everything else about her was wrong. Her heavy knit sweater was on backwards and the side buttons of her skirt were only half done up. On her feet were bedroom slippers that looked like rugs. But it was her roving, loose-muscled eyes that were most wrong.

"Before you have breakfast, could I talk to you?"

I hesitated.

"Could I talk to you?" she shrieked, planting a strong, big-knuckled hand on my arm, advancing so rapidly that she stepped on my foot. "NOW!"

"Later, I have to go," I said sliding my foot out from under her slipper and running toward the center of camp, dreading that she had something to do with Padma's death, hoping she didn't, wondering how I could protect her and wishing I didn't have to. Most of all, wanting to get away from her implacable will. Didn't she realize, romantic old fool, that I must choose Wylie myself and not have him thrust upon me like some sort of fate?

15

The perfumed aftermath of the night's rain mingled pleasantly with the odor of frying bacon as I headed toward the tables set up outdoors near the grill.

At the table most removed from the others, Ron and two uniformed black rangers were eating bacon and eggs. Driscoll stood over them gesticulating with the coffee pot in his hand as he spoke in rapid Swahili. The passionate forward thrust of his shoulders contrasted strikingly with Hitsai, who sat alone several tables away, looking like a stricken bird. She held a glass of pineapple juice to her mouth, but did not drink, nor try to conceal the huge tears coursing from her dull black eyes. Farah and Elsa were eating at a table facing the swamp. I could hear the cereal crunching in their mouths as I passed.

Seeing me approach, Ron got up wearily to greet me. There was a tinny look in his eyes. It was still unclear to me what this middle-aged man owed Wylie. Something to do with a bar fight long ago in Saigon. Where Ron had been a mercenary? Dealing? Wylie had swept through the story at a fast clip. The most I had gleaned was that there had been knives, a man's eye lost, Ron accused, then exonerated, thanks to Wylie's intervention. All of it sounding very macho, 'sixties and loathsome.

"These guys want to speak to you," Ron said, motioning me toward the table.

"Where's Wylie?"

He frowned at my use of his friend's name. "At the Research Station. Best not to talk about that yet."

We walked over to the table. The ears of the two officials had not been pierced, nor had their lower incisors been removed, which meant they were probably not Masais. This would please Ron since the Masais, our landlords, hated the camp for hiring men of other tribes.

"This is Caleb Mutua and Daniel Kibera," Ron said, pulling

out a chair for me. "Mrs Cavanaugh is the organizer of the
safari group."

They nodded at me imperiously. It was their country. I had
had the temerity to have one of my group murdered in it. If
nothing else, I was guilty of the gravest imbecility.

Mutua, the older of the two, spoke first. "I want you to know
how much we regret this – uh – regrettable occasion."

"A very sad incident," Kibera mumbled.

That little comedy finished, Mutua launched quickly into the
meat of the matter. "This is a fact-finding mission today only."
As if on cue, Kibera whisked out a pencil and held it poised over
a hand-sewn notebook. "My man will take notes."

Grabbing an empty chair from behind him, Mutua stretched
his right arm along it, the better to display his broad capable
shoulders and khaki epaulets. His stern demeanor looked like
an elaborate mimicry of white bureaucrats. But I suspected
that under his performance there was more than a little compassion for any animal that kills.

"Mr Watkins tells me that you believe the Indian woman
killed herself," Mutua barked at me. "What we question is the
use of a spear."

I was too stunned to reply. It had not occurred to me that
Ron would persist with the suicide story.

"Using a spear would have been in character," Ron said
smoothly. Kibera's pencil started moving the minute Ron spoke.
"Mrs Sarup was given to the grand gesture."

"The what?" Kibera asked.

"She was depressed and refused to join the others on the
game rides," Ron explained.

"And being an Indian, I suppose she was isolated from
the others . . ." Mutua gently rubbed his thumb and index
finger together, as if testing how far the truth could be ground
down.

"But why would she choose to kill herself out of doors?"
Mutua asked. "On a path, wasn't it?"

"Was it outdoors?" Ron looked at me, his face round with
surprise.

I nodded dumbly. Kibera drew a jagged doodle on his
pad.

Ron shoved some toast into his mouth. "Her political connections were not the best."

"The Indian community is not going to ignore the murder of a rich Indian woman just because she was a Communist, Mr Watkins."

"They might," Ron said, but not with much hope.

Mutua's chin jerked up two notches to show his irritation. "So what other explanation can you give them?"

Mutua made a tent with his fingers. "You can tell us who killed her."

"We know who killed her. She killed herself."

"I don't like it," Mutua said with an air of finality.

Kibera coughed politely and looked past us at Mrs Obie who was walking down the grass path like a crab. One step to the right, two forward, one to the left. Seeing me with the policeman, she turned away and pretended to be engrossed in the animals in the swamp. She looked drunk, but I knew she wasn't. There had been no smell of liquor on her breath when she shouted at me in that harsh, determined voice. I winced as I remembered her slippered foot on mine. The strength of her gnarled red hand. Which could have heaved a spear into Padma's warm Brahmin flesh? Because Padma threatened to denounce her and Wylie to the other women? Or had Mrs Obie truly gone mad and simply felt like killing someone?

Mutua turned to Ron for information on this disheveled creature.

Ron shrugged nonchalantly. "Just one of the members of the group. Very upset about the suicide."

Sensing that the men had lost interest in her, Mrs Obie lurched to the nearest table and beckoned listlessly to Driscoll who ignored her.

Rocking the empty chair under his arm, Mutua addressed me in the semi-drone of an official delivering a report. "When an abnormal death occurs, the normal procedure is to have an autopsy. Facilities for doing so are not available here. We are therefore taking the victim to the missionary hospital." Planting a large brown hand on the table-cloth, he hoisted himself up from his chair. "We will take two cars. Our own and one of the camp's vehicles."

"Where is Padma's body now?" I asked.

"In the camp vehicle," Kibera said, shooting a piece of bacon into his mouth.

"Is there anything I should do? Any papers to sign?"

"All documentation must be handled in Nairobi," Mutua said.

"The Indian Embassy . . ." Ron mumbled.

"We've got to inform her family right away," I said. "Can we send a telex from here?"

"Tomorrow," Mutua said quickly. "Mr Watkins can telephone from Narok tomorrow. You and your group will leave tonight for Nairobi to be questioned by the police. The Narok force doesn't have the authority to conduct an investigation of this nature."

"But this is where the mur . . . where she died."

"I've already telexed your travel agent's representative to make reservations at the Norfolk Hotel," Ron said in his helpful-innkeeper voice.

Mutua turned his broad khaki back to Ron and marched off in the direction of the parking lot. We could sleep in the street for all he cared. Kibera followed close at his heels, smiling with his teeth clamped shut.

"Eggs, Mrs Cavanaugh?" Driscoll was standing before me with a platter in his hand.

I shook my head and stared at my empty plate. "Padma was murdered. You know it, I know it and they . . . those policemen know it."

Ron's eyes widened. "Do they? I got the impression they hadn't made up their minds."

"Driscoll. *Service!*" Mrs Obie's spoon came down hard on the table. Hitsai jumped.

"Before you do anything, you better take care of her," Ron grunted, jerking his head in Mrs Obie's direction. Behind her, I could see Mabel, her lumpy shape clad once again in safe potato colors, approaching our table.

"Look, I'll see you later," Ron said worriedly. "I've got to make sure those two clowns know what they're doing."

16

"Finally flipped, huh?" Mabel asked, sitting down in the chair Ron had just vacated. She had taken one look at Mrs Obie's back to front sweater and mouth groping the rim of her coffee cup and sized up her condition immediately.

"Yes, I'm afraid she's going to cause a scene. She was already screaming at me this morning."

"I can handle that." She thumped the satchel in her lap. "Valium. Fifty grams the first go around."

"You think she'll take them?"

"Like a baby. She loves pills almost as much as booze."

"Good. She's better off asleep."

Seeing Elsa and Hitsai coming towards me, questions shooting from their eyes like hooks, I got up hastily. "Tell them I'll talk to them in the main house in a half hour," I said and fled.

Back in my tent, I flung the covers over my bed, doused my face with water and tried to collect myself before I spoke to the women, but I couldn't stop going over the events of the night before.

Any one of the women could be a killer, but which? With no real clues, it was useless to speculate and only made me more frightened and nervous than I already was. It was vital that I stay calm. I was responsible for the women's presence in this savage place. My first priority was their safety. My second: to disband the group before another murder occurred.

The rest was a blank. If I'd remembered how to pray, I would have. To the God with the mud-caked thumb.

Realizing that the women were waiting for me, I ran back to the center of camp.

Wylie was standing at the door of Ron's office. "Could we see you for a minute?" Wylie asked in his stiffest Bill Spears manner.

"Why? Has something else happened?"

"Not yet." Seeing Jean and Carol on the lawn, he sent them a polite, employee's bow and followed me into the office.

I sat down on the typist's chair. Ron was behind his desk. He made me wait while he lit a cigarette and studied the walls. "Mutua doesn't want a murder," he said at last.

"I gathered that. Why?"

"To keep it out of the press. The Asiatic community is still very stirred up by the rapes and looting that went on during the Air Force rebellion. If they hear that an eminent Indian intellectual was murdered in the Mara, they'll be enraged and accuse the government of engineering it."

"Maybe they did."

"No. Mutua would have known."

"Then who killed her?"

"If we knew, the publicity wouldn't matter. But an unsolved murder could keep the story alive for weeks."

"So?"

"Mutua has decided that the best thing all round – for you and his government – would be for it to be an accident."

"With a spear?"

"Not exactly." He pushed some unanswered mail around his desk. Blew at some dust. "Suppose Padma decided to disobey camp rules and took a vehicle into the bush alone without telling anyone. Say that vehicle ran out of gas and she started walking. At this time of year, game is scarce. Chances are she would be attacked almost immediately."

"But she didn't do that."

"We would organize a search party of course as soon as we realized she was missing. But the Mara is very big. It would take at least a day to find her. By which time, the scavengers . . . well, there would be no question of a spear wound."

It took me about thirty seconds to understand. *"No. No, you can't."*

I remembered the maribou storks I had seen in the bush, red pouches hanging from their ugly necks, torn, black feathers, dull philosophical eyes. Park cleaners, they were called.

"I won't have it," I said, walking around to face Ron, pressing the opposite side of the desk, wanting to ram it into his belly. "It's a horrible, heinous idea."

"Look, I tried to talk Mutua into the suicide theory. You heard me, but he said it wouldn't wash." The distress in his voice seemed genuine.

"Get Mutua back here, now. With the body. At once."

"We can't," Ron muttered. "He didn't tell us where they were going. Why would he?"

"Oh my God,"I closed my eyes. *Don't visualize, I ordered myself. Keep it abstract. Don't hear the rip of flesh, the chomp of blood-drenched beaks.*

I turned to Wylie. His eyes were as neutral as the TV screen in my tent. "Did you know about this when we were talking this morning?"

"How could I? Mutua didn't get here until seven thirty. I don't like it any more than you do. But Ron had no choice."

"He could have stopped them."

"At gun point?"

"I'm telling the women and then telling the police in Nairobi." I turned towards the door.

"You're free to do what you like, but think first," Wylie said, slipping slowly in front of me, his hand raised in the gentlest of staying gestures. "If you contradict Mutua's story, he could detain the group or refuse to protect it. Right now we've got his word you can leave Kenya tomorrow night. And what proof can you give the Nairobi police that she was murdered? The body's gone."

"I *saw* the spear wound."

"And Mutua will see something else. It will be your word against his."

"But can't they tell from the . . . bones whether a person was killed by a spear or an animal?"

"Not after Kibera is finished with them," Ron murmured.

"The women will tell the police that she was murdered."

"They can tell them whatever they like. They'll be Mutua's boys and fully briefed."

"And when the Communists wake up to the fact that one of their agents, assuming she was an agent, has been murdered? You think they'll take that lying down?"

"She wasn't murdered. She was attacked by wild animals."

"She has a husband and two sons."

"Her remains will be sent to them."

"But when the women find out what her family's been told?"

"When they find out – I'd wait until I was in London before I told them, if I were you – they'll have had time to figure out that there's no point in taking on the whole Kenyan police system. Also, involvement in an unsolved murder is not something they want in their dossiers."

"They need high security clearance to get government jobs," Wylie murmured.

"That's hardly Theresa and Claire's problem," I said, glaring at him, furious that he was siding with Ron.

"There was no love lost between them and Padma."

"Artists don't kill."

"Janet, everyone here is suspect. Even Mrs Obie."

"And you."

He sighed. "Where were you at six o'clock?"

"Oh stop it," I groaned. "Please just stop it."

Ron looked at his watch; he had no interest in our family squabbles. "Look, the women know the body was taken out of camp. We better stick to the autopsy story for now."

"To be performed by maribou storks?"

"And other scavengers. At this time of year, it's difficult . . ." Ron's voice trailed off reflectively.

"What will the staff say when they find out her body was put in the bush?"

"They won't. Driscoll is making sure all the vehicles are inoperable."

"But one of them could hear about it later and tell the authorities in Narok."

"No chance. A murder in camp would give the Masais an excuse to close us down. The staff knows this. The continuation of the camp means a lot more to them than the murder of an Indian tourist."

"Of course, the continuation." A cloud passed into my head. Then a green and yellow El Greco sky ablaze with haunted, ancient oils, bound together by a mystic's spittle.

Perhaps I fainted, sitting in that chair. I don't know. Neither of them seemed to have noticed. They were both looking out the window at Jean and Carol, who were walking toward the main house. Their faces were drawn and anxious. Were they already seeing the headlines: "KGB Agent Murdered in Millionairess's Think Tank. All Scholars Suspect"?

"Okay," I said at last. "I won't tell the women until we get to England."

"Good." Two beats later, Ron was pushing himself out of his chair. The machine within the stocky legs and chubby hips had been switched on and the affable smile was already agitating the cheek muscles. "You better tell the ladies to start packing. We've got a busy day ahead. I'll telex for extra planes right now."

He walked hurriedly around his desk, pausing only to give Wylie a clap on the arm. He might have been a team-mate congratulating another for a match well-played.

17

The women were waiting impatiently for me in the conference room. Their expressions ranged from hostile to fearful and threatened. Even the camaraderie of the Drudges and Creatives had broken down. No one was talking to anyone.

I didn't speak for more than ten minutes. Just stated that the conference was over, that Padma's body had been taken to the missionary hospital and a couple of planes would come that evening to take us to Nairobi where the police would interrogate us.

They reacted to the news that the conference was over and they would be immediately leaving the camp with graceless relief. Which was understandable. They were desperately afraid there would be another murder and felt as distrustful of each other as they were of the staff. Everyone – from the elderly Susan Wu to the wild-eyed, gun-carrying Claire – was capable of lifting the spear Padma had been killed with.

"Why won't the police be talking to us here?" Ann Peabody asked.

"Because the local police aren't qualified to conduct an investigation. The Nairobi police will question you instead. You are, of course, encouraged to tell them all you know. However, there are two things I think you should be aware of. One is that Padma was working for the KGB."

About half of them looked surprised. The rest knew.

"The other," I went on, "is that Ron told the Rangers that he thinks she killed herself."

"But Janet, don't you think she was murdered?" Farah whispered. It was a conspirator's whisper that implicated everyone in the room.

I looked at her straight in the eye. "I am not a detective. If you think she was murdered, you should inform the police. It's their job to follow through on that. Mine is to get us safely out of camp before anything else happens."

"Whose spear was it?"

"David's, the young tent attendant down in my area of camp. He is as innocent of murder as I am. He brought it with him when he was hired, thinking he would be a guard."

"What will the police ask?" Farah wanted to know.

I tried to phrase my words carefully: "They're probably hoping you'll agree it was a suicide. They don't want a political scandal any more than we do. But if any of you are suspicious of someone, you should say so. Of course, it could detain us. I mean, we can't expect a Third World police force to solve this murder overnight." I was meandering and sounding as slippery as Ron and Wylie.

"How can we expect anyone to believe a woman killed herself with a spear?" Theresa's baritone cut through the slush of my words like a shovel.

"We can be grateful that it was a frontal wound," Ann Peabody said in her odd, elusive way.

No one reacted. It was as if she hadn't spoken.

"What proof do you have that she was working for the Russians?" asked Carol Schumacher, tense and distrustful as ever.

I repeated what Wylie had told me in the early morning hours. "She was reporting to a contact in Nairobi. The Kenyan secret police raided his place about a week ago and found her correspondence with him. They informed the Indian Embassy who told Mr Zareda who told Ron."

"Why didn't they tell you about it right away?"

"Apparently Zareda told Ron they mustn't get involved. They're only innkeepers, remember."

"Was she reporting on our discussions?" Claire asked angrily.

"One would assume so. They didn't tell Zareda the contents of her messages."

Murmurs of disgust over Padma's betrayal filled the room and would probably have gone on longer, had they not been stopped short by Dorothea's next question.

"Did Ron mention if the Kenyan secret police thought there

were other agents among us?" She raised her long neck high above the others, but looked at no one, not even me.

"If there are, I haven't been told. Actually, I don't want to know. Not now. Do you?"

Dorothea didn't answer. No one moved.

"Then my idea could never have worked. The Soviet Union would have known about it from the start," Claire said, breaking the silence.

"Correct."

I moved toward the door. "If there are no more questions, I think we should all start packing. A couple of Cessnas should be here around five to take us to Nairobi."

There was an ungainly rush to sort out possessions and pack. We had only six hours before the planes arrived. Everyone had problems. Typewriters had to be placed in boxes with proper padding. Wooden statuettes they'd bought in the nearby Masai village had to be given away or properly labeled for future shipments.

Mabel supervised the dissolution of the library. To avoid confusion, she labeled some heavy cartons with the women's names, placed them on the lawn just outside the library and instructed them to put their books into the appropriate cartons.

Most horrible sight: one box labeled Padma Sarup. In it were only two books. The rest – she had brought at least twenty-four – had found their way into her colleagues' boxes. No one remarked on it. Not even Mabel, who expected and accepted such things.

During this commotion, I spoke to Wylie only once. He came up to me just as I was walking away from the library.

"After I've wound up things here in Kenya, I'm going to London. Would you like me to look you up?"

"Yes of course. Definitely. How can you even ask?" I replied, grinning like a school girl. Or maybe just feeling like one. "I'll pick you up at the airport in London. You can stay with me."

"It wouldn't be for a week or so."

"Fine. I'll be there."

He started to say something, but Driscoll was running toward me with a ledger book in his hand. "Mrs Cavanaugh, about the batteries. You have several cases left . . ."

Barbara Howell

"See you in London, then," Wylie said softly and left me to deal with Driscoll.

Lunch was a hasty affair. Travel was the most discussed topic. When they were permitted to leave the country, would they be able to get plane reservations easily?

"Not to worry," I replied. "My travel agent will handle everything."

When could they contact their families?

"You can call them from Nairobi," I said, thinking that Mutua and his men would never permit this.

Would they be going on to Little Middletowne to finish out their contracts?

"No, the electrical work isn't finished. But of course, everyone will get her salary for the full three months."

Through all this, Padma's name did not come up. No one mentioned her last idea which would never be presented, nor questioned how she, a mystic, could also be a Marxist. Nor why, instead of having a couple of investigators fly to the scene of the crime, we must fly to the investigators.

Don't think, don't sink below the surface seemed to be the protocol for the day. None of them seemed aware of the dimming of their powerful intellects. Yet it was painfully evident in their limp, expressionless faces and audible in their monotonal voices.

When in danger, play dumb. *Of course.* Theresa was right. Panic, whether caused by Nazis, phony space invaders or a brutal murder in an alien land, makes the mind stop functioning. Truth becomes irrelevant and complex, intelligent human responses like guilt, self-interrogation and compassion are abandoned the way drowning men abandon their shoes.

If I sound disdainful of the women's behavior, it is because I am. But no more disdainful than I am of myself. Nothing they did exceeded my cowardice. I had loved and respected Padma. Most of them had found her, at most, amusing.

But she was dead and we were fated to stay alive, to thrive, to get out of Kenya and continue like Camp Urudu and the smiling natives who waved us off at the airfield.

Only Mabel spoke up for Padma. Once. And only to me. We were in a camp vehicle waiting for the last plane to return

212

and take us to Nairobi. Mrs Obie was sleeping on a stretcher beside us.

"If Padma was a Communist, wouldn't it have been smarter for her to pretend to be for the hoax idea and *then* tell the Russians what was being plotted? It just doesn't make sense that she tried to talk you out of it."

No sense at all. Yet three of the most brilliant women in camp had bought it. "Maybe she did that to protect her cover," I said and sighed a deep, authorial, Theresa Crater sigh. How convenient those exhalations are. Might not primitive man have made such a sound as he ate his king and remembered sadly what a wise ruler he had been . . . most of the time?

We never spoke of Padma again.

Only when flying over the escarpment, radiant with sunset reds and purples, did I remember that I hadn't left any instructions on what to do with Padma's personal belongings. Would Ron have a member of the staff pack them up?

I pictured her saris being distributed to the girls who did the laundry. For months, the finest silks of India would flutter around the Kenyan women's shoulders in a little corner of the Mara and no one would ask why, because everyone would know why.

18

The old Norfolk Hotel's wide, matronly, colonial shape beckoned like a long lost relative as we drove up in the ambulance that had met us at the Nairobi airport.

Excited, self-conscious tourists in safari suits were on the veranda drinking Pimm's and clearly enjoying the titillating aura of white supremacy that still hangs over the place.

While Mabel oversaw the hoisting of Mrs Obie from the ambulance to the room they would share, I spoke to the travel representative, who was waiting for me at the reception desk.

The conference finished up early, I explained brightly, million-airessly. The rains were so tiresome and the women weren't so young. Mrs Obie, poor dear, had had a nervous collapse.

When the travel agent asked why one of the scholars on her list was not traveling to London, I explained that Dr Sarup had chosen to stay at Camp Urudu to complete her studies. The agent nodded absently as her nimble black fingers danced across her calculator. For a tourist to prolong her stay in the bush often happened and did not require further explanation. Besides, her main concern at the moment was the breakdown of the hotel switchboard which occurred, oddly, just as the first plane load of women from Camp Urudu had arrived in the hotel.

That evening, I had dinner with the group in the dining-room. At any time, they could have contacted the police or the Indian Embassy or left. There was a cab stand right outside the hotel. But they did none of these. They stayed and co-operated.

Seated at a long table in a corner, they displayed a united front of sedate, husbandless tourists chatting about animals and local customs in low, cultivated voices. No one could look at us without yawning.

The following morning, three of Mutua's policemen in im-peccable uniforms with little gold insignia pins gleaming from

214

their starched collars, came to interrogate the group. With their twenty-four inch necks and bulging military chests, they exuded a fearsome law and order which no one in the group questioned.

As far as I know, the women stuck to the suicide story. It didn't matter, since whatever they said would be ignored.

While they were talking to the police, Mabel handled the Mrs Obie problem with her usual skill, once again displaying her ability to adapt to whatever moral environment she happened to find herself in on a given day.

All she required from me was the name of a physician in London whom I had seen. I could think of no one except a Dr Paddington, a gynecologist on Harley Street. "He'll never remember me," I said.

"He'll remember," she said tersely, which, indeed, he did. I had forgotten during my time in the bush how a female who arrives in a chauffeur-driven car and leaves a sable coat in the waiting room sets off pleasant, long-lasting reverberations in the memories of people in the service professions.

The phones still being out of order at the Norfolk, I went to the Hilton Hotel to call him. When I described my housekeeper's condition and hinted at the disturbance she could create at Immigration, he got the picture with remarkable speed. What is needed, he said, are an ambulance and a certified psychiatrist to meet you at Heathrow and a reservation in a private clinic in London. We could discuss commitment later. For now, a little Thorazine. The hotel physician could ring him. Under the circumstances, it was perfectly correct and yes, most effective.

We left Nairobi on an 11 p.m. flight. Although the women had all traveled tourist class when they came, I offered them first class tickets for the return trip, but none accepted except Mabel. During the long flight back to England, no one came forward to First Class, nor did I go back to them. Failure, that great catalyst for dispersion, had already halved the world we had shared.

When we arrived at Heathrow, Mrs Obie was immediately carted off on a stretcher to a London clinic.

When I informed the group that we would go directly to an airport motel for one last meeting, they resisted valiantly. They had phone calls to make, people to see, things to do, but most of all, they could no longer stand the sight of me or each other. Flight was the order of the day: from fear, self-recrimination and, above all, the lies that flowed from my mouth in such a steady stream into their welcoming ears.

Fortunately, the promise that travel agents would be at the motel and the knowledge that the last third of their salary had yet to be paid, convinced them to get into the Daimlers waiting outside the terminal.

The morning was chilly, gray and British; the porters and receptionists at the motel, the palest of Aryans with cheerful cockney voices. Dressed in skirts, with lipstick on most of our mouths, we were in another state of mind, another hemisphere: closer to the bomb, but further from the beast.

I was relying on that change of perspective to give them the willingness to listen, and me the courage, to tell them of Padma's last excursion into the bush in the company of Mutua and Kibera.

The women expressed horror, then anger, over the brutality of Mutua's act. They were, I believe, sincere. But there was little they could do. Padma's burial was a *fait* mercifully *accompli*. Proof that she was murdered had been destroyed. And to expose the cover-up would mean exposing themselves to interrogations, the press, scandal . . .

And Padma, after all, was a Communist and a spy. There was a kind of justice there.

Would I be wanting to form another conference some time in the future so that they could continue to develop their ideas? asked Carol Schumacher, who had by no means relinquished her dream of female supremacy.

"How can there be another conference?" Hitsai snapped. "Who could ever speak freely now that we know we've been infiltrated?"

"Or may be killed," Susan Wu murmured.

"Even if you don't hold another conference again, I for one have not given up the search for a solution," Farah declared loudly and decisively.

The others applauded and seconded her resolve. One murder would not deter them. They would all keep trying. On their own, of course. Groups, especially international ones were "impractical" and "not really effective". Everyone was cordial. But the fear and distrust of each other that lay under their brave conversation was almost palpable.

Not wanting to prolong our last moments together, I summoned the travel agents who were waiting in the lobby. They set up extra tables in the suite and immediately got to work writing tickets. To increase the brisk, impersonal mood they had introduced into the room, I, the eternal hostess, had drinks, coffee and sandwiches sent up.

Soon there were rolling food carts, several sets of extra ears and such clinking of ice, glasses and forks that any mention of Padma's fate was out of the question.

Only Ann Peabody, cautious, silent Yankee, who could easily be affiliated with the CIA, wanted to probe further. Touching my arm, she motioned me to go into the bathroom adjoining the sitting room. I followed her wearily. The last lap.

Arms crossed and leaning against the towel rack, she asked: "Won't Padma's family go to Kenya to investigate her death?"

"They might. Yes."

"Well then, they'll find out it was a cover-up and we'll all be prosecuted."

"Maybe. But it would really depend on the word of the staff at Camp Urudu, wouldn't it? And before they talked to anyone, Ron would be in the picture. He'd tell them it was a trick to blame the murder on them or some such story."

"But there might be one honest man among them. What about Driscoll?"

"He was the one who emptied the gas tanks in all the vehicles so the staff couldn't go into the bush the morning they took her body."

"It's so terrible, so completely barbaric and awful. How could you have let them do it?"

"I told you. They did it without asking me and I couldn't stop Mutua after he had left."

"Indian detectives might come and question us at home."

"I doubt it. I really think her family will believe it was an accident. She abandoned them every winter, remember, when she went to America. It would be consistent for her to abandon camp and go out alone."

217

I stared out of the window at the gray parking lot and the cars' faint, plump shadows under the blank suburban sky. The African bush was not going to pursue us into this bland, concrete ordinariness any more than Padma's family would.

Ann bent over the teal blue sink and ran some water over her hands. "So you think we're safe?"

"Would you feel safer going back to Kenya – assuming they let you in – and reopening the case?"

"Do you think anyone in that room out there did it?"

"Not really. But I'll never know, will I? That's the trouble with cover-ups. One is never completely safe and one never finds out the truth."

When Ann and I returned to the room, Mabel came up to me with that agitated, housewifely air that gives so many people the impression that she is a lightweight. I had already told her the whole story while on the plane. In my shoes, she would have done exactly the same thing, she had said. Nevertheless, there was a distance between us.

"I've got the checks ready," she said. "Do you want to pass them out?"

"God, no." Visions of Henry Ford handing out dimes to the poor. "Give them their checks after I've said goodbye."

And so, amid the clatter of trays and murmured discussions with the travel agents, I walked around the room, shook hands with each of the women and thanked them for their co-operation. They knew there was no hope of asking any more questions with the travel agents in the room and didn't try.

A few memories stand out: Theresa's dream-like stare as she drank her tea. She was clearly writing the book that could be made of our adventure – with Padma and the bomb neatly excised, of course.

Claire, beautiful Claire, the only one of us to remain in safari clothes, explaining to one of the travel agents that she wanted a flight to France. She had a month to kill before she went into rehearsal and wanted to spend it at her agent's villa in Juan-les-Pins.

A glimpse of a black leatherbound Bible in Elsa Heinzelmann's satchel. Would she still continue to apply that great brain of hers to St John the Divine's savage, meandering prophecies?

Dorothea, drumming her fingers impatiently as the travel agent slowly ran her finger down a column of figures.

For one moment, they were individuals to me again and I wanted to weep, plead with them, one by one, to mourn with me, and somehow throw off our humiliation. But there was no opening for such an emotional display in that solid phalanx of women bent on escape.

And in truth, I didn't want to create one. I wanted to get away too.

I picked up my briefcase and purse and slipped out the door. By the time I was in the limousine heading for Eaton Square, they had become a cold, comfortless blur that I hoped I would never have the motivation to sort out.

Eaton Square

1

Thus ends my account of what happened in Africa. I finished it sooner than I thought I would. Wylie is still upstairs. The fever is almost gone, but he's still not ready to get up.

I could stop writing now, but don't want to. How can I when there's more – so much more – to understand?

After seeing the women off at the airport motel, Mabel joined me at Eaton Square. Although anxious to return to New York, see her daughters and grandchildren and give them a slightly censored, but still rousing account of her adventures in the bush, she agreed to stay for a week and help with the bills and correspondence waiting for me in London.

There was a permanent job open as my secretary-housekeeper, but it held no interest for her. She didn't like London, hated its weather, the lack of shops in Belgravia, and René and Marie Dupont, the French couple whom Mrs Obie had hired to watch over the flat.

But most of all, Mabel was a little afraid that if I got myself into such a pickle in Kenya, this propensity for trouble might become a life pattern and, well, she would rather work for someone with less complicated aspirations.

She was delighted, however, when I told her that Bill Spears was Wylie Cavanaugh.

"The old man's son? Would you believe . . ." She laughed and puffed out her curls. "You know I kind of liked him as Bill Spears. A little dull, but nice. Good looking too. What a character he must be."

"Sometimes I think I'm in love with him," I said. "Do you think I'm crazy? I wouldn't even mind marrying him. I don't know at all what he thinks of me."

"Don't worry, you'll get him."

"I'm afraid he won't come to London. We only spoke that once outside the main house before I left."

"He'll show," she said with a shrewd chuckle. "If he was smart enough to make you fall in love with him, he's smart enough to marry you."

When I called Tom O'Riley, I did not tell him about Wylie, only that the conference was over and why. As I was describing Padma's "accident" in the bush, I realized how much more believable it sounded than the truth.

Tom had no trouble accepting it. Hadn't Moriarty said the bush was dangerous?

"You still going ahead with the Little Middletowne thing?" he asked.

"I haven't decided yet. Aren't you curious to know if we got anywhere with the nuclear problem?"

"I figured you'd tell me if you had."

"How are the tomatoes doing?"

"A few snags, but coming along. Great growth potential there."

Next, I called Hal Palmer. He sounded delighted to hear from me.

"When are you coming to New York?" he boomed. He missed me. He would never forget the Regency suite. I was great. Life was great and Reagan was a political genius. His voice was louder than a year before. It was as if his letter cutting me off had never been written.

As for the group not finding a solution to the nuclear problem, what difference? The project had never been publicized and we never really thought the women would come up with a truly viable idea, did we?

When we talked about Padma's death, he quoted Murphy's Law: "If something can go wrong, it will."

After I hung up, it occurred to me that he might have engineered Padma's murder himself. His government clients might well have requested it. The presence of a Soviet agent in MIT's department of astrophysics would be intolerable. Had Hal asked – paid – one of the scholars to eliminate her? Could that have been part of his contract of "a confidential nature"? I began to feel sick.

*

A week passed. I alternated between longing to see Wylie and brooding over the cover-up and the absolute failure of my magnanimous dreams. I felt morally and intellectually dead.

I didn't speak to Susie Raintree, Lady Whitmore or any of my friends in London, except Nigel Draycott and only once. He had been in touch with the Duponts on and off all year and been calling every day since my return.

When I finally took one of his calls, he told me in his usual, indirect, sensual way that he had drifted away from Horace Leone, was now attached to a married woman of some substance, but was willing to come back into my life, or at least my bed, at less than a half hour's notice. He had taken a flat on Lower Belgrave Street and was only ten minutes away.

Though I wouldn't have minded seeing him, I didn't take him up on his offer. I had this adolescent, paranoid vision wherein Wylie suddenly arrives in London with no warning, comes to the flat and finds me sitting in the drawing-room talking to Nigel. Upon seeing me thus engaged, he leaves in a rage, condemning me for ever to a lifetime of Nigels.

I visited Mrs Obie twice in her rest home in Kent and sat with her in the patients' lounge sipping tea the color of decaying limes. She didn't mention Padma, nor did I. I didn't stay long. The perpetual flicker of the television on the floorboards, grown raw from listless shuffling feet, was almost as depressing as the inmates. "And the food is execrable," she told me more than once.

I asked her if she would like to move to a better home. Perhaps one in the United States, a country place, somewhere like Little Middletowne. She wouldn't hear of it. She was waiting for Wylie to come and tell her what to do. "He promised we'd go back to the South of France and reopen the house. You heard him say so. He's got his communications all wrong. That's all. The radio isn't functioning," she said, tapping out some private morse code with her foot on the disreputable wood floor.

I didn't have the heart to tell her that the villa was rented for three years and that she herself had arranged the lease.

That her madness is permanent doesn't make sense. She was never that fragile. Yet the three psychiatrists who examined her at the London clinic say she is and that she must be incarcerated until she shows a "marked improvement".

Two weeks passed. I began to think Wylie would never come.

Most of the time I read the papers, watched the news on television and thought about the bomb. How could I not with Pershing 2 and cruise missiles about to be deployed in Europe at the end of the year and the President announcing that he wanted to extend the arms race to outer space?

I also found myself thinking more about God. How could He want his beautiful experiment annihilated? I kept wondering. Because He couldn't.

If my time in the bush taught me nothing else, it was that life was too beautiful – too balanced and green and finished – for its creator to want to destroy it.

We were aiming the weapons, not God. Which meant, as I'd always known, the problem was, had always been, our freedom. For if we were pawns of the life-force, how could we have the power to opt for our own extinction?

Wylie said we didn't have that power. But what if the next Hitler tried to prove him wrong? When had mad men ever obeyed the natural law?

Perhaps the real culprit is Copernicus. If people still saw the earth as the center of the universe, we wouldn't be living on the brink of a holocaust. It's this idea of the earth being an insignificant *speck* in a vast, unknowable galaxy that makes us irresponsible and silences our artists and philosophers.

Can you imagine an Aristotle or a Michelangelo taking the possible annihilation of mankind *by* mankind sitting down?

Maybe we aren't insignificant. Maybe that's the truth we have to rediscover.

2

At the end of April, Wylie called from Nairobi only minutes before he stepped on the plane for London. When I asked him why he was so late in coming, his only reply was: "Things to do." As elusive and mysterious as Toto.

I waited for him behind the arrivals barrier with the rest of the crowd. Waited two hours. Didn't dare leave even to get a cup of coffee. I was afraid that if he didn't see me standing there, he'd wander out of the airport and my life for ever.

I almost missed him. He was wearing a torn safari jacket and dingy jeans. Pushing his luggage cart ahead of him, he gazed around the terminal with the wan neutral look of a traveler who doesn't expect to be met, though I had clearly told him that I would be there. His lumpy army surplus duffle bag and canvas suitcase were half open.

I pushed through the front line of people and leaned across the barrier waving my arms. "Wylie, I'm here."

He tilted his head quizzically. The lights in his eyes were dimmer. His hair and beard disheveled. Even his skin had turned an unbecoming gold color.

"Janet. Say there. Hi!" He stood behind the luggage cart and sent me a vacant smile. If I had wanted to kiss him, I would have had to walk around the cart. I didn't. Perhaps I should have. But I was suddenly very shy.

"I've been waiting for hours. What happened?"

"They took me apart at customs."

I laughed. "A beard, jeans. They probably thought you were smuggling thirty pounds of heroin in that duffle bag."

"I'm glad I didn't try to take a gun out."

"So am I. Let's get out of here."

He followed me like a dazed, distracted child. I had no idea how sick he was, just accepted this new child-like dimension as eagerly as I'd accepted all the others.

*

"Why would an American want to live in a place like this? I don't understand it," he said when we were seated in the drawing-room on Eaton Square, surrounded by oil paintings that museums coveted, and drinking coffee from porcelain cups.

His denim covered legs and suede desert boots invaded the middle of the seating area like long unpredictable weapons.

"Because it's here and there's nowhere else I want to go right now."

He stared at the creamy, sculpted ceiling and tremulous, crystal chandelier overhead. "I feel like I'm in the middle of a movie."

"What would you prefer? A ranch house in the middle of the Cavanaugh oil fields?"

"No. I just like rooms that are a little simpler." He nibbled on one of the tiny crustless sandwiches prepared by Marie Dupont. "Anyway, I won't be imposing on you for long. I'm on my way to Tibet to do a film."

"Tibet? What for?"

"I've been thinking about going there for a long time. It's very wild, very empty. They say the light there changes your thoughts."

"A film about what? The Dalai Lama? Growth cycles of bamboo shoots?" I shuddered. "The air there must be so thin. All those barren mountains. Everything about it seems forlorn and lonely, like a living death."

"And what is a living life? If you could tell me, I'd do it."

"Me. I'm a life."

He saw my longing and his face took on a teasing, elusive expression that, for lack of a better word, I can only call the objective correlative of the spirit that was Toto.

René Dupont came into the room to pour more coffee and brush some crumbs off the serving tray. "Anything else?"

"Could I have a beer?" Wylie asked turning sweetly to René the way Americans who have been brought up by servants often do.

René frowned, bowed and left. After living alone with his wife in the flat for over a year, he had a lot of adjusting to do. I waited for his footsteps to fade down the hall.

"Now tell me everything. Did you learn anything more about Padma and the KGB? Will her family start an investigation?"

"I doubt it."

"Ann Peabody is terrified that one day she'll open her door and see a small dark man standing there who wants to ask her a few questions. So am I, but I don't have to look for a job with the government."

"When Ron called Mr Sarup, he didn't question the story of the accident."

"Mutua was lucky that it was so like her to go out into the bush alone. What about the KGB?"

He studied the turbulent blue-black seascape over the sofa. "Padma wasn't working for the KGB."

"But the Indian Embassy said . . ."

"They made a mistake and confused her name with that of another character, P. K. Harup. He was the double agent sending messages to the first guy they caught. They nailed Harup a week after you left. She probably wasn't even a Communist."

"But there's an enormous difference between the letters H and S, between a man and a woman. How could they be so dumb?"

"Not they, Zareda. Ron was only repeating what Zareda told him."

"But in something as serious as this, you'd think Ron would have checked."

"But it wasn't serious to Ron at first. He didn't give a damn if you had any spies in the group. He and Zareda just wanted the money to keep rolling in."

"Then you should have checked."

"He didn't tell me about it until after she died and I believed it."

"And I believed you. Since all my information was coming from you, what else could I do?"

"What does that mean?" he asked testily.

I switched course. The last thing I wanted at that moment was a confrontation. "It means that Padma didn't betray the conference. We betrayed her."

"You didn't betray anyone. You had no choice after Mutua took the body."

229

René was standing at the door with a little tray in his hand.

"Ah, my beer. Nice and cold. Terrific, René."

"Will that be all?" René grimaced at my untouched coffee.

"Yes, thank you," I said. "And could you shut the door, please?" I felt Wylie studying me. Seeing how I handled servants would, of course, interest him.

"I had begun to suspect Hal Palmer of having arranged Padma's death," I said when the door clicked shut. "But if she didn't work for the KGB, there'd be no motive, would there?"

He didn't answer. Just drew his legs in and stared at his desert boots. I wondered if Mrs Obie had told him about Hal and me.

"Do you still think Mrs Obie killed Padma?" I asked after the silence had gone on long enough. (On the way home from the airport I'd told him about her institutionalization and he had agreed it was probably for the best.)

"Not anymore. But if you'd seen the fit she had the day after she told Padma about the transceiver rig, you'd think her capable of murder, too. She ranted on about how Padma hadn't understood and laughed at her. How I would be disgraced and how you'd hate her and me. I didn't think much of it until after Padma was murdered. Then, I thought well, yes, maybe old Mrs Obie did fling a spear into her. When Ron found out she was carrying a switchblade, he thought so too."

"Just to protect her plot with you?"

"It's possible. I've been the center of her life since the day she met me."

"I've often thought of that."

"Of what?"

"Of you on Astor Street when your mother was dying – a sad, spooky little boy playing with the elevator. How could she not love you?"

He frowned. "Maybe too much. When I left home, she never stopped writing to me. If I'd kept her letters, I could fill six volumes. She was always trying to patch it up between me and my father."

"Why did you hate him so much?" The words just popped out. I hadn't wanted to talk about Cy so soon.

"You've got it all wrong, Janet. He hated me." He took a long gulp of beer.

"He talked about you all the time. He said that the prodigal son came home and so would you. He wanted to see you."

"He could have found me. He could have bought and sold every detective agency in India."

"I asked him to hire a detective agency, but he kept saying you'd show up or write. You always had before."

"How was I to know he was dying? When I last saw him he was a strong healthy man with more stamina and appetite for life than anyone I'd ever known."

"You got Mrs Obie's letters saying he was dying."

"No, I didn't. I had already gone to Nepal without leaving a forwarding address. I don't know if you can understand this, but I wanted to get away from her letters. They were driving me crazy. I'd leave them unopened for days and feel guilty. They were so full of this cloying common sense and cajoling. 'Just call him once in a while,' she'd write. 'He's an old man, one of the richest in the world. You'll regret it for the rest of your life.' When they tracked me down and told me he had died, I . . . Yes, I felt awful. But it was too late. There was *nothing* I could do."

"Did you love him at all?"

He lowered his chin, clasped his elbows and retreated into himself for a private consultation with Toto, Bill Spears and other assorted selves. "He was a big, important, fleshy man who was condescending to his wife and deeply disappointed in his only son. He was impossible to love."

"And you? Were you so lovable?"

"Not to him. I was everything he loathed in people. Quiet, withdrawn, no ambition. I was also afraid of him. Roll all those traits together in an Irish, self-made millionaire's brain and what you come out with is 'weak'. A loser. 'A goddamn, fucking hippie freak loser,' he said when he saw me in India."

"Well you'd been to an opium den. You were dirty. You told him you were an addict. How could he not react that way?"

"I never said I was an addict. Granted, I didn't look like the Ivy League ideal he had wanted to spring from his loins, but it was a phase and I was broke. I had no money after I was

231

Barbara Howell

discharged from the army. He never gave me a nickel. Did he tell you that?"

"Why should he give you money if you were only going to use it to fuck up in India?"

"Right, you're right. I didn't deserve any money, though it would have been nice to have had just a little. But forget that. After the war, I admit I was behaving like a delayed adolescent. I was a type, a victim of my class and age. But I wasn't a loser. I wasn't even weak. Every moment I was in India, I was studying, learning, earning my living, shedding layers and layers of Irish American snobbery and intellectual paralysis. Look, I didn't become the wisest man on earth. I'm still nowhere. But at least I know that."

"You are somewhere. You're in this house with me."

He sent me a wild disoriented grin. Half-Toto, half lumpen nature guide from the bush.

"You're also intelligent. You could help me figure out what to do with the money."

"Mrs Obie says it's destined for the city of Chicago if you die without getting rid of it. Is that true?"

"Yes."

"That's really very funny. You realize it shows how desperately unimaginative he was. He didn't even have one friend, not one real friend to give it to."

I wanted to cross the room and start hitting him. To scream and tell him what a spoiled, stupid fool he was. But I did none of these. I poured myself more coffee. "Listen, I'll say this only once. I loved Cy. I don't know anything about this person you're describing. All I saw was a sensitive, lonely man who was in deep trouble, struggling with death all alone because you weren't there. That's what I saw and that's what I'm going to remember. You're not going to change that no matter how hard you try. He wasn't lying. And I don't think you're lying, either. The trouble is that both of you got it wrong. You didn't hate each other. Feared, maybe. Were disappointed in. But not hate. And now he's dead and there's not a damn thing that can be done about it except . . ."

"Love each other?" His tone was mocking. But I didn't believe the tone. I believed the words.

232

His head dropped as he reached for his beer, but was too weary to pick it up.

"You're tired. Let me take you to your room."

He rose obediently and followed me up the stairs and down the corridor. When we ended up in the guest room, there wasn't even a glimmer of disappointment in his eyes. Clearly sex between us was not going to be rushed.

"It's one of the nicest rooms in the house. It faces the square," I chirped.

"My father had taste in houses," he said, studying the beautifully proportioned windows. "The villa in France is lovely. And even though the house in Chicago was too dark, it was a little Georgian marvel."

"Maybe I'll go back to Chicago and put a skylight in the house. They're doing that with a lot of older dark houses."

"You could." He ran his fingers over the brass headboard of the twin bed near the window. "Were my mother's crucifixes still on the landings?"

"I don't remember." I hadn't seen anything like that.

"She had a prie-dieu in the bedroom. But he would have thrown that away too, I guess." He tugged feebly at the covers on the bed. I helped him turn them down.

"Well, I'm glad you like the room," I said. "Mine is at the end of the corridor. I face the back."

He nodded weakly. The geography of the flat held no interest for him.

"Do you know where my duffle bag is?" he asked. He was practically sleeping on his feet.

"I told Marie to take it and press your clothes."

"Really? Thank you." He sounded surprised, but surely such small luxuries were a part of his Chicago past.

"So I'll leave you." It was only two in the afternoon. He would sleep for hours. How could I get through the whole afternoon? I kissed him lightly – sisterly – on the cheek. It was burning. "You have a fever. Why didn't you tell me?"

"Because I wanted to talk to you."

Closing his door, I tiptoed down the hall and thought not of him, but of Cy: hands clenching the heavy French linen sheets. His skeletal, pain-whipped face. The poorly concealed, very

233

real, desire in his eyes not for me – never really for me – but for death. And then, my mother, entwined in rubber tubes, staring at the door, waiting for me to walk in.

Why had they come back? Wylie was here. I could stop running. We were in this together: ungrateful children who had defied the old laws. Giving nothing. Received everything. Deprived our parents of all that was good in us. Could we make up for it now by loving each other? Did Wylie somehow see it that way too?

When I tried to wake him that evening, he was delirious. I called the doctor who said it was probably some form of jaundice, complicated by malaria. The next day the blood tests showed he had Hepatitis B and would be in bed for at least three weeks.

3

Wylie is better and London is warm and sunny. Yesterday, June 2nd, he came down to the drawing-room twice. The bones in his face are sharper. The better to catch his swift changes of expression. Sullen, then laughing. Wise, then foolish. Different from me, then so similar I feel that I'm living with my twin.

He asked me what I was doing in the study all day. I told him I was finishing an account of what happened in Africa. Would he like to read it? No thank you, he said and went back to bed. I wonder if he will try to read it anyhow.

Tonight when he came down for dinner, his scraggly beard had vanished. Also the jeans. He looked like a clean-cut, well-bred American in gray wool pants, an Oxford cloth shirt and v-necked sweater. With a dimple.

That dimple, which was also Cy's, is a gift from the lower, earthier gods: a light-hearted agape signal of sensual joy that tells more about him than anything else.

René took one look at the new, well-dressed, fully recovered Wylie sitting happily in the drawing-room, and glowered. Nothing irritates and disheartens a certain type of Frenchman more than American good looks, especially when ensconced in old-world opulence.

"Now I see why Mrs Obie told you to grow a beard. You look incredibly like Cy."

"I must go and see her. Is she all right?" he asked, ignoring the mention of his father.

"She's okay, but in the wrong home. It's not comfortable and I want to move her. But since I haven't decided where I want to live, I haven't done anything yet."

"I could visit her tomorrow." He glanced at his watch as though he were on a schedule so tight every hour had to be programmed.

He laughed when I led him into the dining-room. Marie had

lit all the candles and put us at different ends of the ten-foot-long table. I picked up his place mat and put it next to mine.

His table manners are early-'sixties hippie. He eats with his head down, ignores the butter plate and puts his bread on the table. His left arm lies motionless between him and his plate, like an extra utensil.

He was famished and had two helpings of everything. The gleam of approval in René's eyes as he watched Wylie heap his plate with Marie's *choucroute garnie* makes me suspect that the Duponts will come around to accepting this handsome stranger sooner than they think.

"When did you first start getting really curious about me?" I asked, putting my elbows on the table and feeling somewhat the same satisfaction as René as I watched him eat our good food so voraciously.

"When Mrs Obie met me in Ireland," he said cleaning his plate with his bread. "She told me terrible stories about you and this guy, Nigel, who did coke. She was appalled."

"Poor Nigel. Nothing he did could win over Mrs Obie."

"But the more she said against you, the more I could tell she kind of liked you. Little things she said betrayed her. It was beginning to make you very fascinating. I figured if you had won her over, you must be out of the ordinary and not the grasping opportunist who'd conned a dying man out of his money whom she had originally described."

"Is that how she saw me in the beginning?"

"What else could she think when my father arrived in France thirty pounds thinner with a redhead on his arm saying he wanted to get married?"

"Why did she come to work for me in London if she thought I was so awful?"

"How could she bring us together if she didn't keep an eye on you?"

"Are you glad now that she did?"

"I'm very glad." He grinned. "I haven't eaten this well since before I left for Vietnam."

"Oh Wylie, don't say those things."

He put his fork down. "I'm sorry. I shouldn't tease you. I promise I'll stop."

4

Four days have passed.

He went to see Mrs Obie yesterday and came back looking depressed. "She's not crazy," he said. "If she were here at Eaton Square she'd get well. It's that place that's driving her nuts."

"The doctors don't agree with you," I said.

"They don't know."

"Is she glad you're here with me?"

"I'm not sure."

"Has she admitted anything about Padma?"

"I didn't ask."

"If you don't think she killed Padma and if Padma wasn't with the KGB, who do you think did it?"

"I don't think we should speculate."

"Why? Why won't you tell me everything you know?"

A long macho silence. Better that way. I don't want to have known a killer. Or fear one.

He has taken to circling me when we stand in a room, coming closer, moving away, coming closer still, then grabbing my arm when he wants to make a point. Yesterday, he held my hand when we crossed the street.

My response to this is instant, electrical, crazed, animal hunger. I long to touch him, squeeze his hand, no, to be honest, to fling myself on him, beg, do whatever is necessary to get him to move closer. But something holds me back. You have done enough doing and influencing, my unconscious seems to be saying. Let the prince come and wake you. You have too much power already. He must assert his.

5

Which he finally did. This morning. He came into my room while I was having breakfast in bed, talked about something, I have no idea what, and then, with an urgency I didn't think he was capable of, he was on the bed, arms winding, legs winding around me, energy pouring out of him, and longing, equalling mine, burning Nigel out of my imagination for ever.

Not because Wylie is a more skilled lover than Nigel. No one is. No, it's the mystery in Wylie. His eyes. That grin. The feeling he gives me that I'm participating in something greater than just sex. Something magical. And like all magic, mixed inextricably with a desire to be more than we are.

Oh, I shouldn't be describing this passion. To put what I'm feeling into words might subdue it. And I have no intention of subduing what I am feeling right now.

"I am in love, listen, Wylie, I am in love," I said, melting my body full length against his. The happiest woman, if only for that second, in the world. "You can't leave me now. I need you too much."

"Oh yes, darling," he said. "Yes I can." His voice was sad. His face full of love. Should I believe the voice, the face or the words?

6

Britain is obsessed by its general election though everyone is predicting a landslide for Margaret Thatcher and her pro-nuclear policy. Like Kohl in Germany, she's got a winning issue. Which means American cruise missiles will probably be in England by the end of the year. The Russians are threatening to walk out on the Geneva talks, but no one seems to be listening.

At least twice a week on the news, they show women peace demonstrators being carted off Greenham Common Air Base and dumped somewhere off screen. I think this process is televised more for its entertainment value than for anything else.

I miss Kenya.

"If only we could have just met like two ordinary people," I said this morning, feeling his belly, hard, smooth and warm against mine. "Without the money or your father coming between us. If only you weren't so poor and I wasn't so rich."

"Dad knew what he was doing when he disinherited me. It was an act of genius."

"And giving me the money? Was that an act of genius?"

"We'll only know later. But he knew his wife's son. He knew I'd hate the money as much as my mother did and see it as a kind of curse."

"Do you still really think she died of a broken heart?"

He turned to lay on his back and put his hands behind his neck. I looked at that taut-skinned, beautiful profile and felt weak. "My grandmother thought so. Those were her words at my mother's wake, over and over. My aunts tried to shut her up. It wasn't right for her to say such things in front of me. Or to show how much they hated Dad. He was very proper that day. Sat for three hours during the wake. Shook hands with the mourners with those soft palms of his. Looked solemn, if not sad. Kept his mistress under wraps. He stayed home for a whole week. Not to be with me. The Boys came every night and he held his usual little court in what he called his den. A month later he told me I had to go to boarding school."

"Did he send you to a Catholic boarding school?"

"No, the religious thing was her baby. My father had no interest in the Church and had always insisted I go to secular schools. She'd gone along with him, convinced that I'd keep my faith no matter what. But that was the first crack in her heart. After that, it was just a matter of chipping away at it in little pieces."

"I simply don't believe that. Cy was not a cruel person. Your grandmother made it up." I tugged at his shoulders and made him face me.

"My grandmother said it was his denial of the faith that broke her heart. My aunts said it was his women. But it wasn't either of those."

"I know. You're going to tell me it was the money."

"Right. She saw it carrying her towards a freedom she didn't want and couldn't comprehend. She didn't need millions of dollars or a house on Astor Street with an elevator. He did. Her dreams revolved around words like cozy and togetherness. She really believed things like: 'A family that prays together stays together.'"

"Probably does." I smoothed his hair and moved forward so that his mouth was touching mine.

"A lot of Americans go nuts when they get too rich. Too much heaven on earth. It's the antithesis of life."

"Come on. Just getting enormously rich and knowing your husband is having affairs does not kill a woman."

"Maybe, but it killed her."

"And you've always wanted to avenge her. Is that it?"

"No, more than anything to understand him." He pushed me gently on to my back. Smiling, determined.

"And do you understand him now?"

"Knowing you, yes. I'm beginning to." He slid on top of me and his tongue sank into my mouth.

7

Hours and hours, turning, twisting. Slow, then fast. The air is warm, the window open. It is June and June is for lovers. I don't want to think of the world, especially not this world.

But last night I saw Padma who has not gone away. Why did she have to die? Who stole her papers? And what did she mean when she said only trust could save us? How could the predators she so dramatically described ever stop being suspicious of one another?

She called the killing of one's own species for gain the original evil. Did she mean that when we began to prey on our own kind, and not just on the animals we depended on for food, that real evil began? Suspicion began? And we headed down the road that has brought us to the brink of a holocaust?

But trust doesn't work. Never has. Neither does suspicion. Suspicion feeds panic. Trust allays it. There's an idea there that I'm not grasping. Too many nightmares. Too much fear.

When I finally fell asleep, I dreamed of atoms, bulging with neutrons and protons, trying to get out, pulsating against a thin wall. I saw the strong force sweeping across the globe. Fusion and fission, faster than sound, faster than light. Until finally, the earth was as silent as the sun. Nothing remained. Not even the original handful of dust.

I turned on the light, woke Wylie up and told him about the dream. He cradled me in his arms. He understands. He loves me.

The next morning, I sat in the bathtub and watched him shaving over the sink. He looked like a sculptor putting the finishing touches on a very precious piece of work.

"Do you like yourself?" I asked. He had only a towel around his waist. One abrupt move and it would fall off.

"The outside? It's all right. Inside, I'm not so sure. I worry. I

241

want to be clean. That's why I dream of Tibet. I'd like to spend a year tracking and filming snow leopards. They're such solitary animals, they're hard to find."

"Lonely animals."

He glided the razor carefully across his chin. "Yes, very. After they mate, they don't stay together. They each go their separate ways."

"Is that how you see us? As snow leopards?"

He laughed. "We're not innocent enough." He tapped his razor on the sink and the towel slipped to the floor. An erection.

Without a word, he grabbed both my hands, pulled me out of the tub and dragged me, wet and slippery, into bed. Oh God, he is good.

8

He found an old ivory chess set in the study and has taken to playing by himself. He can sit for hours scowling at the board. Thinking, delving. I want to drown inside his mind and explore every wave and undertow. Find out what he knows that I don't know. If I could learn and understand his contrary view of things, I would be whole.

Yesterday, when I asked him to teach me how to play, he did so, very patiently.

When I started to make a stupid move, the look of distress in his eyes warned me to think again. Underneath the demons, there is a gentleness.

He still occasionally says he wants to go to Tibet. But I don't think he will. I think he'll stay for ever.

I think he is one of the loneliest men in the world. How could he not be after all those years of running and running from Cy's love, all love?

"I've been obsessed with you since the day I first heard you existed," he confessed last night.

He didn't have to. I already knew. (Hadn't I been obsessed with him, too? Was that why Cy pitted us each at different ends of his huge fortune?)

In my imagination, I had often seen Wylie standing alone in the post office in Katmandu, Tom O'Riley's letter in his hand. "Regret must tell you your father . . ."

Suddenly, for the first time since he left home, there was no more love to reject. No father eventually to come home to. No one and nothing remaining except me, this journalist from New Hampshire his father had left behind.

"Who is this woman my father loved more than me?" he asked – must have asked – in the deepest part of the soul where we all speak the language of children. "Why did he give her all the money that was supposed to go to me?"

He could have hated me. He could have wanted to kill me.

243

9

He doesn't know what to do about me. He wears his ambivalence like a flag.

I can see it in the way he observes me, tests me, tries to free himself from me. But I rather think he can't. I think he knows that if he throws my love away, he may be rejecting the last good that will ever be offered him.

Maybe Mrs Obie knows this, too.

But how can I ever know what Mrs Obie knows?

What did she want to tell me that morning after Padma died and I ran away from her?

If she knows why Padma was murdered, she must know who killed her.

10

Margaret Thatcher and her pro-nuclear policy have won their landslide victory. The people of England are calling for our cruise missiles. The Queen is silent. Andropov is dying. And the world is a little more terrified than it was the day before.

But all I see and feel in the morning are strong white-hunter hands that wander the length of me like angel wings, the pat-pat of wake-up kisses, skin against skin against silk.

In the corridor, the Duponts tiptoe across the heavy carpets. Serving us when we want to be served, leaving us alone when we want to be alone. For lovers, there are no better servants than French ones.

Sometimes I talk about the bomb, but he remains the same cheery fatalist he was in Africa. Sooner or later, a lie or illusion will be born that will prevent a holocaust. The life-force will make sure it will.

In other words, Mother Nature will take care of her vicious children no matter what.

Though he'd never admit it, Wylie's fatalism is a type of faith. A fine virtue, but maybe not applicable here. Maybe lethal here.

11

Museums and movies. Tickets for Glyndebourne. Walks in St James's Park, then down Piccadilly, over to Old Bond Street to look in the shops. London is full of flowers and ladies wearing hats. We talk of the beautiful countryside. Lady Whitmore knows of three stately homes for sale. Why not buy one, Wylie? Why not ten?

I am courting him in my old way, the only way I know, the wrong way. I bought him a Jaguar which he was embarrassed about accepting, but finally did; he hadn't owned a car since he left Chicago. But when I took him, a few days later, to a tailor on Savile Row for some suits and he had to look through 400 swatches of pinstripes and twills, he rebelled: "Never, never take me into that place again."

I love his asceticism. I love in him what is not in me. I want to hide all my fur coats. I want to do everything for him except let him go.

12

"Listen Wylie," I said as we were walking across Eaton Square last night. "I love you. I want you to marry me. I want to share your father's money with you."

He sighed. Sisyphus pausing to adjust his rock. Could he, would he ever give it up?

"This morning I thought that that's why Cy left me the money. So you would find me. Maybe he even chose me for you. He knew you could only accept it if it came through me."

"Accept what?"

"The money. And his love. He did love you. But since you didn't come to him, he worked through me. Don't you see?"

"No, I don't see. And you don't see. I'm not interested in the money. I never have been. That's your and Mrs Obie's fantasy."

"Okay, so you're not. You're above materialism. Fine. I wish I were. Forget the money. Think about me, about loving me. Think how happy we'd be if we were married."

"I can't give you an answer to that. I'm not at all sure I'm suited for marriage. You've got to give me time."

He has taken to going out for long drives in his car. When he comes back, he is distant.

"Are you seeing someone else?" I asked gaily, doing a terrible job of pretending I thought that was the most natural thing in the world.

"No, just driving. Driving helps me think."

About what?

When will he just speak openly with me and stop being so guarded? There's still too much he hasn't explained.

Why, for instance, did he stop talking to me through the

television on the very same day Padma died? And since he didn't go to Narok with Ron that night, where was he?

If I were sure he loved me, I could trust him.

But since I'm not, I don't.

All I know for certain is that I never want to be alone again.

13

We're getting too social. Days have gone by since I've written in this journal. Must learn to be more disciplined.

I invited Susie Raintree over for drinks. Her affair with John, the Pentagon man, finished months ago, when he went off to help deploy the Pershing missiles in Germany. "He was definitely a dead end," she said, laughing at her pun, always brave.

When I introduced her to Wylie, she was enchanted by him and loved his being Cy's son. "It's so incredibly romantic. You do see that, don't you?"

She and Wylie chatted together about life in London. Somehow he sensed her unhappiness and was kind.

"Do you ever think about going home?" he asked in a way that made me wonder if he might be missing America, too.

She shook her head and laughed. "No, the men are better here." Meaning Wylie was better.

He enjoyed the compliment but looked embarrassed. He doesn't know how to handle repartee with women. But then what man who loves snow leopards would?

Last night we went to one of Susie's dinner parties. Her guests liked Wylie well enough. He was polite, but when we left, he said: "This isn't your world, Janet, or mine. I'm going along with you now, but don't get your hopes up. Really, don't."

14

This morning, I asked him if he would like to go to see Mrs Obie with me. No, he said, he was coming down with a cold. In truth, he did have a kind of sniffle. I didn't argue with him. His relationship with his oldest, most consistently loyal supporter was undergoing some delicate adjustment I was not qualified to understand.

I left him in his bed looking like a bad imitation of Proust and had René drive me out to Kent.

Like so many British institutions, the outside of the mental home, with its ancient gardens and stately gothic windows, is excessively beautiful and betrays none of the yellow-lit bureaucratic folly within.

In spite of the chill in the air, we decided to sit in the garden on a stone bench under a white flowering tree. She wore a tweed jacket and sensible skirt and had a new sprightly manner. Her face was powdered. Sanity seemed to be reigning at the borders of her mind.

Wrapping a rough Shetland wool blanket around her knees, she said: "How many times I've wanted to sit in Hyde Park with a blanket around my knees! But I thought I would look too old and depressing to all the young passersby. But now that I'm mad, I can do whatever I like. There are advantages, Janet dear."

"I like you calling me Janet. May I call you Madeleine?"

"Oh yes, you may. Janet and Wylie. I've waited a long time for this. Will you two marry?"

"I want to, but he's so evasive, so hard to trust."

"The rascal. He would never commit himself to anything. He says his father killed his mother, but I'll tell you, *entre nous*, Wylie helped speed up his father's death."

"He says his father hated him."

"No. Cy loved him. But, oh dear, he was a difficult child.

250

When his father said, 'do this', Wylie would do the opposite. If he told him to turn out the electric lights, the lights would stay on all night. When he was sent back to boarding school on the train, he'd stop off somewhere and drive us all mad with worry. And so messy, dressing like a dustman all the time. Oh, he was impossible."

"But you loved him."

"Well, yes. You see he never played any of his tricks on me. He knew what side the love was buttered on. I mean . . ."

"Which side his bread was buttered on?"

"Yes, only I don't mean butter. I mean love."

"Did he hate his father?"

"Well, people might have thought so. But I think he wanted Cy to love him more than anything in the world. He just couldn't admit it. Don't forget there were all those aunts and the grandmother telling him what a cruel man his father was."

"Wylie said you were always on his side."

"I was. But I was also thinking of myself. I didn't know it then, but sitting here in this garden, the truth is not as difficult to face as it is on the outside. You see things from a distance."

I made a little pile of gravel with my toe as I waited for her to go on. She didn't. "How were you out for yourself by befriending Wylie?" I asked.

"It stopped me from falling deeper in love with Cy. Imagine how ridiculous that would have been. I was seven years older than him, English, a servant, an old maid in love with her master. So I chose the son and mother love."

Then you were never married? I almost said, but didn't. I had only half-believed she had been married. The sailor husband had always smacked of myth and need.

"Mother love suited me better," she went on. "You don't have to ask for much love back. I didn't know I was choosing it then. But I did. Oh Janet, Cy was a powerful man when he was younger. When he came into a room, people would stop talking. He was like a walking earthquake. A sensual bloody man. Any woman would have been susceptible to him."

It was hard reconciling this picture of a vibrant, domineering man with the frail, unhappy person I had known in Crete, but I was beginning to believe it. "Was he nice to you?"

"Gallant. He treated my vulnerability with respect."

"Like Padma did?"

Her head swung around swiftly. "What, is Padma here?" she croaked.

"I just suddenly thought of her."

"Where is she?"

"In India by now. Her body would be in India."

"She is a good woman."

"Was."

"Why do you say was?"

"She died. Don't you remember? You were the one who came and told me about it."

"Padma is not dead."

"But I saw her body."

"Let me tell you, she is very happy where she is. We had long talks about that. We were friends."

"What else did she tell you?"

"That she loved her sons more than any people in the world."

"Did you tell her you had a kind of son of your own? Did you tell her Bill Spears was Wylie?"

"I don't remember." Her eyes lurched right to left. "It's all gone away. She's not dead," she said in a crazy sing-song voice. But this time, the madness didn't quite ring true. Her legs moved nervously, loosening the blanket around her knees. It dropped on the gravel. She wore no stockings and her legs were blotched with bruises.

I shivered. A mean little breeze was gathering. The tree behind us swayed, sending white petals and yellow pollen to our feet. "I just wonder how she died."

"Don't wonder that."

"Because you think Wylie killed her?" I gripped her arm. For comfort more than for anything else.

"No, that's not possible. Whatever motive would he have? He would never kill a woman."

"But you worried that he might have? Is that why you're pretending to have lost your mind?"

"Of course not. I'm cuckoo as a cloud. Mad and bad."

"Well, just for the record, Wylie was in the Research Station talking to me on the television when it happened. I know he

252

didn't do it." But I didn't know that. Not at all. The last time he spoke to me *qua* Toto was on the morning of the murder. In the evening, he could have been anywhere.

"Was he? That's very nice . . . Mind you, I never thought . . ."

"Do you think one of the other women killed her and stole her papers?"

"How do I know? I was staff. I didn't mix with your geniuses."

"You talked to Padma."

"She was different. She had wisdom."

Tears started in her pale uncertain eyes and wandered through the wrinkles on her face. Red hands folded tensely in her lap, she watched a white petal land on the sleeve of her rough tweed jacket.

As I picked up the blanket, I noticed a woman patient in a black gabardine raincoat walking towards us.

"Hi Maddy! Nice pretty day," she shouted in a thick Australian accent. She had gruesome yellow eyes and thick copper-colored hair.

Mrs Obie didn't acknowledge the other woman's presence. Looking straight ahead of her, she said: "I did the right thing."

The lunatic stood directly in front of us, feet spread apart, hands on her hips. "Maddy killed a moth for us last night. Didn't you Maddy?"

Mrs Obie's hands clenched into fists. "Padma told me that she wanted to die. She said the life-force was wicked. That's what she discovered in the bush."

"But later she discovered something else. Another idea. It was written in her manuscript that was on her desk."

"Maddy, the moth killer." Copper hair whipping against her face, the madwoman rocked on her heels, crunching the gravel with her ugly black suede shoes. The wind had turned nasty. Thick raindrops plopped on my hands and forehead.

"Let's go inside before it pours," I said briskly, grabbing Mrs Obie's elbow and trying to make her stand up, but she wouldn't budge.

"Maybe Padma had to die. How else was the conference to end? Everyone talking about scaring the world to death with space invaders. You saying it had to be unanimous. Padma was the opposition." She looked at me with a grin that made me think of Wylie. "Maybe Claire Montmorency killed her."

The lunatic put her hand over her ears. "You tell her Maddy. Tell her about the moth." Her thin legs twisted in a little dance under the black raincoat. Tapping her ankles and clapping her hands, she ran across the lawn to the patients' dining-room.

"We're going to get you out of here," I said leading her away from the bench. "Either we'll find a home nearer to London or you'll come back to Eaton Square. Wylie wants you there."

"No, please. I'm fine here. That redhead doesn't bother me. I did kill a huge moth. Scared the daylights out of her, poor thing. I can cope." Wrapping her arms around her tweed bosom, she gazed at me with dry, emotionless eyes. "When I die, I wouldn't mind having my ashes scattered in the bush in Kenya."

"You're not going to die," I said, guiding her through the French doors that led to the dining-room. You're going to live with us and be happy."

"Mrs Obie still talks in circles. None of it makes sense," I said, walking into Wylie's room as soon as I got back. I hadn't felt so depressed for weeks.

He was sitting up in bed reading Schopenhauer. On the bedside table were two nosedrop bottles and five different kinds of vitamins.

"It makes perfect sense. She's in love with me, thinks she has lost me to you and has had a nervous breakdown."

"She's not 'in love' with you. She loved Cy."

"Really?" He looked genuinely shocked. I don't believe he has ever suspected that Mrs Obie was anything but a servant. I said nothing more. It was not for me to interfere with whatever decision or vow she made – or might have made – so long ago. She had suffered enough.

"She also thinks you might have something to do with Padma's death. Or half of her does. That's why she's acting insane. To protect you and make me think she did it. The other half says no, you could never kill a woman. Is that true?"

He reached for my hand and kissed the tips of my fingers. "Of course it's true."

I pulled my hand away angrily.

"Maybe it's time I tell you my other theory about Padma's murderer. Do you want to hear it?"

"I want to hear the truth."

"Well, in lieu of the truth, I'll tell you what I think. From there we can discuss if it's plausible. I think that Padma was killed by a thief and that the thief was David."

"David would never kill someone. And anyhow her diamonds and ivory jewelry were in her tent. Only her papers were missing."

"I know. Which is why Ron and I assumed that robbery had nothing to do with it. But after you and the women left Urudu, Ron discovered that Padma had $600.00 on her when she died. She had taken it out of the office safe that morning, even signed a chit for it. We'll never know why. Maybe to buy some artifacts from those con men in the Masai village. In any event, the money wasn't on her body or in her tent after she was murdered. My theory, which is as valid as any, is that she caught the thief, who was probably David, in the act of stealing. He was so frightened, not so much at the thought of losing his job, but of *her*, that he panicked and killed her."

"With a spear he happened to be walking around with?"

"It was his. He had a right to carry it. If someone stopped him, he would have said he was taking it to one of the guards."

"But David was so sweet. Like a child."

"Whom Padma could easily terrify. Just before I left for England, Ron met me for a drink in Nairobi and told me that David had gotten so insolent he threatened to fire him. And what do you know? David turned on his heel without a word, marched out of camp and took the next plane to Nairobi. Tent attendants can't afford to take planes. He made $80 a month tops."

"Does Ron think he did it?"

"He'd never admit it. More than anything he wants to forget the whole thing ever happened. His only worry would be that one day David will start feeling guilty and confess to a murder that has already been reported as an accident."

"So if what you say is true, all that lying and spiriting us out of Kenya and putting her body in the bush was done to protect a thief."

He sighed. "I know. It makes you almost wish Mrs Obie had done it."

"Is that why you didn't tell me about David right away?"

"Partly. I also don't have any proof, which makes anything I say just speculation. It's still possible someone in the group did it, like that little sneak Ann Peabody."

"If Padma wasn't with the KGB, why would anyone want to kill her?"

"I don't know."

"I've always thought that whoever took her papers killed her. It just doesn't seem possible that it was David. Do you think anyone else on the staff thought he did it?"

"We'll never find that out."

"It would explain why they went berserk the night she died."

"And why Ron was so anxious to cover it up. He could have suspected it was someone on the staff from the start. You realize that if they discovered that a crazy tent attendant killed a tourist, the Narok Council would close Camp Urudu the next day."

"Oh Jesus, the women will suspect each other for the rest of their lives. And all of it just to protect a thief!"

"You mustn't think about that."

"But I must." I wanted to cry. To wail and cry and mourn. Not just for Padma, but for ourselves and our stupidity. Our incredible stupidity.

"The humiliation of it. The lies I told. You told. The horrible way they got rid of Padma's body."

I went to the window, pulled the curtains open, looked at the gray, glowering sky and drew them closed. "If Claire hadn't put her on the defensive with the space invader fantasy, *your* fantasy, she would have presented her idea about trust before she was murdered. She was ready to show it to me. But with everyone against her, she felt she had to perfect it."

He threw the covers off the bed and patted the spot near him. "Come sit down. You look so miserable, little stepmother."

"Nothing's changed," I groaned, but the sound I made was nothing like the desolation I felt in my chest, my bones. I lay down on the bed next to him, but with my back turned. I didn't want to see his eyes. "Everything is the same. I've still got $250 million dollars which has probably increased to $255 million since I last looked at the Boys' statement and the world is still threatened by the bomb and I'm still wondering what to do with my money and the world is as vicious and predatory as Padma said it was and, oh God, I'm back where I started and I'm so alone."

"You're not alone, Janet. Please stop."

"I am. Who are my friends? You, threatening to leave all the time? No, I'm more alone than I was. At least before, I had Mrs Obie, now I don't even have her."

"She might get better. In fact, I'm sure she will if we get her out of that home."

"But I don't want her. I mean, yes, great if she gets well, but that's not the point. I want *you*. Why don't you love me?" I asked, suddenly remembering how wonderful rage was, how great to throw off the controls after months of worrying about the world and hostessing for geniuses and trying to get him to love me. "What's wrong with me? Why won't you marry me?" By then I was shouting.

He froze. Flight, every tortured Toto membrane in him seemed to dictate. *Don't let this woman catch you.*

"I don't think I'll ever be able to marry my father's wife. But that doesn't mean we can't . . ."

"FINE. DON'T," I screamed, flinging myself off the bed with one adrenalin-filled leap. Now everything was rage. Rage at the lies, at Padma for dying, at the utter imbecility of my fate that decreed that someone as inept and weak as I would become one of the richest women in the world. But rage mostly at this teasing, wily, stubborn, mind energy creature from nowhere, with his stories and theories coated in grease.

"You come. You go. You're hot, you're cold. You change your mind. First Padma's a KGB agent, then she isn't. Then Mrs Obie killed her, now David did. But no proof ever. Just lies and theories and doubts. No wonder your favorite theory is that only lies motivate people." I started pulling at the bed clothes. I wanted to tear the room to shreds. "No wonder Mrs Obie thinks you killed Padma."

"Shhhh. Shhhh." He grabbed an arm, then the other and slowly pulling me, guided me back into bed. "Easy . . . it's okay."

257

All calm. All soothing man. All wily wunderkind. Whom, it seemed, I was doomed to love. He pulled me closer, eyes glowing, dimple gleeful. Happy. My anger, which he knew could only be because of my love, was making him happy.

Oh it shouldn't be this complicated, but it is.

"Janet," he was saying, "I'll go, but listen first. I have been thinking of how we could work out our lives. Listen to me. Don't turn away."

"You said that when you were on the television screen. You said listen and I did and all it brought me was one murder and a thousand lies."

"Shhh. Come back." His hands went around my shoulders, gentle muscley, warm strokes, soft, patting and coaxing. Wylie does lovable, is lovable again and knows it. His victim, I, cling to a pajama button. Since there's no hope at all, may as well enjoy this last moment, a muddled tear-drenched voice inside me murmurs, as his arms wind around me. Later, I'll go and join Mrs Obie in the nuthouse, the voice says, but for now, let him engulf me, let me fall down, down into love again.

When he fell asleep, I got up and went to my bedroom which is where I am now. It is four o'clock and raining and all the colors have left the room. If Wylie is lying about David, he could be lying about everything. Suspicions are crawling around in my head like worms. If only I could trust him. But when has he given me any reason to?

15

At dinner he was flying high on Toto wisdom. He was going to console me, you see, vanquish my despair, make me love him and his lies, no matter what.

"Your think tank was not a waste, Janet. Not even Padma's death was. We learned a lot."

"We learned to save our ass. We were cowards and I was the most cowardly of all."

"Of course you were a coward. So was I. But we were human. We acted like human beings who were scared, whose only thought was to survive. We learned the power of lies."

"Oh shit."

He picked up a chicken leg, ripped the meat from the bone with his hands. A leprechaun grin. The usual Celtic knowingness: half clown, half prophet. "Just look who was lied to: some of the most hard-nosed, brilliant representatives of humanity. First they believe that Padma worked for the KGB. Then that her body has been sent to the missionary hospital for an autopsy and finally that the police can only question them in Nairobi rather than at the scene of the crime. And they bought it all. They followed us through that labyrinth of lies like children following the Pied Piper. Proving that survival will always be more important than truth."

"All the women proved was that in a panic the mind stops functioning. People get *dumb*. Which is what world leaders are now. Dumb with panic. They suppress it, of course, but every time there's a crisis that could lead to a nuclear confrontation or they find out that the other side has a newer bigger bomb, what they feel is panic. And what they are is dumb, dumb, dumb. Because they won't face the truth that unless there is total disarmament, sooner or later, there will be war."

"No one will ever face the truth when there's a lie around that's more appealing," he said, still picking at his chicken.

"Either a madman will come to power in one of the nuclear states or someone will panic and there'll be an accident. These are simple, easy-to-understand truths. Why can't anyone face them?"

"Because they're unbearable. Truth is unbearable. Padma saw it. We are all predators and victims. We don't know if there is a God or not or whether we exist for a purpose. We strongly suspect we may be here just so DNA can make more DNA. But what will save us from the terrible despair these truths bring is an illusion or lie that will convince us to stick around and not blow ourselves up."

"*No*. It's illusions that are killing us. That's what Padma saw. She knew only truth can change people. That's why she scoffed at the space invasion hoax and said only trust would save us." I pushed my plate away. After so many weeks of brooding over Padma's words, their meaning was finally coming clear. "Oh Wylie, I think I see what she was getting at when she was talking about trust. She meant I should give the money to the peace movement. Trust is what the peace movement is all about."

"Trust in what? God?"

"No, plain, simple trust between Russia and America – which is what total disarmament would require. Nothing else – no lie, no illusions – will work. And the only people laying the groundwork for that kind of trust are in the peace movement."

He laughed. I can still hear his laughter. "They're the most naive of all."

"No, they're realistic. Padma was realistic," I said when his last chuckle had petered out. "She saw that today the odds have changed. That the risk of an accident or a maniac coming to power is far greater than the risk of invasion by either side. Don't you see? Multilateral disarmament is a terrifying risk, but not as great a risk as maintaining our nuclear arsenals in a world where one itchy finger or an accident can destroy a country in eight minutes."

I got up from the table and began pacing around the dining room. Finally, finally something decent and valid was taking shape in my mind. "Instead of mucking around with think tanks, I should have been pouring money into the peace movement. I should have been marching. I thought that being so rich, I could do better than that. But I can't. No one can. I'm sure that's what Padma wanted to tell me, but she felt she had to perfect her arguments first. She knew just saying I should put the money toward something so ordinary, so *real*, would never have the glamor of the other women's ideas. That's why she delayed so long. But it's not too late. I've still got $250 million to spend." I was smiling, feeling something like enthusiasm again, maybe hope.

Which he was not sharing. Not at all.

"Even if America and Russia were miraculously swayed by the peace movement and disarmed, that doesn't mean the nuclear nut fringe would. Places like Libya and South Africa would never give up their nuclear capability."

"But they might. I believe they would. Russia and America are the leaders of the world. People *follow* leaders. If the two greatest countries disarmed, smaller countries would be so stunned by the sheer moral power of such an act, their attitudes about war could be completely reversed. It could be the start of a new age."

"And humanity would move one step up the ladder of evolution?" he asked, smiling dreamily, skeptically, condescendingly.

"Why not? Listen, humanity could change. If it changed from being matriarchal to patriarchal, it could change again."

"You don't know that for sure."

"But it makes sense. Real discoveries like men impregnate women or the earth is round or all men are equal convulse and change the world. Illusions like God is merciful or angry don't. They preserve the status quo. And the *truth* that trust in a nuclear world is a better gamble than suspicion could make us evolve to a higher plane. The trouble was that until now, trust wasn't reasonable. It didn't pay."

"It still doesn't."

"But it could. You know it could. The people in the peace movement think it could. It's bigger than it's ever been in the history of the world. And if I donated $250 million, it might grow that much more."

"Go ahead," he said distantly. "But you know a quarter of a

billion would just be a drop in the bucket. You'd see it evaporate in a year on committees and free-loaders. You'd be photographed at peace marches as another millionaire eccentric."

For a second, I felt as though I were back in Kenya and talking to Toto on the television. But he wasn't Toto. He was Cy's disinherited son and telling me that anything I did with the money would be ineffectual. The same thing he had been doing since the first day he spoke to me: laughing, mocking, discouraging.

"I know exactly how limited the money is. And that there's a good chance we'll be blown up before anyone seriously considers disarming. But at least I'd be investing in something I believed in. It would have some impact."

"But not enough." He stared at the candlesticks and caught a piece of dripping wax. He was there and not there. "Why bother putting your money into something that you aren't sure will ever succeed?"

"Because I don't care if it's a dream. All I know is that if one day I look up in the sky and see a fireball, I want to be able to look at God and say I was on your side, life's side."

"You have no idea if there is a God or not."

"That's right. I don't. It's Pascal's wager all over again. If there is a God, I'm backing him. If there is no God, I've wasted the money. But since I may go up in a fireball anyway, I'm willing to take that gamble."

"Suit yourself." His voice was dull. He didn't like this wager. Didn't seem to like anything I was saying. Especially he didn't seem to like hearing that the whole $250 million might be going to the peace movement and that he might not get the half I had offered. Which he had refused. Because he didn't want to marry me? Or because he was somehow planning to get all of it?

I headed for the door. My heart was beating too fast. Must think clearly, I ordered myself. Must stay calm. *Must not panic.*

"You're not going to finish your dinner?" he asked. His expression was bland and remote. I wanted to shake him, let him know that he couldn't dismiss my ideas and hopes so callously, tell him I hadn't bought all his rubbish about David killing Padma, show him I wasn't as dumb as he thought I was.

"I told Mrs Obie that you were at the Research Station the evening Padma was killed." My legs were trembling.

"Thank you." Very cool.

"Were you?"

"No, I was in camp, fixing one of the Land Rovers, then in the bar." He picked up a salad leaf and nibbled on it as if it were a piece of toast.

"And you never read Padma's papers?"

"I never saw them. What are you talking about?"

"Why did you suddenly decide to leave and 'return to your star' on the very day she died?"

He raised his voice. "Because Ron wanted me to. He saw Farah snooping around his office and thought she'd seen the amplifier."

"Really? Is that the only reason?"

"*Yes, that's the only reason.*"

I left him to his lettuce leaf, ran upstairs, locked my bedroom door and pulled out my notebook.

I am writing this in bed. I'm exhausted and want to go to sleep, but I can't stop being afraid.

Not just of him. Of the evil in that fear. Of a larger and more lethal thing with icy palms and demon fingers, clutching the earth, squeezing and squeezing the life out.

The other force.

16

I am not a philosopher. My thoughts are only glimmers in a vast night. My thoughts are stories. Here is the thought I dreamt last night:

Suppose there are two gods, not one. Both lonely. Both equal. Both free.

Call them M and E.

Suppose also, that eons and eons ago, M (whose real name is perhaps Mind, but could also be Mass, or simply the person whom we call God), decided to take the stuff that was the universe and create a companion for himself who would be similar, though perhaps not as great as he.

He started by locking a small amount of energy into atoms which combined into molecules, then cells, plants, and animals. Until finally, millions of years later, a creature evolved who could form abstract ideas, knew right from wrong and was free.

If all went according to plan, this human creature would one day evolve into a true companion for M, perhaps by combining with other human souls and becoming one great soul, far away, somewhere else, in the future, millions of years from now. When and where and how that would happen is a mystery. And this is a story with a mystery.

E the other god, whom we might call Energy, hated this life experiment and had only two desires: to see this potential companion turned back into energy and the original loneliness restored.

Wylie must have finished his breakfast. I can hear him pacing around upstairs. Surely he slept as poorly as I did. He knows he has shown his hand and is nervous. How could he expect me to believe David murdered Padma? Lies upon lies. How can he hope to make me think he's not interested in the money when all he does is find arguments against my giving it away?

I want to lock the door of the study, but if I do, he will know I am afraid. And I don't have time to get up. I must finish what I'm writing before he destroys it. If need be, I'll throw it out the window like a message sent out to sea.

Through the ages, we were always aware of E. The Christians called him the devil (though he was much greater than any fallen angel), envisaged him roaming the earth and described his home as a place of brimstone, fire and chaos. Other cultures and religions gave E other names, but all identified him as evil. Though no one knew E's true intention, which was the destruction of man, they were aware that wherever hate and suspicion were, so was evil.

Nevertheless, we believed that goodness would win over evil and that, overall, we were safe and watched over by M. And we were, very closely, but his plan had one vulnerable aspect. His humans were free. They had to be. Pawns or slaves could never develop into a true companion for M.

In this freedom, E saw his chance to tempt humans into reconverting themselves into energy of their own free will.

We don't know when E first introduced the idea of men using their predatory skills on other humans for the sake of gain. All we know is that at some point, men and women bought it. Freely. And knew it was evil because they had long since discovered that other humans were sovereign.

Padma called this the original evil. Humans called it war and declared it inevitable. (Though they knew it wasn't because, unlike other creatures, they were capable of freely choosing good over evil.) But the first killings for gain bred so much hatred and suspicion, it *seemed* inevitable.

Soon people started calling war part of the natural order.

And having been thus transformed, it was often considered noble, sportsmanlike, even good.

You can't really blame people for not guessing where war would lead. It didn't seem to be doing any irremedial harm. In some ways, humanity thrived on it. The human population burgeoned and knowledge increased a thousandfold: fire was discovered, the wheel invented, electricity harnessed, the atom split and outer space explored. Life never seemed to have so much going for it. Humankind was incredibly smart.

But E just waited and laughed. For he knew that with each scientific breakthrough, men would – of their own free will – invent new, more lethal weapons (their suspicion and hatred would never permit them to ignore the inevitable business of war), which would culminate in the creation of nuclear weapons and a final war in which there would be no gain, except for E.

Meanwhile M, who was committed to the idea of humankind's freedom (why bother with the project at all if there were no freedom?) stood by and watched generation after generation choosing war and marching inexorably towards the annihilation of all life and the extinction of his dream to create a companion who was as free as he.

People said – I said – that M had forsaken humanity. Others thought he was passive or powerless over E. But that wasn't the case. It was human freedom causing the problem. Or, to be specific, man's freely choosing war over peace, suspicion over trust, hate over love.

Again and again and again.

Wylie is knocking on the door.

He's gone.

"What are you doing in there?" he wanted to know.

"I'm going over the Boys' last statement. I'll be finished in a while. Why don't you ask René to make you more coffee?" I called through the door in a voice filled with solicitude.

"Money takes up all your time," he said petulantly.

"Be glad I have it."

The halls are so thickly carpeted, I can't hear his footsteps, but I think he has left.

I now see that his disdain for the money is an elaborate pretense. He has always wanted it and for three years, he has carefully planned how to approach me, seduce me with words, get into my house and violate whatever was good in me. I think he has chosen evil and only evil which is what he meant when he told Cy that he wanted to experience the lowest grade of life on the human spectrum.

Cy understood this, hoped that Wylie would change, but would not force him, waited for him to come to him of his own free will. And when Wylie did not, Cy left his money to me. In me, he saw a tiny hope. Not a great one. A little beam. All there was.

And for a while, I justified his hope. I was on the right path. Starting the think tank, going into the bush, finding Padma – all that was correct except that Wylie had infiltrated and beside me, at all times, was Mrs Obie, helping him, not knowing why.

He gave Claire the idea of the outer space hoax. Poor Claire, she was completely beguiled. And why not? It was a playful idea, a lie that could never work. But it worked for Wylie. It distracted me and made me stupid enough not to insist that Padma show me what she had written that gray morning in Kenya.

He was very busy, Wylie was. But that's how evil works: busily, from all angles – dividing the group, flirting with Claire, tempting me with his propaganda. "DNA will win out. The life-force is stronger than any human invention," he said, then accused me of wanting to be God, which I readily admitted. What he didn't admit was that he wanted to be God, too.

How clever, how apt, how satanic of him to invent the idea of a mind energy. No weight, no size, only intelligence and an ever-increasing mobility. Whispering, tempting, sweetening my fears by telling me to trust in an amorphous, invisible life-force which would insure our survival even as it allowed us to continue to be vile.

Padma saw the truth. Saw that, in order to survive, the nuclear powers must learn to trust, not fate, not some life-force, but each other. But knowing how alien such an idea was, she called it a dream. A better dream.

Like the marchers' dream. Plodding, tiny people in an enormous world, sowing hope, promoting the only wager that matters.

Which is why, if Wylie read her manuscript, he had to kill her. He knew that if she had lived, she would have ultimately convinced me to give the money to the peace movement and the promulgation of her glorious, magnanimous dream.

Which is why, the morning after her death, he immediately

267

went to work on me: deriding her mysticism, pushing his theory of lies, mocking the peace movement.

"As long as the world lasts, there will be marchers," he said. Oh, he is so seductive. In one brilliant stroke, he made them sound futile.

And I bought it. I bought his lie and forgot the dream.

Until last night, which is why he wants to kill me now. He knows I know he wants the money.

He must think fast. And will. Just as he thought fast when he saw Padma was getting somewhere, which is why he, not Zareda, planted the rumor that she was with the KGB. Why he, not Mutua, plotted her grotesque burial.

He can't kill me here with the Duponts in the flat. It will have to be elsewhere and will probably seem like an accident. Yes, an accident like Padma's death supposedly was. Most likely in the car I gave him . . . those long drives alone. Oh God, he's been planning how to do it for days, no years, *three years*.

After he has killed me, he will produce a will, typed on my typewriter, forged with my signature, stating that I have left him all the money. Who would challenge such a will? He will claim that we were going to be married. Susie Raintree will testify that we looked like we were in love. The Duponts will confirm that we slept in the same bed. If he bribed them enough, he could get them to sign the will as witnesses. What judge would deny him the money? He is Cyrus Cavanaugh's son. Who would suspect him? The only person who knows he is capable of murder is Mrs Obie whom he has said he wants to get out of the rest home – so he can kill her, too.

Poor Mrs Obie. She should have only loved Cy.

But I think I won't make it that easy for him. I'll give him a run for his money. The phone is beside me and Nigel is on Lower Belgrave Street. "Only ten minutes away," he said.

Dear Nigel with Oriental eyes, indeterminate loyalties and a mind full of secrets. He has no time for peace marches, but he is all I have and good enough.

To get him to come, all I have to say is that my stepson, Wylie Cavanaugh, is here. He'd understand instantly how dangerous Wylie is. How could Cy's disinherited son not be?

I saw it for two years when I told the Boys not to let him near me. And in the bush, Mrs Obie saw it too, but could not say no to him. Though I'm sure she tried. Which is why she started to behave so strangely after I bought Little Middletowne. She knew he would be joining us and dreaded what he would do.

He is back. I'll open the door. I want to face him.

It's over. Done. He's gone upstairs. No sound above me. An awful stillness.

"Why won't you speak to me?" was the first thing he asked. I think. I'm not sure of anything. "Are you still working on your accounts?"

"No, I'm calling Nigel Draycott and asking him to come over."

"Why?"

"Because I've decided that you're not going to win this round."

"You think someone like Nigel will make you happy?"

"Nigel doesn't want to kill me, Wylie. That's a big plus."

"What are you talking about?" He sounded peevish as though this were some sort of silly game.

"Look Wylie, I know you killed Padma. I'm on to you."

"Are you crazy? Why would I kill someone with a spear? You've gone mad."

"Yes. Like Mrs Obie is mad. Look, I see you for what you are and you'll never get the money. It's a bitter pill to swallow, I know. If you had been just a little less careless, I might still be upstairs in bed with you dreaming of our wedding. But you told too many lies once too many times. There's no use hiding anything any more. You want the money before it goes to the peace movement and the only way to get it is to kill me."

"I have never killed anyone and would never kill you. You're completely paranoid." He was not wheedling. He sounded strong and filled with conviction, but a day before he told me not to depend on his love.

"How will you do it? In the car I gave you? Is that what you've been planning during those long drives alone?"

His face changed. Horrible anger. "What kind of monster are

you?" Eyes black and crazed. Mouth twisted. "From the start you've humiliated me with your suspicions. Why can't you trust anyone?"

"But I did. I trusted you. Not knowing who to love and who to fear was my Achilles heel, but I was rich and lonely. It's my only excuse. If Cy had given the money to another woman, maybe she would have acted differently. Maybe Padma wouldn't have died. But life is the way it is and I was the woman in Crete at the time and so I was the one who had to make the mistakes."

"I wanted to love you. I tried to. I even admired you. But even when you were begging me to stay with you, you never stopped suspecting me – the person you claimed to love – of one evil thing or another. How could I ever be sure you wouldn't turn against me?" Hurt in his eyes. Real pain. Or was he just acting?

"Go away, Wylie. Pack your bags. If you don't my next call will be to the police."

"Christ, Janet, how can you speak to me like that? I despise the money. I don't give a fuck if you give it to the peace movement or not. Money ruined my father and it's ruining you."

"Have you finished?"

"No, I haven't finished. I haven't told you that I hate you. Hate. More than anyone on this earth. Hate you."

He has started moving around upstairs, opening drawers, packing, *leaving*.

And the terrible thing is that I still love him.

Oh God, maybe he isn't interested in the money and never has been. Maybe he's really a fatalist and honestly thinks the peace movement is futile.

Maybe David did panic when Padma caught him. Maybe *I'm* panicking.

Maybe all this time I've gradually been getting more and more paranoid. Maybe he couldn't love me because I was always so suspicious of him. I didn't hide it. The questions I asked. . . .

And now he hates me. Hates me.

Since Cy left me the money, have I trusted anyone? I thought my friends in New York had abandoned me and that the Boys were fixing the books. I couldn't believe Nigel loved me and I even suspected Hal Palmer of arranging Padma's murder.

But how could I not be suspicious when there were so many unknowns, so many people and things to fear?

Or is suspicion the real demon? Is my fantasy that there are two gods just a reflection of the fears and oppositions in me? In everyone, including good people who want to be good, but can't?

Is there only one god? No god?

Does it matter? Knowing won't help us. Never has. The only thing that will save us is trust. Not in God. In us.

And the only way to get it is to choose it.

But it shouldn't be up to me to make such a decision. I am no one. I am scared and alone. I hate him for making me afraid. Love him for getting angry. Don't want to lose him. Don't want to die.

I hear the thud of his luggage on the stairs. He is opening the front door.

I can see him from the window. He's walking towards the Jaguar. The car he would kill me in. Not kill me in.

He knows about cars. I don't. He knows about violence. I don't. I'm terrified.

I must get into that car, risk my life, prove that I trust him.

I can't. I must.

I am all he has. He is all I have, my love, my mind energy, Toto, all.

He's loading his bags into the trunk. I must stop writing, must put my pen down.

Will.